Return to Me

MAE ARCHER

MELBOURNE, AUSTRALIA

https://www.pishukinpress.com/

Cover design: Created using Canva elements

Previously published 1st September 2013 by Momentum Books

Paperback ISBN: 9781922871022

Chapter 1

If Lana Walters had ever thought about dying, she'd have assumed it would hurt more. Instead, when the bus hit her, the lights simply went out. One moment of inattention and then, nothing. Next she knew, she was weightless, flying above Boston.

Lana saw her body lying on the street. Her best friend, Vanessa, was on the sidewalk, her screams shattering the silence that had descended on Newbury Street. She wanted to tell Vanessa not to cry, that it couldn't be good for the baby, but she was being dragged higher and higher. The street disappeared from view and she was lost in a blanket of clouds.

Time didn't exist in the great blue sky. As Lana frolicked among the clouds she remembered Frank and wondered if she would see him, but she was caught up playing with the cloud wisps that curled around her in tendrils, and this thought passed by quickly.

She was just getting used to flying, tumbling about in the wind, when the clouds parted and the strings holding her in the sky were cut. She hurtled down, her eyes stinging as the world flashed past her. Prickles of fear made her feet tingle as the ground rushed up toward her.

Her fall slowed abruptly and she found herself floating above a street. There was a crowd gathered, watching as firefighters and paramedics swarmed around a crumpled car, its front folded into a accordion against a tree. Shards of glass glittered on the street.

She landed gently among the crowd. The firefighters shouted at each other, then there was the grinding sound of the saw. Lana winced and covered her ears, squinting as sparks flew around her. A firefighter shifted and she glimpsed the woman in the driver's seat, her blood-streaked hair covering her face. As a paramedic smoothed the blond hair behind her ear, the woman's eyes fluttered open.

She looked at Lana.

·♥·♥·♥·♥·♥·

Lana woke, gasping, her heart galloping in her chest as she looked around wildly. She was alone in the hospital bed. She took a shuddering breath and counted to ten, her hands clutching the sheet.

'It's just a dream,' she murmured, the sound of her voice soothing her. Forcing her hands to unclench, she sat up slowly, her ribs aching faintly with each movement. She pushed her hair away from her face. She'd had the dream every night since she'd been in hospital and each time it lasted longer; last night she'd woken while floating above the street.

The door opened and Bess, her nurse, walked in. 'Are you ready, Mrs Walker?'

Lana nodded hesitantly. Even after a week of being told she was Alannah Walker, she was shocked each time she was called by that name.

'Why don't you change in the bathroom?' Bess handed her a lemon and white plaid wool suit.

Lana closed the bathroom door behind her and leant on the basin. Looking down, she touched her bare ring finger. A light flashed across her eyes and her vision swam then cleared to reveal a rose-shaped ring on her finger. She blinked, and her hand was bare again.

Goose pimples broke out on her skin. Her hands tightened on the basin as her legs shook. Breathing shallowly, she waited for her strength to return. She turned on the tap and washed her face. She looked at herself in the mirror and saw a stranger with the same pale blond hair and blue eyes, but where her own face was round and rosy-cheeked, making her look younger than her twenty-five years, this face was angular and had a sickly pallor. She ran her palms over the sharp planes of her cheeks. Her skin felt papery and blue veins could clearly be seen the surface. What had happened to her?

She pushed away from the basin and stripped. As she pulled on the skirt, she became aware of the tenderness of her bruises. The suit was closely fitted and the waistband cut into her, pulling on her skin and making her ribs hurt. Thankfully the piercing pain she'd felt upon first waking in the emergency room had settled into a dull ache over the past few weeks. She looked down as she slipped her feet into white shoes and saw her smooth, bare calves. It all felt so … wrong.

She smoothed her damp palms on the skirt, a nervous flutter beginning in her stomach, before she turned the doorknob.

Bess greeted her with a smile. 'Your husband just left.'

Lana exhaled at the reprieve. She knew she was being a child because she'd have to see him eventually, but not yet. She needed more time.

'I'll go tell Dr Chaine you're ready.'

Lana nodded and sat down, her body protesting with each motion. Shifting in the seat, she tried to find a comfortable position. Her toes were squashed in the pointy shoes and she couldn't wiggle them. She hated pointy shoes. Closing her eyes, she tried to force a concrete memory of her own shoes, but it danced away. She lifted her hands to her face and rubbed at her temple. Why couldn't she remember?

Hearing footsteps, she turned as Dr Jeremy Chaine arrived by her bed.

'So how are you this morning?'

Lana forced a smile to her lips. 'Fine.'

He wrote a notation on the chart and looked at her. 'Have you remembered anything further?'

She shook her head.

He must have seen the apprehension in her eyes, because he continued. 'Don't worry, everything will be fine. I have every confidence that your memory will return once you're in familiar surroundings.'

At this point, the Jeremy she'd known would have reached out and touched her gently on the arm, giving her the comfort of a physical touch. But this Jeremy turned to speak to Bess as if Lana wasn't in the room.

Lana kept her gaze on the doctor's bare left hand. She was finally starting to believe that he really didn't know her.

Her memory was like Swiss cheese, tangible certainty filled with bubbles of blankness. When she'd seen Jeremy for the first time, she'd instantly had a flashback of her friend Vanessa. Seeing his left hand unadorned, and Bess's possessive looks when Lana had tried to convince Jeremy he was married to her best friend, she'd thought she was in the midst of a nightmare. It was only when she'd felt the sharp pinprick of a needle in her arm, and that Jeremy clearly didn't recognize her that she'd realized something was terribly wrong.

'Any questions?'

Out of the corner of her eye, she saw Bess tensing. After a week of testing him by describing his and Vanessa's wedding ceremony and reception, and tossing out the stray bits of information she'd known about him, Lana was ready to give up the quest.

She shook her head. She was beginning to believe that either she was crazy, or the car accident they told her she was in had damaged her memory. How else could she explain the flashes of recall that were totally at odds to what they told her was her life.

'I'll show Tristan in.' Jeremy looked at her, waiting for her reaction.

Lana returned his gaze impassively. He turned away and ushered in the man they said was her husband. She held her breath as the black wavy hair came into view and she had a faint sense of recognition but when she saw the stranger's thick eyebrows and taut face the sensation faded. As he approached her, she clenched her hands in her lap and held her panic at bay. His sharp eyes were intent on her face and she knew he was watching for signs that the she would lash out at him again.

He bent to kiss her. She kept still, aware of Bess's and Jeremy's suspicious eyes on her. The man must have sensed her reluctance because he hesitated, his lips hovering just above her cheek. She put her hand on his arm and pulled him toward her. His kiss was perfunctory, and when it was over he placed his arm around her shoulders and turned to face Jeremy.

'Bess and I will give you some time alone.' Jeremy held the door for the nurse.

As soon as the door closed, Tristan removed his arm and moved away. 'Are you ready?' He lifted her suitcase.

She nodded, looking at the floor. He started walking to the door, but she tugged at his arm, stopping him. She felt his muscles tense under her fingers and quickly removed her hand.

'I wanted to apologize,' she said to his back.

He turned to look at her.

'For the way I reacted.' Her throat dried and she swallowed rapidly. 'I was confused after waking —'

'No explanation is necessary, Alannah.' He placed a hand under her elbow and helped her up effortlessly. His strength made her shrink within herself. But she didn't resist as he pulled her to him and led her out the door.

She realized that Tristan was matching his long strides to her short, tottering steps– she was walking as if she'd never worn heels. His arm tightened around her shoulders and she felt his patience, smoothing her awkwardness until her steps lengthened and she walked with assurance.

The smell of sweat and wood rose from his skin. His skin was tanned, as though he worked in the sun. The first time she'd seen him, she'd been struck by a sense of déjà vu. She'd seen the shimmer of another face with paler skin and gentler features. She winced to herself as she remembered her hysterical shouts of denial when he'd told her he was her husband.

Tristan walked to a red Ford truck in the hospital's car park and placed her bag in the back before opening the passenger door.

'Sorry, I just came from work and didn't get a chance to go through the carwash this morning.'

She frowned. Why would she care if the car was dirty? She'd started shivering when they walked outside, her stockinged legs exposed to the crispness of spring. He looked at her as she rubbed at her arms and reached into the front seat to retrieve a coat then bundled her into it.

She glanced at the step to the cab, and he bent and placed his hands behind her knees, lifting her in his arms. Panic seized her and she tensed.

He carefully placed her on the passenger seat. 'I won't hurt you, ever.'

She saw his frustration in his eyes and lifted her hand, wanting to place it against his cheek and comfort him.

He stilled, waiting for her touch, the look in his eyes softening.

Her hand hovered, but in the end she couldn't. She made a fist and lowered her arm, flinching when he closed the passenger door with a slam.

The wind billowed his Celtics T-shirt against his broad chest as he circled the car to the driver's door. There were smudges of dirt on his jeans. He wasn't the kind of man she was usually attracted to – she liked men who were less visibly masculine; a man who didn't make her aware of her vulnerability with every breath. Someone who was tender, someone more like Fra—

Pain cut through her temple. She cut a quick look at Tristan. He was looking out for oncoming traffic. By the time he'd turned into the street and was staring through the windshield, she was sitting with her hands on her lap, gritting her teeth until the pain eased slightly.

As they wound through the streets to what was supposed to be her home, her already tense muscles clenched tighter. Unclenching her hands and stamping her feet did little to ease the tension. As Tristan turned the truck into the driveway of an apartment block, dread settled in her stomach.

Tristan parked the truck in the building's basement and lifted her out, his touch impersonal. He set her on her feet and went to get her bag from the back. She swayed, her hand hitting the side of the truck with a bang as she tried to stop herself from falling.

'Alannah, are you all right?' He put his arms around her.

'I'm just feeling a little faint,' she murmured into his chest. She tilted her head to look at him, overwhelmed by how tall he was. Even though she was wearing three-inch heels, he still had ten inches on her, much taller than — She clutched her head, a gasp of pain escaping her lips. Only when she heard the ping did she realize they were in an elevator, and that she was being cradled against Tristan's chest.

'Put me down, I'm too heavy.' She weakly pushed at his shoulder.

'You wouldn't weigh one hundred pounds if you were wet.' He shifted her and pressed the button.

She laughed faintly, her head falling back as she looked at him. 'I haven't weighed a hundred pounds since I was fifteen years old.'

Tristan slid through the open door. 'You haven't weighed over a hundred pounds since you were fifteen.' He spat out the words, his hazel gaze full of simmering resentment.

Her smile faded and she tucked her head under his chin. She felt a sting of betrayal, as if the family pet had taken a bite out of her.

Tristan stepped out of the elevator and stopped at an apartment door. He set her gently on her feet, his hand caressing her back, as if in apology for his sharp tone.

As he unlocked the door, she felt her breath speed up and her palms bead with sweat. He pushed the door open and swung her again into his arms, the apartment flashing by in a blur of movement. She saw glaring whiteness before she had to shut her eyes.

He set her on the sofa, kneeling before her as he placed a cushion behind her back. 'Okay?'

His hands were on each side of her, but instead of feeling caged, she felt sheltered. She avoided looking around. She nodded.

'I'll get some water.' He stood and disappeared through the entryway.

Her hand hung limply in the air, too slow to catch him. She kept her eyes on the white carpet, fearing the memories that might leap out to knock her over. Clenching her hands on the cool leather of the sofa, she realized she was leaving a smudge of sweat. 'Damn.' She tried rubbing at it, but made the mark worse.

She looked for tissues, and stared in amazement. She was floating in a white cloud: white furniture, white drapes, white carpet, white walls. It was like being in a sterile cell. She was fascinated by the decorating, and didn't realize immediately that the room evoked no sense of recognition.

Tristan returned with a glass of water.

She sipped, her eyes on the white leather sofa on the opposite wall. She placed the glass on the white maple coffee table and quirked her lips. 'Someone really likes white.'

He looked around him with a raised eyebrow. 'You decorated it.'

She stilled, shaking her head in instinctive denial.

'Oh, of course.' He bent and lifted the glass off the coffee table. 'You don't remember.'

He walked out, leaving her staring after him. She couldn't decide what scared her more: that she was supposed to be a person whose idea of decorating was space age meets insane asylum, or that he thought she was lying about her memories.

When Lana realized he hadn't returned, she stood on her trembling legs and followed. Reaching the kitchen door, she saw he was bent over the sink. She walked through slowly, taking in the white laminate cupboards with chrome door handles. Wobbling slightly, she reached out to the dining table, her fingertips leaving a smudge on the spotless glass.

He turned to lean against the sink, his arms folded over his chest. She wanted to retreat, her mouth drying of saliva under his gaze. Remembering she had nowhere to go, she decided to tough it out.

Straightening her shoulders she met his gaze. 'You think I'm pretending to have amnesia?'

'Let's just say that your amnesia ploy is convenient.'

She stared at him uncomprehendingly. He pushed away from the sink in frustration and stalked toward her. She stepped back, losing her balance and almost falling.

He reached out to catch her. She flinched and grabbed hold of the chair, her foot hitting the chrome leg and making her wince in pain.

In the sudden silence, she heard her heartbeat.

'I have never in my life hit a woman and I'm sick of having my own wife treat me like a wife-beater.' His voice was full of frustration. He ran his hands through his hair and took a deep breath before softening his voice. 'Alannah, I know that you think that your amnesia ploy will put a stop to it but —'

The phone rang, halting his words. They stared at each other, and she waited for him to finish his sentence. The phone rang again, its shrill tone demanding attention. With a sigh of frustration, he answered.

She pulled out a chair and sat. She was trembling with relief, feeling she was on the edge of a precipice and he'd been about to throw her down. His voice intruded on her thoughts, and she cocked her head to listen. A stab of jealousy cut through her, startling her in its intensity. He hadn't spoken so tenderly to her yet, he'd only been strained and abrupt.

He was standing in profile to her, his face transformed as he smiled gently. Recognition hit her. She'd known this man. Fondness filled her and she wanted to go over and lean into him. Instead she looked at her hands on the table. She knew with bone-deep certainty that she'd loved that man with the gentle smile and been loved in return. Her eyes teared up as she felt the pain of loss. What had happened to them?

'No, she's okay.' He looked at her, the smile fading and the hardness transforming him into the remote man she was familiar with. Seeing the tears on her cheek his eyes narrowed.

She looked away in embarrassment, awkwardly wiping her face.

'Here she is.' He handed the phone to her. She took it, looking at him questioningly. He covered the handset. 'It's your mom.'

She tried to thrust it back.

He covered her hand and squeezed gently. 'You will speak to her, and you will apologize.'

She put the phone against her ear, her hand trembling from the effort of not flinging it across the room.

'Hello,' she said into the handset, her voice cold.

'Alannah, honey, I'm so glad to hear you're okay.' Her mother's voice cut out and Lana heard her gasping for breath as she suppressed her tears. 'Tristan tells me you're going to be just fine. That the doctor said you would make a full recovery.'

She felt his hard gaze on her, but refused to look at him. 'That's right.'

Silence filled the line. 'Well, I guess I'll let you go.'

Lana pictured Tammy as she'd been the last time she saw her at the hospital: her glossy hair gleaming with blond highlights, her eyes supposedly full of pain and hurt when Lana had told her to leave and never come back.

'I just wanted to see that you were okay.' She paused, as if searching for courage. 'I love you, baby.'

Lana's hand tightened on the phone, anger coursing through her. 'Thanks for calling.' She stood and hung up the phone gently.

Even with her back to him, Lana felt the anger snapping around Tristan. She turned to face him, a smile of bitterness tilting her lips. 'Let me guess. You're on Mommy's side, right?'

She felt the change in him; the frustration and anger withdrew. 'Don't you think it's time to let go of your childish grudges?' His unconcerned voice raised goose pimples on her skin. 'So she hospitalized you when you were seventeen. Grow up. If that's the biggest betrayal you'll face from a parent, consider yourself lucky.' He walked out of the kitchen, speaking over his shoulder. 'I'm going to have a shower.'

Her hands dropped and she looked at his back in confusion. What was he talking about? She looked at the phone, raising a finger to her lips to bite her nail.

'Oh, God,' she whispered, sitting on the chair. She raised her hands to her face as terror took hold. Could her memory be so damaged that she didn't even know what the truth was?

She looked over her shoulder at the door Tristan had disappeared through. Tammy must have lied to him. She'd always been good at telling stories that suited her.

She stood, the now familiar weakness washing over her and leaving her swaying. She had to find Tristan and tell him the truth. With determined strides, she followed Tristan down the hallway. Brightly colored frames caught her eye.

Her strides slowed, familiarity taking hold as she stared at the sketches. Each house had been lovingly detailed, evoking the feeling of security and comfort. She frowned as she looked closer. They were almost like architectural drawings. The broad pencil strokes looked just like — Pain cut through her temple, cutting off her thought.

She winced, blinking. In the blackness behind her closed eyelids she saw herself lying against bright cushions. She was nude, warm patches of sun shining through the window and creating patterns on her skin. He sat on a chair holding a sketchbook, his face in shadow.

Lana opened her eyes and looked around. She shook her head dazedly, feeling like she'd been jerked back to another time. Tristan – she had to find Tristan. Hearing the shower behind the closed door to her left, she turned the doorknob and stumbled inside.

'Tristan.' Steam rose around her, hiding the floor.

'Alannah.'

She turned to his voice. The water cut out abruptly and he stepped out of the shower, water sluicing down his body. 'What's wrong?'

Her eyes traveled over the drops glinting on his skin. As he lifted a towel off the rack, the light fell on the scar that ran down his chest. She focused on the pale line then looked up at his face. 'What's that?'

'Is that what you interrupted my shower for?' He ignored her as he dried himself.

'You had a heart operation.'

He lifted an eyebrow. 'You don't say.'

All sound disappeared. His lips were moving but she couldn't hear him. Her ears popped, as if she was in a plane that was taking off. Pressure built in her chest until she couldn't breathe. She closed her eyes, images flashing like a DVD switched to fast forward. Snapping her eyes open, she looked at him in disbelief. How could she have forgotten?

'You came back,' she whispered brokenly. He put his arms around her as she fell into him. She smiled tremulously, her hand cupping his cheek. 'You're not dead. I love you, Frank.' She saw was his irises widen, then blackness descended.

Chapter 2

In her dream she was sitting on a chair beside a hospital bed, holding Frank's hand. She eased her grip. His hand was narrow, with long, delicate fingers. It was the hand of an artist. His face was pale, his body thin and frail beneath the sheet.

She leant over him and gently pushed his dark, wavy hair off his forehead. Brushing a kiss onto his sunken cheek, she whispered, 'I will always love you, Frank.'

Grief rushed over her and she gasped for breath. She lifted his hand to her cheek, remembering his tender touch. Turning it over, she kissed his palm, tasting her salty tears.

A woman's arm went around her shoulders. She turned and saw Vanessa sitting beside her, eyes red-rimmed and face pale. She was in the backseat of a car. An elderly man and woman sat across from her – Frank's parents. Kevin had his arm around Lillian, his hand stroking her back. Lillian stared out the window blankly, her hazel eyes full of pain.

Following Lillian's gaze, Lana looked through the window too, and saw they were traveling slowly through a cemetery. Black marble headstones glinted in the weak sunshine. Color photos and gold lettering told stories of pain and loss. The car stopped and they got out. She followed Frank's parents, nudged along by Vanessa.

She was staring at the ground, her black, dirt-covered shoes peeking out from under her black skirt. The sun glinted off the rhinestone butterfly pinned to her jacket; Frank's present to her on their first wedding anniversary.

She breathed in, her nose filling with the scent of freshly dug soil. A man was praying, his voice deep and resonant. The voice faded and she heard a whirring motor and creaking wood. She lifted her head. A casket was lowered into a deep pit.

She gasped as she realized Frank was in the casket. Her head dropped back and she looked at the sky, the bright sunshine burning her eyes.

'Lana, Lana,' Vanessa called.

Her best friend was waiting for her on the sidewalk. She was on Newbury Street in front of Vanessa's boutique. Hearing a metal ping, she looked down. Her butterfly brooch sparkled in the sun as it slipped off her jacket and onto the street.

She leapt after it, picked up the brooch and smiled in relief. Vanessa screamed her name over the screech of tires. Lana looked up. A bus was sliding toward her. She raised her hands to shield her face.

Frank, where are you?

Her body flew through the air, leaving her spirit hovering above the street. Lana watched her body land with a thud, face-up on the hard asphalt. The butterfly brooch sat on her palm, as if perched to take off.

Vanessa's screams of anguish shattered the silence on the street, as Lana was pulled higher and higher until she was surrounded by clouds.

Then the clouds disappeared and she was above the street again. Everything moved so quickly. Hearing shouting and the grinding sound of the saw, she looked ahead to where paramedics and firefighters stood around a crumpled car.

'I've been here before,' she said.

She realized no one in the crowd had heard her, their eyes were on the firefighter wielding the saw. He shifted and Lana saw the woman in the driver's seat. Her heart sped up as she recognized her own face.

She looked back at the car. The woman's eyes opened, then glazed over.

A paramedic shouted, 'We're losing her!'

The woman was pulled out of the car and laid on a stretcher. She disappeared from sight as paramedics bent over her. Lana moved closer and looked down at the woman's serene face, her eyes staring at the sky, a bruise appearing her forehead.

Vapor rose from the woman's body and as it touched Lana, she felt anguish and guilt. It detached from her and she watched as it disappeared into the sky.

She turned back to the body. A paramedic was pumping the woman's chest. 'Come on, dammit. Fight!'

A force like the sucking of a tornado surrounded Lana. It lifted her, pulling her toward the body on the stretcher. She reached out, desperately trying to grab someone in the crowd. Her hands disappeared through them.

The paramedics worked on the woman, until one of them said, 'She's gone.'

Lana fought with everything she had but she was pulled inexorably toward the body, her vapor form drawn into it until she was one with the dead woman.

She lay with her eyes closed, her ribcage aching and her head pounding. She blinked and realized she was on the stretcher.

Her eyes met the paramedic's and he smiled. 'You're back.'

·♥·♥·♥·♥·♥·

Lana's eye was pried open and Jeremy's face appeared. He flashed a bright light into her eyes, making her squint. 'And then she fainted?'

'Yes.' Tristan's voice sounded strained.

She felt them move away but could still hear snatches of their conversation.

'I didn't believe her ...' Tristan continued, but the rest was indistinct.

'You can't tell her until she remembers ... big trauma ... needs to recover.'

She opened her eyes a crack and saw Jeremy snapping his bag closed before leaving the room. With a last look at her, Tristan followed.

She tried to sit up, but fatigue weighed her body. With a sigh, she gave up the fight and surrendered herself to sleep.

·♥·♥·♥·♥·♥·

Tristan closed the apartment door after Jeremy and went back to the bedroom. He stood in the hallway and watched Alannah. The light spilled over her, making her blond hair glow on the pillow, framing her pale face.

He sat on the edge of the bed and traced the scar under his shirt with his finger, feeling the raised and rigid tissue. He'd told Jeremy of Alannah's last words before she fainted; Jeremy had said it was a positive sign of her regaining her memory.

But Tristan had never told Alannah about Frank.

He felt her hand around his. Her lips curved into the sweet smile he hadn't seen in a long time.

'Frank,' she murmured as she tugged his hand.

He jerked, the name he hadn't heard in years reminding him of the past he wanted to forget. He hesitated when she opened her eyes and he saw the love shining in them. Tristan didn't know who Alannah thought Frank was, but he was certain she didn't know his secret.

She frowned, her hand restlessly moving on his. He lay down beside her and she arranged herself to lay her head on his shoulder. He stared at the ceiling and felt her breath on his neck as she slipped back to sleep. She lay against him in total trust, her hand curved over his heart. Her need was like a boa constrictor crushing his chest.

As soon as he could, he tried to ease out of bed but her hand tightened on him. He gently removed it and placed it on the pillow beside her head, holding it until she calmed. Her eyes fluttered but didn't open. Her breathing deepened and he sighed in relief.

How could he have been so wrong? He'd been sure that she didn't have amnesia and was faking in another bid to manipulate him. His guilt surged as he remembered how he'd behaved toward her. Jeremy had told him he had to let her heal in her own time. Until that happened, Tristan had to behave like the loving husband she expected.

Remembering her smile when she'd called him Frank, he frowned. Where did Frank fit in this scenario? He rubbed at his forehead, feeling hemmed it. His questions would have to wait. He pulled the duvet over her shoulders and closed the door behind him.

·♥·♥·♥·♥·♥·

At first when she woke up, she thought she was still among clouds. The bedroom was filled with bright light that shone through the sheer lace curtains.

She propped herself up on her elbows and looked around, blinking in wonder. She was in the princess room of her dreams. Every night as a child, while she'd slept on the living room sofa wrapped in a scratchy blanket and enveloped in cigarette smoke, she'd dreamt of the bedroom she'd have when she grew up.

The walls and carpet of this room were pure cream and the furniture was wrought iron. Glancing at her feet, she saw that the coverlet was satin with lace ruffles. There was a butterfly curled into the iron at the foot of the bed, and she automatically reached for her butterfly brooch.

Feeling only the soft cotton of a nightgown under her finger-tips, she collapsed back onto the bed. Images flashed through her mind: Frank's death, his funeral, the bus. A tear slid down her cheek as she remembered his beautiful eyes, closed forever. Sobs broke from her and she huddled deeper into the pillow.

She lifted her head when the door opened and watched as Tristan approached the bed, his brow knitted in concern. A sob froze in her throat as he sat on the bed, his weight dipping her toward him.

'What is it, Alannah?' His hand smoothed her hair. 'Are you okay?' The aloofness was gone and his gaze was filled with tenderness.

'You're back.' She threw herself into his arms. 'Frank, I knew you'd come back to me.'

She felt him flinch before he returned her embrace. 'Every-thing's going to be all right.' He gently rubbed her back as she sobbed on his shoulder.

With a shuddering sigh, her weeping stopped. She realized that Tristan had arranged himself so that he was sitting in the bed, while she lay across his lap.

She pressed her face against his soft cotton shirt and stroked her hand along his arm. Feeling the bulge of muscle, her dis-quiet grew. She closed her eyes, and breathed in Frank's scent. Smelling wood instead of turpentine, her eyes snapped open and met Tristan's hazel gaze.

She stilled, her eyes moving to his lips and back to his eyes. When she examined each feature separately, she saw Frank so clearly: the wide forehead, thickly fringed hazel eyes, full lips. It was the differences that caused her stomach to hollow out in uncertainty. The lines cutting into the tanned skin in the corners of his eyes, as if he squinted a lot in the sun. The scar dissecting his right eyebrow. The overall harshness of his face emphasized by his stubble-covered cheeks– a harshness she had never seen on Frank's face.

His hands clasped her shoulders. 'Are you feeling better?'

She looked into his eyes, and her uncertainty left. She smiled and nodded.

Tristan placed one hand under her knees and the other around her back, lifting her in one smooth motion as he stood. Her grip tightened on his shoulders. He let go of her legs and she dangled in midair, pressed against his chest. He bent and placed her feet gently on the ground. She held on to him until her world stopped tilting. As she stood before him, his strength and vitality subdued her memory of Frank's quiet spirit.

She stepped away, not meeting his eyes as he walked around her. 'Have a shower while I make breakfast.' He left the room. The door behind him shut with a sharp click.

She shuddered and sat on the bed, her legs turned to water.

The euphoria she'd felt upon seeing Tristan faded as the reality of her situation hit her. Even though she knew that Tristan was really Frank, she still didn't know how this had happened. How was it possible they'd both died and yet they were reborn again?

Frank had contracted rheumatic fever when he was eight years old. At first the doctors assumed he was suffering from the flu. Months later, when he was correctly diagnosed, his heart valves were already scarred and permanently impaired–only surgery could correct the damage. His mother, Lillian, became ill from worry. His father, Kevin, took time away from the company to care for his family, leaving himself vulnerable to embezzlement by an unscrupulous partner. With the money gone, Kevin and Lillian's medical insurance lapsed and they couldn't afford surgery to repair Frank's heart.

She frowned as she thought of Tristan's robust body and extra inches. How was it his parents had had the money for the operation in this life? He was almost a completely different man. She shook her head fiercely. No. He is the same. He is still Frank. All that mattered was that Frank was back with her. The how or why wasn't important.

Hearing the clanging of pots she remembered Tristan's order. She walked to the bathroom. In the shower, as she lathered the soap over her skin, she saw the bruising on her ribs was still livid and painful to touch. She frowned as she toweled herself dry. She should have healed by now.

Returning to the bedroom with her hair wrapped in a towel and another around her torso, she crossed to the closet and pulled the doors open. She switched on the light and hesitantly ran her hand over the garments on the left-hand side of the closet, rubbing the softness of satin, silk and linen between her fingertips. The clothes were sorted by color with matching shoes stored on the built-in shoe rack below.

Lana had never been one for anal-retentive tidiness: Frank had teased her that she was the original artistic-pack-rat chick. And her idea of coordination was choosing two similarly colored pieces of clothing and tossing them on. Rifling through the hangers, she stopped when she reached the lace and satin lingerie.

This wasn't right. She rubbed her aching stomach as her gaze ran over the clothes again. She'd never been much of a clothes horse and her purchases were motivated by comfort rather than aesthetics. She frowned, quickly flicking through the hangers again. The only pants she could find were black with a logo on them. There were so many skirts: short skirts, long skirts, skirts with side splits, back splits, front splits, A-line, straight –but absolutely no pants.

She stepped away, and jumped when something brushed her hand. She turned and saw she'd walked into Tristan's clothing. Her agitation calmed when she saw the familiar wool jumpers, cotton shirts and jeans on his side. She pulled his shirt to her face, breathing in the fresh scent of washing powder. She mustn't let the strangeness confuse her. All that mattered was she and Frank had a second chance together.

She collected a sweater, a pair of tracksuit pants and a T-shirt and dropped them onto the bed, closing the door to the closet. She released her hair and hung the damp towel on the bedhead. Undoing the towel around her torso, she tossed it onto the satin coverlet. Seeing movement from the corner of her eye, she quickly covered herself. Looking over her shoulder, she expected to see Tristan and her heart skipped a beat.

She was looking at herself in the mirror on the closet doors. With slow movements she turned fully, taking in the sight. It was the first time she was seeing her body all at once. She was delicate and frail, without the voluptuous curves and golden skin she was used to seeing, her ribs and hipbones jutting out. She peered closer at her shoulders, running her hand gently over downy hair. This body was starved, and had begun to turn on itself in its battle to survive.

Her legs collapsed and she curled up on the floor by the bed, her back pressed against the damp towel, the hard ridge of the iron bedhead imprinting itself on her back. She wrapped her arms around her legs, and pressed her temple against her knees, she started to rock. 'It's not me. This isn't me,' she muttered between gasps.

She heard thudding footsteps. The door opened and Tristan called her name. She lifted her head.

'What happened to me?' She raised her arms, looking at her bony wrists. 'Why do I look like this?'

Pity filled his eyes. 'Oh, baby.' He reached for her, but she shrank back.

'No, don't touch me. I'm ugly.' She put her head down, hiding from him.

He placed something around her shoulders. Seeing it was the T-shirt she'd chosen, she put it on properly, tugging it down to cover her legs.

He sat beside her, leaving a few inches between them. She felt his gaze on her, but continued to stare at her feet.

'I guess you don't remember.' He cleared his throat. 'You're sick, Alannah. You suffer from anorexia, but you refuse to accept treatment.'

She shook her head, lifting her hand as if to ward him off.

His hand gripped hers. 'Yes,' he insisted. 'You've been sick since you were fifteen years old.' His voice softened. 'Tammy didn't realize that it was more than teen dieting until you collapsed at school.' He paused, letting her take it in.

She squeezed his hand, encouraging him to continue.

'You were in hospital for a year and after that you learnt to eat just enough not to have to be admitted again. After we got married you were better for the first few years. You ate more, filled out, but then.' He let go of her hand, using it to rub his temple. 'Well, then it got worse again.'

The questions tumbled to the tip of her tongue but went unasked when she saw his hands. She looked closer at the thickened fingers. Without a thought she reached for his hand and turned it palm up, rubbing it on her cheek. Instead of the smoothness of Frank's palm, she felt the callused hand of a man who labored for a living.

She let go abruptly and stood, her head swimming as her weakened body struggled to keep up with her emotions. At least now she knew why she'd been so tired and lethargic at the hospital. As she stretched, there was a tightening across her ribs. And why her injuries were still so tender.

She noticed Tristan's face as he stood, his jaw clenched and his mouth flattened.

She lay her hand on his elbow. 'I'm sorry. I didn't mean to throw off your hand.'

He didn't look at her as he shrugged off her touch. 'We'll talk about that later.' He walked through the open door. 'Hurry up, breakfast is getting cold.'

She didn't understand what was going on. In a heartbeat he'd changed from Frank's sweetness to a cold stranger she was wary of. She took a deep breath and started dressing. By the time she finished rolling up the legs of Tristan's tracksuit, she was panting slightly with exertion. She straightened up, her hand reaching for something to hold onto. It was scary to have her body betray her in this way. She remembered Frank's frailty, the way every sniffle and cough was an enemy to guard against because it could take him away. Her immune system was probably destroyed and incapable of protecting itself. First chance she got she would visit a health shop and buy an armful of vitamins.

Feeling the cold touch of glass on her palm she realized she'd grabbed the vanity table to support herself. It was covered with top-of-the-line anti-wrinkle creams, skin recovery creams and plush make-up bags in varying sizes. She was about to turn away when she noticed the jewelry box. She flicked the top open. Tears sprung to her eyes when she saw the ring. She took it out and gently ran her finger along the curve of the diamond petals of the rose. With a smile, she slipped it onto her finger. It had been a clear sunny day in the park when Frank had placed it on her hand for the first time. She closed her palm and breathed out her relief.

Here was proof that this was where she was supposed to be. This was the ring she'd dreamt about since her fifteenth birthday, when she'd seen a similar design in a jewelry brochure. She'd refined the drawing, doodling in her notebook at school as she dreamt of her Prince Charming. She pressed her hand to her heart, humming slightly.

She'd shown Frank the design and he'd had the ring made for her by a friend of his who was a jewelry maker. It hadn't been as elaborate as the ring she was holding – her wedding ring had been made with silver and decorated with rhinestones – but it was the same ring. Her eyes snapped open as she realized: she was Alannah. Only her fifteen-year-old mind could have created this. She glanced around the princess bedroom again. That's why so many things were familiar

She stilled as she remembered the rest of her dream. Goose pimples rose on her skin at the memory of looking down at the dead woman with her face and being sucked into her body. Had she crossed over to an alternative reality after dying? The theme song to the Twilight Zone started up in her head.

She gulped and laughed shakily, her gaze catching on the ring. Plucking a tissue from the box on the vanity, she shredded it and padded the loose ring so it wouldn't slide off. Enough with the science fiction. All that mattered was that she was back with the husband she loved – the how and why wasn't important.

Chapter 3

When she walked into the kitchen, Tristan was dipping toast into his egg. He didn't look up but continued reading the paper as she sat down to her breakfast. She ate the two slices of toast, half an egg and one rasher of bacon.

Picking up her empty plate, she stood and put the skillet back on the stove.

Tristan looked at her. 'Are you still hungry?'

'Hmm,' she murmured, as she collected eggs and bacon from the fridge. He was staring at her as if he'd never seen her before.

She placed the bread in the toaster. 'I need to regain my strength.'

Tristan came to stand beside her and sliced the bacon before placing it in the skillet. 'Just be careful not to overdo it. Your stomach has shrunk and can't take much food in one sitting.'

She nodded as she buttered her toast. Two more slices of toast and one bacon rasher later, Lana realized she'd been too ambitious. Her stomach was stretched to the brim and would burst if she swallowed another bite. A burp fell from her lips. She belatedly covered her mouth and glanced at Tristan.

He was smiling indulgently at her. 'You want me to finish that?'

She passed the plate to him and watched as he cleaned it. When he finished, he put his elbow on the table and cupped his chin in his hand. 'I see you've changed designers.'

She glanced through the glass tabletop to her tracksuit pants and thick socks. 'That's right. Its fashion a la Frank.'

His smile faded and his scowl returned. 'I'm not Frank.'

She swallowed the protest rising to her lips. 'All right, Tristan.' She forced his name out.

She wanted to ask why he'd changed his name. Looking at his scowl, she thought better of it. It didn't matter what he called himself. A rose by any other name was still as sweet.

He stood and started clearing the dishes. She desperately cast around for a way to salvage the light-hearted mood she'd ruined. 'Why don't we have your parents over for dinner?'

He gave her a blistering look over his shoulder. She realized she'd blundered again.

'My parents are dead.' He threw the tea towel he'd used to wipe his hands onto the dining table and left.

She blinked, trying to absorb his words. Dead. She would never again feel the comfort of a mother's hug when Lillian embraced her. She would never again see the look of a father's pride in Kevin's blue eyes.

She stood, looking for Tristan, absently wiping her face before allowing her feet to lead her through the living room in the direction Tristan had gone. She entered the hallway and pushed the slightly ajar door of the second bedroom.

Tristan looked up from behind the desk, his eyes narrowing. He stood and came to her, his hand reaching for her cheek before checking himself. He clenched his hand into a fist and dropped it by his side.

'I'm sorry.' She wrapped her arms around him, burrowing into his warmth as she tried to block out the world beyond the door. His arms came around her slowly, and he pulled her firmly against him with a deep sigh.

She listened to the sound of his heart, the strong beat reverberating through her. He was alive. Frank was alive. And they were together forever. When the image of Lillian and Kevin rose before her eyes she banished it, her arms squeezing his ribs tighter. She couldn't think about that, not yet, or she'd sink beneath the weight of her loss and pain.

She breathed in deeply, her breasts pushing against his chest, and their embrace changed, became charged with sensual tension.

She splayed her hands on his back, feeling the firm muscles. She shifted, rubbing herself against him. She could feel him hardening. Warmth pooled between her thighs. Keeping her eyes closed, she rubbed her face against his chest like a kitten. His erect nipple brushed against her cheek through his shirt.

He tensed beneath her touch and took hold of her hands, holding them against his chest. She kept her eyes closed, waiting for a kiss. As the moment stretched out, she opened her eyes and frowned. Tristan's hard jaw was just above her face. The languorous desire that had awakened disappeared in a heartbeat.

He released her without a word and returned to his chair behind the desk.

She hadn't meant to get carried away, but when she was near him, he was Frank. And when she saw that he was different it was always a shock, bringing to mind the reality of her situation. She opened her mouth as she looked at Tristan's dark head bent over the computer keyboard, the words of explanation ready, then she closed it abruptly. What was she going to say?

I'm not really your wife Alannah, but I am your wife in another world. As it was he was tiptoeing around her thinking she was fragile from her accident. All she needed was for him to think she was crazy.

She started to apologize. 'Tristan —'

'I'm busy. Close the door on your way out,' he snapped. He didn't look up.

She stiffened at his dismissal and her perversity kicked in. Spotting the sofa against the wall, she sat down. She him pause, his chest rise as he breathed in deeply. His hand clenched the pen, then he continued writing.

She smiled to herself, settling deeper into the sofa. He'd have to acknowledge her presence sooner or later and give her the chance to clear the air between them.

She looked around in surprise. This was one room where there was color. The bottle green walls, wooden floor-to-ceiling shelves filled with books, and lots of light gave the study a feeling of warmth and comfort.

She felt herself relaxing. She hadn't realized the cold sterility of the apartment had been affecting her until now. She glanced back at Tristan. He ran his finger down the page and then turned and scanned the monitor, seemingly immersed in his work. He scowled and lifted his hands over the keyboard, typing with two fingers.

Lana sighed. She stood and ran her hands along the bookshelf. As she glanced over the titles there was a catch in her throat. Her fingers gently caressed the spines. *The Old Man and the Sea*, *The Catcher in the Rye*, *One Flew Over the Cuckoo's Nest* – all books that had sat on her bookshelf. Books lovingly thumbed by Frank while he sat in his favorite chair.

She glanced at Tristan, holding *The Old Man and the Sea* against her chest. *Look at me, look at me*, she chanted in her mind. His hands hesitated over the keyboard, then he continued his work.

She sat on the sofa and adjusted the cushions beneath her head before flipping through the novel's pages. Soon she was lost in its words. The ringing phone brought her back to the present and she looked up, holding her place with her fingers. Tristan tapped on the desk with his pen as he talked. He looked at her pointedly. She returned to her book, pretending to read as she eavesdropped on his side of the conversation. When he hung up, he stared blankly into space.

Lana sat up, placing the book face down on the sofa. 'Is there a problem at work?'

He grunted without looking at her.

'If you need to go, I'll be all right.'

'No, you won't.' He spoke as if she was a child.

'I don't need a babysitter,' she snapped.

He turned back to the monitor, ignoring her again.

She picked up the book and lay back on the sofa, blindly staring at the page as anger coursed through her. If he was going to be stubborn, then he deserved what he got. She glanced at him as he doggedly continued with his two-fingered typing. What if Tammy came to stay with her? She'd have the opportunity to find out information and stop constantly making blunders. She gripped the book tighter as her excitement mounted. Then she'd gain the upper hand and learn how to ease the tension between them.

She sat up again. 'What if Tammy stayed with me?'

'I don't think that's a good idea.' He continued typing.

'But I'd like her to come. I want to apologize for how I behaved toward her.'

He looked at her with a quirked eyebrow. 'You didn't want to apologize when you spoke to her on the phone last night, yet now you've had a change of heart.' He shook his head and looked back at the monitor.

She felt her cheeks warm up as she realized how inconsistent she appeared. *I won't have to tell him I come from another world – he'll just think I lost some brain cells in the accident and became terminally stupid.*

'I– I've realized I shouldn't be holding a grudge against Tammy for putting me in the hospital. She just did what she thought was best.' She rubbed at her lip, waiting for his response.

He stopped typing and seemed to be considering her idea. 'No, I can't take the chance that you'll hurt her again.'

She looked at him in disbelief. 'She's my mother. I can speak to my own mother.'

'Not until I can be there to supervise, you can't. Tammy's been through enough without having to undergo another barrage of insults.'

'What are you, the mommy police?' She regretted the words as soon as they left her mouth, wincing as she heard the echo of her snide voice.

He turned to look at her, the full force of his anger in his eyes. 'Tammy has done nothing but love and care for you and at every turn you have rejected her. And when she came to the hospital after your accident, fearing that her only daughter might die, you repaid her worry and fear with scorn and anger.'

Lana looked down at the book in her lap, feeling ashamed as she remembered the way she'd twisted from Tammy's embrace. She couldn't even remember much of what she said, she just remembered the hatred in her voice and the way Tammy's eyes filled with pain.

She took a deep breath. Feeling sorry for herself wouldn't help. The fact was she'd treated Tammy based on her past memories, and now she had to fix it.

She left the study and crossed the hallway to the bedroom. Opening the closet doors, she scanned the shelves until she found what she was looking for. She lifted the camel handbag and opened it. There was a wallet and address book inside, among other things, and she pulled out the address book and found Tammy's number.

Tammy answered on the fourth ring. Lana hesitated, her throat choking up as memories tumbled over her.

'Tammy– Mom. It's Lana.'

There was a silence and Lana feared that Tammy was going to hang up. That she'd pushed her away once and for all.

Tammy cleared her throat. 'Hello.'

'Mom, I'm so sorry about the way I was at the hospital. I haven't really been myself since the accident. I'm sorry I hurt you.'

'That's okay, baby. I'm just glad you're okay.'

Lana heard Tammy's gasps as she cried and her hand clenched on the handset. Her heart suddenly cried out for her mother's soothing touch. 'Mom, can you come over? I need you.'

'Oh, baby. Oh, my beautiful baby. Of course I'll come. I'll be right over.'

Lana hung up slowly. She looked at her trembling hands, wiping them on her tracksuit-clad thighs. She stood and paced the bedroom in agitation. What had just happened? Tammy had betrayed her when she was sixteen years old and she'd learnt she could never depend on her. That she could only depend on herself.

She stopped abruptly as thoughts swirled in her mind. This Tammy hadn't betrayed her, it wasn't fair to judge her by the other Tammy's actions. Lana looked at the phone, hearing again the happiness in Tammy's voice when she said she'd needed her. This Tammy loved her daughter and was willing to put her life on hold with just one phone call.

She ran a hand through her hair, gripping it in her fist as though ready to pull it out. She was so confused. Her emotions were see-sawing from one extreme to another and she didn't know what was wrong or what was right in this upside-down world.

She smoothed her hair behind her ears, calming herself. She had to be rational and think logically. She picked up Alannah's wallet and searched it, finding her driver's license. She traced a finger over the birth date. Even though she'd known it, seeing the truth hit her hard. They shared the same birth date. Lana looked around. They had started as the same person, yet somewhere along the way a major change occurred, and they took separate paths.

She frowned, tapping the license against her hand. That must be what had happened to Tristan too. He'd had the heart operation that Frank hadn't. Remembering that Lillian and Kevin were dead in this life, pain stabbed her. Tristan's parents had died whereas Frank's had been a strong and united presence, giving him the love and care he needed.

She stretched, her back aching from sitting hunched on the closet floor. As she turned her head to stretch the crick in her neck she saw a white photo album with *My Wedding* embossed in gold on the spine. Her eyes widened and she opened the album. Tristan and Alannah had married on the February 12, and their second wedding anniversary had just passed. They had found each other later than she and Frank, who had married when she was twenty and he was twenty-five.

As she glanced through the photos, other changes became apparent. Alannah and Tristan had married at the Town Hall, shunning a traditional wedding. Alannah wore a cream suit with a knee-length skirt and a small hat with a veil. Tristan was in a pin-striped suit.

There were no wedding guests. Their witnesses were a woman with a vivacious grin and waist-length blond hair and a man with moss green eyes who rarely smiled. They seemed familiar but no details were forthcoming, so she looked closer at Alannah and Tristan. They looked happy and in love but there was something that bothered her about them.

She closed her eyes and called up the memory of her own wedding photos. She and Frank had married in a park in Brockton and had a small reception at Lillian and Kevin's house. Even though they hadn't been able to afford much, they had hired a suit and wedding dress. The day had been full of laughter and joy as their small circle of friends and family embraced them in their happiness.

That was it. Her eyes snapped open and she looked back at the photos. Although Alannah and Tristan looked like a couple in love, their kisses were chaste and their touches restrained. On her and Frank's wedding day, they'd been teased by Kevin to stop kissing so the photographer could take some photos where they faced the camera.

She realized that Kevin and Lillian must have been dead for at least two years, but remembering the way Tristan had spoken about them, she thought it was much longer than that. Was that the difference that had changed him into the man she knew now?

She rubbed her hand over the shiny plastic that covered the photos, tracing Tristan's face. He shared the barest resemblance with Frank; it was almost like he was a different person. She closed the album with a snap, pushing the disturbing thoughts away. No, he was the same man, just like she was the same as Alannah. The differences were just superficial.

She glanced down at the license again. Like her first name. She'd always hated being called Alannah and from the time she was old enough, she'd insisted that she was Lana. Tristan's insistence in using his middle name in this life was jarring to her. Why had he made the change? Her eye caught on Alannah's last name. And why did Tristan change his surname from Walters to Walker? The thought unsettled her. There was only one reason a person changed their name: to hide.

Cold fear swept over her. Her hands tightened on the license, nearly snapping it. With jerky motions, she put it back into the purse and walked into the living room to wait for Tammy.

When there was a knock at the door, Lana hurried to open it before Tristan heard. Even though she'd instigated this visit, she was still unprepared for the emotional blow when she looked at her mother – hatred, love, anger and need all fought within her.

Tammy looked at her with fearful blue eyes, her teeth biting her lip as she waited.

'Hi, Mom.' Lana forced herself to pull Tammy into an embrace, bracing for the scent of alcohol and cigarettes. Instead she smelt perfume and face cream. Her rigid arms relaxed and she closed her eyes, taken back to her childhood, when a hug from her mother meant that all was right with the world again.

'Hi, baby,' Tammy said against her neck.

Lana pulled away and looked at her mother properly for the first time. Her eyes were without the redness Lana had come to associate with a hangover. Her skin was soft and clear of broken capillaries from years of alcohol abuse.

Lana had a feeling of déjà vu. This is how she'd felt when she'd recognized Tristan for the first time while he was in the shower, as if she was gazing into a mirror that showed the past and the future.

She stepped aside to let Tammy in. Lana had to focus on the reason for her mother coming over: she needed information. There had to be a something that occurred in Alannah's life to create the divergence and she had to find out what that was.

They sat on the sofa, the leather creaking with their movements.

'Thanks for coming, Mom.' Lana met Tammy's gaze and quickly looked away from the hopeful look she found there. She shifted in her seat, guilt eating at her. 'Mom, I'm sorry for the way I behaved last week in hospital. I—' She stopped when Tammy shook her head.

'You were right. I wasn't really there for you.' She covered Lana's hand with her own. 'I'm sorry I put you in hospital against your will when you were seventeen.' She blinked, tears sticking to her lashes. 'I know you felt that you weren't as important as Michael. I failed you by not being there when you needed me. Can you forgive me?'

Lana looked at Tammy's hand covering her own; she had her mother's hands. When she'd been a little girl, she'd pressed their palms together and checked how much she was growing. She turned over Tammy's hand and pressed their palms together. They were exactly the same.

So much time had passed between the little girl and the woman she had become. She looked into Tammy's face. They could have been sisters. The only thing she'd inherited from the father who'd died when she was two months old was a slight cleft in her chin. Could she lay down the past and start again? This Tammy had made the same mistake, choosing a man over her daughter. Now Lana had to decide if she'd make the same mistake she had in her other life and choose grudge-keeping and righteousness over forgiveness and healing.

The burden of hate she'd carried for eight years eased. She clasped Tammy's hand in her own. 'I love you, Mom.' As the words tumbled from her lips she realized she had always loved her mother. All her hate had stemmed from fear of being hurt again.

Tammy's lip trembled. 'I love you back, baby.' She smoothed Lana's hair behind her ear.

Lana fell into her mother's embrace and gave up fighting her tears. Tammy stroked her back. It had been so long since she'd been her mother's daughter.

'Alannah.' Tristan's voice intruded.

They pulled apart and looked at each other ruefully, wiping their tears. Lana looked up as Tristan entered. He looked at Tammy's tear-streaked face and his lips thinned in anger.

He embraced Tammy gently. 'What's with the waterworks?' He gently wiped her face.

Tammy turned toward Lana. 'We were just clearing the air.' She took hold of Lana's hand. 'I've got my baby back.'

Tristan raised his eyebrow at Lana and she felt his skepticism as if he'd spoken it. She blushed, looking away from him as she remembered her less than noble intent in inviting Tammy.

The phone rang faintly. 'Excuse me.' Tristan left the room.

'That's probably work calling,' Lana said. 'They need him to come in but he doesn't want to leave me alone.'

'Oh, I can stay with you... if you don't mind,' Tammy finished hesitantly.

Lana squeezed her arm. 'No, I'd love for you to stay.'

Tristan returned, his brow furrowed.

'Mom offered to stay with me if you need to go to work.'

He gave Lana a hard smile. 'Isn't that nice of Tammy.' He turned to his mother-in-law. 'Thank you, but I don't think we should impose.'

'You wouldn't impose at all. Anyway, I'd love the chance to spend some time with Alannah.'

Lana put her arm around Tammy's shoulders.

Tristan nodded. 'Okay, I know when I'm beat.' He leant down and pulled Lana into a hug, breaking her hold on Tammy. 'Be nice,' he murmured in her ear. He picked up the truck keys from the console by the door and, with one last look of warning at Lana, left.

Lana breathed out a sigh of relief as the door closed behind him. She turned to find Tammy's gaze on her.

'He's quite a handful,' Tammy said.

Lana smiled weakly and headed for the kitchen. 'Did you want something to drink?' she asked.

'Something hot, please.'

Lana leant on the kitchen counter, getting a grip. It had been almost too easy to manipulate Tammy. She opened the kitchen cupboard and placed two mugs on the counter. She could finally understand Tristan's protectiveness. This Tammy was so vulnerable it would be so easy to hurt her. As she pulled out a block of chocolate and a carton of milk, she hoped that her plan would work.

A few minutes later, she walked into the living room, carefully balancing the two mugs on a tray.

Tammy lifted her mug and inhaled. A soft smile lit her face. 'We haven't drunk hot chocolate since before I met Michael.' Her smile faded, a look of pain crossing her face and her eyes taking on a faraway look. She sipped her drink and smiled brightly. 'It's beautiful. Just the way I used to make it, with melted chocolate and hot milk, and sprinkled with shaved chocolate.'

Lana sipped her own hot chocolate. 'How is Michael?'

Tammy looked surprised, making Lana realize that Alannah wouldn't ask. 'He's good. Busy with the re-election campaign.'

What was he being re-elected for? But she remembered herself in time and stopped the question on her tongue from being spoken.

Tammy picked up her handbag from the floor. 'Before I forget.' She handed Lana an envelope.

Lana opened it. 'Wow, tenth wedding anniversary. Congratulations.' She kissed Tammy on the cheek while she backtracked through her memories. Tammy must have met Michael soon after her last rehab attempt, and rather than regressing with Billy, she'd stayed clean for ten years. She felt as if she was disappearing. If Tammy and Billy had never been together, then it had never ... Her thoughts cut off. No, it had happened. It just hadn't happened to Alannah.

Lana bent the corner of the invitation. 'Tristan and I will be there.' She saw Michael's full name, Mayor Michael Stanton, and kept her face from showing surprise. One question answered, nine hundred to go.

'Really?'

'Sure.' Lana put the envelope on the coffee table, avoiding Tammy's gaze.

'Thank you, baby. That means so much to me.'

A shrill ring cut the air. Tammy lifted her handbag and clumsily rummaged through it, pulling out a slender cell phone and placing it to her ear. 'Hello, Michael.' She smiled at Lana and stood, walking away. 'I have to stay until Tristan returns.' She paused. 'It won't be long.' She looked down at the floor. 'Oh, of course. Yes, I'll be home shortly.'

She turned back to Lana. 'I have to go.' She picked up her handbag and put the cell phone back, before placing the strap over her shoulder. 'Michael needs me to meet with the caterer for our anniversary dinner.'

'Why doesn't he go?'

'Oh, his staff meeting ran over. Time doesn't stop at City Hall.' Tammy kissed her on the cheek and left.

After Lana closed the apartment door behind her mother, she rubbed her head. The constant switching between the old world and the new was wearing on her. It has hard to keep her life separate from Alannah's.

She placed the mugs on the tray and carried them into the kitchen. Seeing the pale lipstick on her mother's mug, she realized what had been bothering her about Tammy. She wasn't a pale lipstick and beige outfit kind of a woman. The Tammy she'd known loved color. Lana shrugged. This must be Tammy's version of the suitable wife. She'd always been a chameleon, changing herself for the new man in her life.

She placed the washed mugs on the dish rack and dried her hands, looking around to see what else she could do. The spotless apartment mocked her. She glanced at the state-of-the-art TV and DVD player in the corner of the room with unease. Her life in this world was very different from the triple-decker attic apartment she'd shared with Frank, filled with secondhand furniture they'd sanded and painted themselves. She looked at the chic room she was in and contrasted it with the wood-en-beamed ceiling and polished floorboards of her other life. They'd created a homey retreat with Frank's paintings covering the walls, enveloping them in a world of their own. In this apartment, she felt uncomfortable and edgy. She had nowhere to hide from the nagging questions circling in her head.

Recalling the book she'd been reading, she hurried to the study. She closed the door and leant against it, feeling like she'd escaped a near disaster. The study could be her oasis from the strangeness surrounding her. It was the one place where she felt secure and sure of herself. She walked past the bookshelves and to the desk. In this room there was tangible proof of Tristan's connection to Frank and the reality of her memories.

She glanced through the papers scattered on the surface of Tristan's desk. Hearing a humming sound, she realized that the computer was on. She shook the mouse and the screen saver faded. Tristan had been using an accounting package to enter the invoices for his material purchases. Glancing through the items, she saw that he was processing building supplies. She alt-tabbed on the keyboard and the home screen came up.

Walker and Co Construction. She smiled, her finger tracing the screen. He was his father's son all right. She sat down and leant back in the chair, closing her eyes. She saw Frank bent over the coffee table they'd bought at the flea market, his face intense as he lovingly sanded the dark stain from its natural grain.

Everything was clear now. Somehow this Frank-Tristan had been more influenced by his father, and instead of dedicating himself to his painting, and doing carpentry as a hobby, he had followed in his father's footsteps and started a construction firm. She rubbed at her bottom lip as she recalled Frank's aura of serenity after he'd completed a painting. Was it possible that he could gain the same satisfaction building ... Realizing she didn't know what he built, Lana scrolled through the screens and read the projects he was working on.

'Car parks,' she exclaimed to the empty room. She shifted the papers on the desk, looking down at its scarred surface. 'Just like his father.'

Glancing at the computer screen again, she rolled up her sleeves and began typing.

The study door opened and Lana looked up. Tristan flicked the light switch as he walked in. She flinched as her tired eyes shut against the brightness; while she'd been working the sun had set. When she opened her eyes, Tristan was standing beside her.

'What are you doing?' He lifted the stacked invoices.

'You left the computer on so I finished your accounts.'

He leant over her shoulder and read the screen. She smelt wood, dust and sweat. She shifted on her seat, her face brushing against him. As the silence stretched out and he didn't say anything, her anxiety built.

He took her hand and gently squeezed it, his lips quirking into a gentle smile. 'Thanks.'

She smiled back, a happy glow filling her chest. This is what it was supposed to be like: the two of them in harmony over the day-to-day details of life.

He stretched, rubbing the back of his neck. 'When did Tammy leave?'

Lana turned off the computer. 'Michael needed her to go home and meet the caterer for their anniversary dinner.' She looked up and met his eyes, seeing her thoughts mirrored in his gaze. He didn't like Michael either. She smiled sheepishly. 'I have to confess, I said we'd go to their anniversary dinner.'

'I'm glad.'

Silence descended between them, but for the first time since she'd returned home from the hospital, it was a comfortable one. She felt herself loosening, a feeling of well-being infusing her. It was going to be all right.

'Your father was such a craftsman.' She touched her finger to the nick in the desk. 'He always loved working at this desk. He said it kept him grounded to what was important in life. I guess that's why you work on it.'

She looked up, her stomach dropping to her feet when she saw his face. He was staring at her like she was a freak in a circus.

'How did you know that?'

'You told me,' she whispered.

He moved toward her. She stepped away.

He crowded her against the wall. 'I never told you anything about my father.'

'I– I —' The words froze in her throat.

He was too close, too big, too threatening. This wasn't her Frank. Her Frank would never crowd her, or make her feel unsafe. She wanted to run away but his arms were on either side of her, blocking her in.

'Tell me,' he demanded, his voice tight with impatience.

Her fear snapped like a rubber band stretched too tight. Anger made her bold. 'Your father built that desk when he opened his construction company. He gave it to you when he went bankrupt.'

He looked at her. She wanted to flinch under his intense scrutiny. Instead she stood straighter and met his gaze head on.

'Close.' He dropped his arms. 'I took the desk when his company was liquidated.' He stepped away from her and glanced at it. 'You're right though.' His dark gaze caught hers, the bitterness and anger making her stomach muscles clench in reaction. 'I work on it to remind me what's important.'

He walked out of the study. Hearing the shower start, her legs collapsed and she sat on the chair. What had she done? She looked at the desk as if it was her enemy. What had happened between Tristan and Kevin? It was as if Tristan hated his father.

Yet Frank had idolized his father and been loved in return. How could things have gone so wrong?

She covered her face with shaking hands. She didn't know how much more she could take. With a few thoughtless words, she'd stirred up echoes of the past and broken the fragile peace that had settled between them. Her guard had been down and she spoke as though it was Frank listening, somehow finding the words that would cause the most damage.

Her stomach rumbled, reminding her she hadn't eaten for hours. She stood and walked into the kitchen. Maybe a hot dinner would be the right peace offering between them.

Chapter 4

Lana walked out of the T station and onto Huntington Avenue. As she entered Louis Prang Street and walked past the Museum of Fine Arts, she began to feel anxious. It had seemed like such a good idea to go to work this morning. She'd have time away from Tristan. She'd immerse herself in Alannah's life. And after staring at the walls for the past week, she was more than ready for a change of scenery. Somehow in thinking about all the pros, she hadn't given any thought to the cons, until now.

She didn't know anyone at work – everyone would think she was Alannah and knew how to do the job, when she was a complete novice. It was only now she realized that in her eagerness to avoid conflict, she was about to face humiliation.

After she'd dropped her bombshell on Tristan about Kevin's desk, he'd avoided her by working in the study. She'd spent the rest of the week in bed recovering from the car accident, and when she emerged from the bedroom, she and Tristan tiptoed around each other like polite strangers.

After Tristan left for work this morning she'd received a call from Siobhan asking Alannah to come into work. She'd understood from Siobhan's side of the conversation that they were understaffed, because some people had the flu and a regular staff member had been in a car accident. She'd been about to interject that she was the one who'd had a car accident, but stopped short. Going to work had seemed like a good way to, well, run away, so she'd agreed without thinking through all the consequences. It was only after she'd hung up that she'd realized her first obstacle – she didn't know where Alannah worked.

After a few panic-stricken moments, rational thought had kicked in and she'd used caller ID to call back. Siobhan had answered with 'Isabella Stuart Gardener Museum', and Lana had gently hung up on her. She hoped Siobhan didn't remember the same trick to identify her crank caller.

As she reached the familiar gray brick building, she was wrenched back to her past life and the wonders hidden behind the nondescript walls of the museum. She and Frank had been regular visitors. He had loved walking through the entrance and into what seemed like a fifteenth-century Venetian palace. Frank would offer her his elbow and tell her they were embarking on their grand tour. They would walk through the floors that housed everything from Italian Renaissance masterpieces by Botticelli and Raphael to modern ones from Manet and Matisse.

With his illness, and their lack of finances, the museum had been the closest they came to traveling. After they'd finished their tour, they'd return to the first floor and the café.

Lana shook her head and returned to the present. Her second obstacle had arrived when she realized that she didn't know what Alannah did. She could have been anything from a gift shop assistant, to a museum teacher who led guided tours. She broke out in cold chills as she thought of a community college high school graduate attempting to fake the knowledge of a BA in art education and in-depth knowledge of the museum history and its collection.

Remembering the filing cabinet in Tristan's office she'd crossed her fingers that she and Alannah shared the same sense of organization. She'd flicked through each drawer until she found Alannah's employment contract, and breathed out a sigh of relief when she read she was a waitress in the museum café.

Her eyes narrowed as she thought about the strange coincidence that both she and Alannah worked as waitresses. She smoothed her damp palms on her pants. After a little more clever deducing, she'd found Alannah's employee uniform of black pants, plain black shirt with Alannah's staff access badge clipped on, black shoes and a long black apron in the closet.

She headed to the west wall and the staff entrance. Her heart sped up as adrenaline surged through her body. What was the worst that could happen? She'd get fired. She turned into the alley and saw a man and woman stood next to the entrance. Smoke curled from the cigarettes they held in their hands. The man wore a security guard uniform and Lana's eyes slid past him to the woman. She seemed familiar. Her steps slowed and she examined the woman. She was wearing checkered pants and a white shirt that usually identified a chef. Except chefs usually wore baggy clothing that allowed them freedom and comfort in the kitchen rather than form-fitting clothing that looked poured onto this woman.

As Lana neared, the woman turned and ground the cigarette butt under her heel. Lana was close enough to see that the shirt curved over high, full breasts and her lacy bra pressed up against the fabric. She looked at the security guard and saw his eyes were on the woman's breasts too. When the woman turned back to him, his eyes snapped to her face.

The security guard spotted Lana. Following his gaze, the woman turned, her brown eyes widening in surprise. Lana gulped as the woman pulled her into a hug. She bent slightly to hug her back, inhaling the scent of Calvin Klein's Obsession.

The woman pulled away and Lana examined her face. 'Alannah, what are you doing here?' she asked.

Lana froze, realizing this was the woman in Tristan and Alannah's wedding photos. An image slotted into place of the woman serving her and Frank lunch in the café. They had visited so often they'd struck up a friendship with the café's chef, Holly.

The waist-length platinum blond braid had thrown her, as the Holly Lana knew had dark brown hair.

Lana smiled in relief. 'Holly.' She glanced at the security guard and noticed his name tag. 'Hi, Charlie.'

Charlie nodded at her.

She looked back at Holly, who was looking at the bruise on her forehead in concern. 'Does your head hurt?'

Lana touched the bruise self-consciously. 'No, it's much better.' She tightened her grip on her handbag. 'I came in to work.'

Holly looked at Charlie in confusion. 'Work. Are you sure you're okay, baby doll?' She brushed Lana's hair away from her face. 'You were in a car accident. You're not supposed to be at work for a month.'

Lana looked at her uncertainly. 'But Siobhan called. She said you were desperately understaffed.'

'That airhead. I swear I'm going to fire her.' Holly put her hands on her hips and blew out her cheeks. 'I told her to contact relief staff and instead she calls you.' Holly started walking her toward the road, her arm firmly around Lana's shoulders. 'You just go on back home and rest.'

Lana stopped. 'I'm fine. I was going stir crazy at home. If you need help, I'd really love to be busy.'

Holly narrowed her gaze. 'You're really and truly all right?'

'Absolutely fine.' Lana smiled.

'Because I'm really in a jam. There's only Siobhan and Shirley serving. Shirley's doing her best but it's too much for one able-bodied person to handle.'

'Where do I start?'

Holly still hesitated, before squeezing Lana's arm. 'You tell me if you get tired and have to leave early, okay?'

Lana nodded and they turned back down the alley. Charlie had returned to his post, leaving behind a smoldering cigarette butt.

As soon as they entered the café, Holly stared at a waitress in the far corner. When the waitress looked up, Holly gestured at her to follow, then led Lana through the curtained doorway. Lana looked at the tiny kitchen in wonder. It was narrow and functional. In her other life, Dave's Steakhouse was a local no-frills steak joint, but the kitchen had been three times bigger. Lana's job had been to cook and serve. Her nervousness abated as she watched a waitress pass by with two plates of quiche.

'Hi Shirley,' she guessed. Shirley smiled at her before disappearing behind the curtain.

The food in the café was pre-prepared and just had to be warmed up before serving. She could do this. The curtain parted and the waitress Holly had gestured to appeared.

'Siobhan, remember how I told you to find someone to come in?' Holly spoke slowly.

Siobhan nodded wordlessly, her blue eyes wide and intent on Holly's face. She reminded Lana of a puppy.

'Remember I told you to call staff on the current roster.' Holly looked at Lana.

Siobhan followed Holly's gaze, her face blank. She picked up the roster. 'But I did.'

Holly plucked it from her hands. 'That's last month's roster.' She lifted a white folder and flipped the pages. 'This is the current roster.'

'Oh,' Siobhan murmured. Tears pooled in her eyes and her lip trembled.

Holly's panicked gaze met Lana's. Lana shrugged helplessly, her lips quirking slightly. Holly narrowed her gaze at her warningly and Lana bit her lip, fighting the smile that was threatening.

'It's okay, Siobhan.' Holly patted her on the shoulder, rolling her eyes at Lana. 'I probably didn't make myself clear.'

After Siobhan left, Holly closed the folder. Lana glanced down and saw 'current rosters' written on the spine. She looked at Holly and giggled helplessly.

Holly saw the spine too and laughed. 'Thankfully her eagerness more than makes up for her flakiness.'

As Holly passed out orders, the petite vixen Lana had observed in the alley disappeared. In her place was a straight-backed commander overseeing her troops with a vigilant eye. Lana frowned. This was a very different Holly to the one she remembered, who was sweet and diffident. She wondered what other changes had occurred in Holly's life.

Shirley entered the kitchen. 'Table nine is ready to order.'

Lana nodded and waded in, carefully mimicking Shirley as she left her orders in the kitchen. The café was small and even with the patio windows open and the outside seating, it could only accommodate under sixty patrons at any one time. Thankfully she remembered being a customer and was aware there was no reservation system; patrons were given a pager and were able to look around the museum until their table was ready.

By her second table, she'd memorized the specials and the hours passed by in a blur. There were only a few patrons left when she returned to the kitchen after clearing a table.

Holly looked up as she placed the dishes on the sink. 'Geez, you're getting really good at the stack and rack.'

Lana looked at Holly blankly as she scraped the leftover food into the bin and put the plates in the dishwasher.

'For someone who's been here only three months, you're my best employee.'

Lana stopped. 'Three months?' She hadn't thought to look at the date on the employment contract this morning.

'Yeah.' Holly smiled wickedly. 'Do you remember when your step daddy came in here after you started?' Holly wiped her hands on a tea towel. 'I thought his head would burst when he saw you carrying the dirty plates. The snob tried to get me to'release' you so you'd go to work somewhere more appropriate.'

Holly hung the tea towel on the hook by the sink. 'No wonder you didn't want to work in his office. Being in his company for ten minutes left me on edge. A whole day would be torture.'

Lana looked down to hide her face as she digested Holly's words. Michael had wanted Alannah to work for him?

Holly's hand on her shoulder interrupted her musings. 'So you ready?'

'Sure.' Lana wiped her hands and followed Holly through the employee entrance.

Once they were outside, Holly pulled a pack of cigarettes from her apron pocket. Tapping the bottom of the packet, she offered the protruding cigarette to Lana.

Great, Alannah smoked. Well, she'd be quitting pretty soon. Lana took the cigarette and bent over as Holly held out a light. After a quick puff, she took the cigarette from her mouth and held it between her fingers.

Holly closed her eyes and inhaled, lifting her head to the sun. 'Tired?'

Lana shrugged. 'I'm okay.' She realized she wasn't feeling too badly. The busy day had given her the chance to have time away from all the stress of leading a double life.

'Well, you were a lifesaver today.'

Lana smiled. Silence stretched out between them. She went over her memories of the the other Holly. She knew she was married and squinted as she tried to recall his name. Alex? Andrew?

'How is Aidan?' She watched as Holly's smile faded. Oh God, did she get it wrong?

Holly took a quick drag. 'Aidan is... well the usual. Inscrutable, unemotional, untouchable. I'd think he was a corpse except I can see him breathing.' She laughed. Instead of the sparkling laugh that turned heads, it was forced and bitter.

Lana looked at Holly out of the corner of her eye. The couple she'd known had been loving and devoted to each other.

Holly looked up. 'What about you and Tristan? Have things eased up?'

Lana felt a chill on her skin. Did Holly think she and Tristan had difficulties in their marriage? 'Oh, everything is great. He's been a dream while I was sick.'

Holly looked at her, skepticism in her eyes. 'I'm glad to hear it.' She smiled. 'Well, onto something more interesting. Let me tell you about my night. Remember I told you about the dancer I met the other night at my new night job? So we went out to dinner and I brought him over to my place.'

As Holly continued her story, Lana raced over the past. In her other life, Holly and Aidan had an eight-year-old son. Joshua. Lana's eyebrows rose as Holly's story continued. It seemed she was a single gal with a very healthy sex life.

'What about Josh?' Lana asked when Holly finished talking about her date.

'He's gorgeous.' Holly spoke in the loving tones of a mother enamored with her child. 'He spent the weekend with his father and they went fishing. When he came back he wanted to tell me in excruciating detail how to hook a worm.'

Lana burst into laughter at Holly's disgusted face. That and relief as she realized there was a pattern to this world. Everyone she knew was the same person, essentially – it was just that they'd gone down a slightly different path.

Holly glanced over her shoulder. She leant forward and tore the cigarette from Lana's fingers, quickly lifting it to her mouth.

Lana turned. Tristan was walking toward her and by the look on his face, he was not having a good day. She gulped as he neared.

Holly walked around Lana and stepped in his way. 'Hello, handsome.'

Tristan kept his gaze on Lana, before looking down at Holly's petite head.

A smile of mischief lit up his face and transformed him into the man Lana had once known. 'How are you, rabble rouser?' He bent and kissed Holly on the cheek.

'Can't complain.'

Tristan looked at the cigarette dangling in her hand. 'I thought you were going to quit.'

Holly looked at her hand ruefully. 'Yeah, so did I.'

He looked at Lana, his face settling into harsh lines. 'Thanks for the note.'

Her trepidation faded. 'I should thank you– I borrowed the wording from your note.'

His eye twitched as her comment hit home. She heard Holly's muffled snort of laughter, before she stepped in, turning Lana to the entrance. 'Why don't we get your handbag so you can go home?'

Lana felt Tristan's gaze burning her as she walked away. When the door closed behind them, Holly squeezed her shoulders and looked at her in wonder.

'Aren't you full of surprises? One day you can't say boo, and now you're a little firecracker.'

After collecting her things Lana stood in front of the door, trying to work up the courage to step outside. She didn't know what had come over her in answering back to Tristan. But then, his tone had been like that of a father reprimanding his child and her words had just escaped.

Taking a deep breath, she pushed open the door. Tristan wasn't alone; three pairs of eyes turned to her. Beside Tristan was a short man with brown hair cut in a severe style and whose moss-green eyes revealed he didn't laugh much, and a boy. He was a miniature version of the man, with the same thick eyebrows, heavy-lashed eyes, sculpted face and full lips. Their squared chins with a faint cleft saved them from prettiness. The only difference was the boy's wide brown eyes, which he'd inherited from his mother.

'Hi Aidan, Joshua.'

She approached them and ruffled Joshua's hair. She met Tristan's eyes and saw suspicion in them. She shook her head wryly and bent down to Joshua's eye level. 'You are the spitting image of your daddy-O. Except for your eyes.' She touched her finger to Joshua's nose and stood, raising her eyebrow in challenge at Tristan.

The door banged open behind them and Holly appeared. Gone was the chef's uniform, replaced by a short denim skirt revealing her muscled legs and a white spaghetti strap top that showed her cleavage. Her hair was flowing down her back.

She smiled when she saw Joshua. 'I'm guessing you forgot this.' She took a Nintendo DS from her handbag.

Joshua took it from her quickly and pulled her into a hug. Holly wrapped her arms around him and kissed the top of his head.

'Mom, do you want to get ice-cream with me and Dad?' Josh leant back to look at her.

Holly's gaze found Aidan and her smile dimmed. 'Sorry, baby. I've got to go to work.' She withdrew from Joshua's embrace.

Aidan pulled Joshua to his side. 'So where are you working now?'

Holly rifled through her handbag. 'At the Red Rose on Franklin. It's a cocktail bar.' She pulled out her keys and posed like a game show hostess. 'I'm the hostess.'

'Congratulations,' Aidan said. 'You're quite the busy bee.'

Holly gave him a hard smile before pointedly looking at Joshua. 'How about we go for ice-cream on the weekend, tiger?'

Joshua smiled, a faint dimple appearing in his left cheek.

'Bye, guys.' Holly stalked off, her four-inch platforms clattering on the asphalt.

Lana looked at Aidan and saw he was watching Holly with what looked like regret. He quickly made his face blank and looked at Joshua. 'Well, let's get that ice-cream.'

'I'll see you at work,' Tristan said to Aidan.

Her brain kicked into gear and she realized Tristan and Aidan worked together.

She watched Aidan and Joshua walk away, their shoulders moving in the same rhythm as Joshua mimicked his father's walk, and remembered the Meagher family from her other life.

She and Frank had been taking a boat ride on the swan boats at the Boston Public Garden when she saw their boat docking at the ferry. She'd been fascinated by them; Aidan had been affectionate and playful with Joshua. While Holly watched Aidan, her face lit up. They had been a loving unit and Joshua had been the sun in their universe. But now there was a painful distance between all of them.

'What happened between them?' She didn't realize she'd spoken aloud until Tristan answered.

'Life.'

Chapter 5

She followed him to the car park and got into the truck without a word. As she watched the passing scenery, Tristan's reply kept circling in her head.

She knew that Tristan and Alannah were different to Lana and Frank. She looked at the shiny interior of the truck and remembered the worn Buick she'd driven. But still, of all the people in this universe, Alannah and Tristan had found each other. That meant it was possible that the love Lana and Frank had shared still existed. She pictured Holly and Aidan as she'd seen them today: standing apart, not touching, carefully avoiding each other's eyes. Their love hadn't survived this time.

She'd been hoping that going to work would provide a distraction; instead it had brought her even more awareness. It was time for a change of topic to stop her swirling thoughts.

'So how was your day?' she asked with forced cheerfulness.

Tristan looked at her quickly before turning back to the road. 'It was pretty good.' He flicked on the indicator and made a left turn. 'Until I came home and found you missing.'

'I had a good day too.' She ignored the sarcastic tone in his voice.

'I'm glad.' He turned into their basement garage. Dark enveloped them as they drove down. 'Because you're taking the rest of the week off.' He parked the truck.

'But I'm feeling fine.' She undid her seatbelt. 'It was great to be busy.'

'That was not a request.'

She watched as he jumped out of the truck and came to her side. He opened the door and helped her out. As he held her hand, she felt the rigid tension as he controlled his anger.

She started walking to the elevator only to realize he wasn't following. She turned to see him pulling grocery bags from the back of the truck. She returned to his side and tried to take a bag but he shifted away, leaving her empty handed. She gritted her teeth and refused to be goaded. If he thought she was so fragile then he could do the macho thing and break his back. At the elevator, she smirked as he shifted the bags against his chest and tried to press the button. She waited for him to ask her to help.

Instead he leant forward, holding the bags up between his chest and the wall, and reached for the button with his free hand. As he entered the elevator she was positive she saw a smile. In their apartment, she followed him into the kitchen, only to be racked with guilt as she saw the sacks scattered on the floor. Tristan must have brought a load up when he came home from work, realized she wasn't home and gone looking for her.

One of the sacks sat in a pool of melted sludge. He picked it up and put it on the sink. Gingerly inserting his hand in the bag, he pulled out a carton of ice-cream. He put it in the bin.

'I'm sorry.' She picked up a bag and started lining up the items on the countertop. 'I didn't mean to worry you.'

'I wasn't worried.' He pulled out TV dinners and put them in the fridge. 'I was pissed.' He closed the fridge door. 'If someone's sick, then they should be home.'

'Well, if someone is sick, then they should have someone to take care of them.' She picked up another sack. 'So I guess I'm not sick.'

She saw she'd scored a hit when he turned away without a word. As they sorted through the rest of the groceries the only sound was the crumpling of paper bags.

Her stomach rumbled as she finished the last bag. She opened the cupboard, looking for ingredients to cook, and instead found spreads and junk food. In the fridge were TV dinners. Tristan reached past her and pulled out the steak and mashed potato dinner. In the past week, Tristan had been making himself a full breakfast and leaving her a plate to eat after he left for work, but they'd been eating take away for dinner.

'Aren't we going to cook?' she asked.

Tristan looked at her and lifted an eyebrow. 'What, you're going to cook?' He turned back to the microwave and pressed the start button, his shoulders shaking as he laughed.

She took a deep breath and fought to keep her voice even. 'I can cook.'

'Of course.' His smile said the opposite.

'Maybe I just never wasted my time cooking for a Neanderthal.'

His eyes narrowed. 'Or maybe the princess can't bear to dirty her hands.'

Her maelstrom of emotions sparked into anger. The only thought in her head was to make him eat his words, literally. She stalked through the living room, picking up the truck keys as she passed. She had the front door open before he cut her off by pushing it closed in her face.

'Where are you going?' His voice was tight with restrained emotion.

She saw the muscles in his forearm clenching. Instead of feeling afraid of the controlled violence he was exhibiting, she was exhilarated. At least he was treating her like an equal, even if he was rabid with anger while doing it.

She slapped at the hand holding the door closed. 'I'm going to get some real food and then I'm going to cook it.' When he didn't budge, she looked at him. She'd managed to wipe the indulgent smile off his face.

'I don't think so.' Tristan took hold of her shoulders and tried to shift her from the door.

She tore herself away and pushed her face into his. 'I do.'

He took the keys from her. 'Come on. Let's cool it ...'

She took the keys back and put them in her handbag. 'You cool it. I'm going shopping.'

She was in front of the elevator before he caught up to her. He looked at her and gently placed his hand on her arm.

'Get your hands off me.' She looked at his hand on her arm, her eyes sharp as glass. Her chest was heaving as she fought for control.

'Look maybe we got off on the wrong —'

'Get your hands off me.'

He let her go slowly and put his hand through his hair. A look of confusion passed over his face. 'We've got groceries. We don't need to go shopping again.'

'That's right, we don't need to do anything.'

'I can't let you go by yourself.'

'Why the hell not?'

'Come on, Alannah, be reasonable.'

'I don't need you to baby me. I'm a grown woman and I don't need a daddy.'

He grabbed hold of her and she stared at him with challenge in her eyes. He let go and held out his hand. 'I'll drive.'

'I don't need you to —'

'Either I drive or you don't go.' He flipped open her handbag and took the keys. 'Lock the door behind you.' He walked into the elevator.

'Wait a minute, Tristan —' Her words were drowned out by the closing elevator door.

·♥·♥·♥·♥·♥·

Tristan stared at the floor numbers, trying to get a handle on his anger. That was close. If he lost it, he knew he'd never be able to stop. He rubbed his hand over his face. What was going on? In the past if he accidentally raised his voice, her eyes had filled with fear and he'd quickly learnt to restrain himself in order not to scare her. Yet now she was in his face, and not shy about her anger.

She had her head bent over a notepad, writing. At a traffic light he leant over and saw it was a shopping list. In the two years they'd been married they'd never written a shopping list. In fact, she'd never even noticed if there was food in the house or not. He'd had to take over grocery shopping out of sheer survival. What the hell was she trying to prove? What was he doing driving for the second time to the shopping mall? He should have just given her the keys and let her go on her own.

She was sick of him acting like her daddy, well, he was sick of being a daddy. He'd love nothing better than to stop treating her like she was made of cotton wool, but she was the one who'd set out the rules long ago. At first he'd tried talking to her in an attempt to understand what was wrong. After her continuous silences and blank expression, he'd given up and they'd settled into the routine of invalid and care giver. If she wanted to the change the rules, fine.

He swung the wheel, hard. Alannah crashed into his side before straightening up quickly and leaning harder into the door. He could see her looking at him from the corner of her eye. It was childish to take pleasure from pettiness, but he figured he was due some satisfaction.

Inside the supermarket, Tristan pushed the shopping trolley, his gaze following Alannah down the aisle. She walked back to the trolley and tossed some items into it without looking at him. His knuckles tightened on the handle and he ground his teeth as she turned the corner into another aisle without checking if he was following.

Her hips swayed as she walked. She reached for an item on the shelf, and he noticed her full breasts and slightly curved stomach. When had that happened? She'd been eating more than usual, but it was only now that he saw her previously dainty curves were developing into voluptuousness. He should be happy she'd put on weight, but he felt uneasy and edgy as hell. Everything seemed slightly off. She was eating when previously she would nibble. She was reading literature where before the heaviest thing she would read was *Us Weekly*. And instead of looking at him with fear and caution, he saw curiosity and hurt.

Remembering when she'd talked about his father, he frowned; she'd spoken as if she knew him. He'd been so disturbed by the memories she'd managed to stir up, he'd retreated, yet now a red flag of warning was raised. But he couldn't push for answers now. Jeremy had warned him to treat her with kid gloves.

She turned to him, opening her mouth as if to ask for something before glancing at him and snapping it shut. He couldn't keep up. Every day it was a different mood, a different personality. Today she was a haughty princess and tomorrow she could be a little girl needing care and attention again.

She stood in the middle of the aisle, her head bent as she perused the shopping list. Suddenly the TV dinners she'd tortured with a fork weren't good enough and La Princessa was going to cook. Yeah, he'd like to see that. One day she can't boil an egg and the next she was looking at the food he'd bought like it was trash.

She reached for a sack of flour, tottering awkwardly on her tippy toes. Without thinking about it, he left the trolley and grabbed the flour. Standing behind her, he breathed in her vanilla scent. Her curved backside pressed up against him. As he lifted down the packet, his arm brushed the side of her breast. He froze.

She looked up at him, her gaze clear and focused. For a minute he saw the woman he'd wanted to marry. The woman who'd had purpose and resolve in her eyes.

Desire twisted in his gut. He leant down, his lips a hair's breadth away from hers when he came back to his senses. He thrust the flour in her hands and walked back to the trolley. He wasn't falling for her tricks again – one step forward, two steps back.

When they returned to the apartment, Tristan pushed open the door with hands loaded with paper sacks. He turned and waited for Alannah. She'd bought so many groceries he'd had no choice but to let her carry a few bags, but he'd still made sure they were the lightest ones. He dropped his burden on the kitchen table and turned to help her. She shifted away.

'That's fine. I can handle it from here.' Her eyes were defiant.

He bit back the words climbing in his throat; it wasn't worth it. He went to his study and lost himself in work. That was one thing that would always be constant. No mood changes there.

His stomach growled and he sniffed as the scent of cooking teased his senses. Checking his watch, he saw it was two hours since he'd come to the study. He walked into the kitchen and sniffed again, his gaze disbelieving.

Alannah was bent over the oven. The table was set with their good china, two lit candles and an open bottle of wine. There was a pie on the counter. He bent and inhaled. He'd never forget the scent of his childhood favorite, lemon and lime pie.

Alannah removed a dish from the oven. Garlic bread. She bent again and golden-topped lasagna appeared. The scents took him back to his childhood. His mother had cooked his favorite meal at least once a month. It was supposed to be a family meal, but his father was always absent.

He was about tell her that her blatant attempt to manipulate him wouldn't work when she bumped into him and jumped, nearly dropping the lasagna. He steadied her arm, his gaze on the dish's golden topping as his mouth watered. Maybe he'd talk to her after dinner.

'Here, let me take it.' He loosened her hold on the tea towel and placed the dish on the table.

He ate with single-minded determination, almost inhaling the food. He felt her at his side, placing more lasagna on the plate, serving him salad or garlic bread, but he only lifted his head to drink his wine. When he was finished, his stomach was stretched to its limits. He looked at the leftover lasagna square. He shouldn't, really. He took it anyway. This was a once-in-a-lifetime feast. Feeling her gaze on him, he looked up.

She sipped her red wine, a smile on her face. 'So who can't cook, Mr Walker?'

Seeing her amused gaze, he realized she was teasing. 'Touché, Mrs Walker.' He lifted his own glass. 'To a phenomenal cook.'

She nodded her head in acknowledgement. His urgency faded and he started savoring the food. A comfortable silence descended between them as Alannah served him a piece of lemon and lime pie.

She watched him eat. 'Maybe I should just serve you the whole pie.' She looked at the empty lasagna dish as she laughed.

His good mood faded, tainted with bitterness. This was what he'd always wanted, a marriage that was a partnership. This was what his parents had, before his operation and the trouble after it. Eating together had been about sharing their day, exchanging stories, enjoying each other. His hand tightened on the wine glass. Instead his marriage had turned out to be an endurance test.

'Tristan, what's wrong?'

He looked at her concerned face, his disappointment too overwhelming to hide. 'What are you up to now, Alannah?' He poured himself another glass. 'What's the new game?' Her smile faded and he could see the bewildered hurt in her face. 'Come on, spare me the waterworks.' He put the glass down and the wine sloshed onto the tablecloth.

'What is wrong with you?' She stood. 'Why is everything about some game I'm playing?'

'Because it is, wifey dearest, I just can't figure out this one. To even go so far as to transform yourself into Susie Homemaker.'

He wagged his finger at her. 'This really must be a doozy.' When he stood he realized, he was drunk.

In one part of his mind he knew he should back off right now. This couldn't end well. But in another, the devil prompted his loosened tongue to say all the things he'd held back. She was looking at him with teary eyes wide with shock and hurt. His mouth formed into a twisted smile of bitterness. There it was — the face that would suck Genghis Khan into tenderness.

'How can you be so cold to someone you love?'

He bent as he poured himself more wine. 'I never loved you. Your little girl lost act played me for a fool.'

He heard her gasp and then she stumbled out of the kitchen. He closed his eyes, his fist tightening on the neck of the bottle. He carefully put it back on the table and punched the wall. 'Shit.' He rubbed his hand over his face. 'What have I done?'

·❤·❤·❤·❤·❤·

Lana closed the bedroom door behind her and twisted the lock. Her chest heaved as she fought to control the pain ripping into her. Why was he hurting her like this? Her legs gave out and she crumpled against the door. She held her jumper against her face, muffling her sobs.

With a last gasping breath she tilted her head back. She'd thought dinner would give them a chance to get closer, and it had seemed to be doing the trick. Tristan had relaxed, losing the guarded expression he usually wore. She'd felt contentment spread through her as she watched the sheer pleasure on his face as he ate. Finally it seemed she'd got something right.

Then abruptly he'd changed. Why was he so hateful to her? It was as if she was an enemy he had to keep at arm's length. If he let down his guard then he had to fortify his defenses by pushing her away.

She heard his footsteps in the hallway and stilled, pulling her knees tighter against her chest.

'Alannah.' He twisted the locked doorknob. 'Alannah, sweetheart, please let me in.'

She bit her fist as she held in her sobs. She didn't want him to hear her crying.

'Alannah, I'm sorry. Please let me in so I can explain.'

'Go away.' Her voice was high pitched, breaking on the last word. 'I don't want to hear what you have to say.'

She waited. His footsteps retreated. She stood and dug through the Alannah's underwear drawer, searching for a handkerchief. She wiped her face and was about to close the drawer when she saw a string. Reaching in, she gently tapped the bottom of the drawer. It gave a hollow thump. She pulled out the drawer and tipped Alannah's underwear on the bed.

Sitting on the floor, she lifted the string and removed the false bottom. She flipped open the first page and smiled as she traced the writing.*Do not read. This is property of Lana Madden. You have been warned.*

She read the date of the first entry– her fifteenth birthday. Tammy had been in rehab and gotten special permission to visit. Lana had been living with the Peterson family. They were professional foster parents and as long as the kids kept their heads down and didn't cause trouble, the Petersons were happy to provide room and board funded by the government.

Tammy had shown up, gaunt and wan but with fierce determination in her eyes. When Lana had unwrapped the journal, Tammy had pulled out a similar red and white notebook from her purse. She'd said that while they didn't have each other to talk to, they could use their journals to express themselves. Lana had kept up sporadic entries while she was a teen, but had left the journal behind when she ran away for the last time

She flipped to the last entry, expecting to read an entry about teenage angst. Her smile faded as she realized what she was reading.

Monday, March 21

Tristan asked me for a divorce. I pushed him away too many times and he got tired of waiting.

Oh God, I have made so many mistakes. It's only now that I've lost him that I realize how much I love him.

What have I done? Please God, don't let this be the end. I have to ask him for a second chance. I'm going to see him and tell him the truth. I can only hope he will forgive me when he knows.

Lana dropped the journal, wiping her hands on her leg as if that would erase the words she had just read. She reeled as the word divorce reverberated in her mind like a flashing neon sign.

She glanced at the date again, coldness descending over her. March 21: the day of Frank's funeral and her death, and the day of Alannah's accident. It all slotted into place; Tristan's withdrawn silence, his belief she was faking, the one-step-forward, two-steps-back dance.

He thought she was trying to hold up the divorce by pretending not to remember.

She laughed, the sound catching in her throat and becoming a moan of pain. She was such a fool. There was no love that spanned two worlds. It was all in her imagination.

There was a thumping noise as Tristan broke the lock on the bedroom door.

'Alannah, what's wrong? Are you all right?' He came to kneel in front of her.

Her mouth twisted into a bitter smile at the concern in his eyes— concern that he'd have to wait longer for his escape. She picked up the journal and flipped to the last entry.

He looked searchingly at her before reading. His lips tightened as he closed the journal. 'I didn't want you to find out like this.' He met her gaze.

'How did you want me to find out? Or were you just going to keep up the emotional abuse until I packed my bags?'

He flinched, reaching for her hands. 'I'm so sorry about dinner. I don't know what —'

She put her finger on his lip. 'I do.' She pulled her hand out of his and stood. 'You're off the hook.'

She felt every twinge and ache in her body, feeling much older than twenty-five. She forced herself to rally and straightened up, nodding toward the closet. 'Feel free to pack.' She chuckled, wiping a tear. 'Or maybe I should be doing the packing.' She sat on the bed limply, all her bravado deserting her.

Tristan sat beside her, careful not to touch her. 'No one is packing.'

She stared at the wall, feeling the tears drip down her face. 'Why?'

She heard his shuddering breath as he inhaled. 'We're just too different. We haven't been happy for a while now.'

She turned to look at him. 'Why?' she repeated, her voice hard and unflinching.

He looked at her. 'I'm tired, Alannah. I'm tired of feeling like an abuser with my own wife. I can't touch you, I can't make love to you – I can't love you ...'

She finished the sentence to herself. *I can't love you, any more.* She closed her eyes, clenching her fist against her stomach as she held in the pain. She turned away.

'I won't leave until you've recovered.' He put his hand on her shoulder.

She knew he was waiting for her to say something. 'It's probably best if you sleep in the study.'

He removed his hand and left.

She fell into the bed, pulling the pillow to her face to muffle her sobs. God help her; even with what she knew, she still felt relief that he wouldn't be leaving her immediately.

Chapter 6

After taking a drive to clear his head, Tristan returned to the apartment. It was dark. He put the truck keys on the console and turned on the kitchen light. The remnants of dinner were still on the table. He walked through the living room and into the hallway where the two bedrooms were. It was quiet. Too quiet.

Fear hit him. What if she'd done something stupid? He pushed open the bedroom door and rushed in. Alannah was sitting up in bed with the lamp on. He breathed out a sigh of relief when he saw her chest moving, her open journal resting there.

He approached and removed it, placing it on the bedside table before lifting the covers over her.

Her cheeks were flushed and she hiccuped as she turned on her side. He sat on the bed and watched her as she slept, stretching out his hand to caress her head. She was getting to him. After all his promises that he'd learnt his lesson and wouldn't let her manipulate him again, he still fell for her like the dumb jock he was.

He looked away from her as he remembered the day he'd asked for a divorce. He'd been standing in front of the open fridge, a pounding headache splitting his head after a night out

with Aidan, thinking guiltily about what he'd done. He remembered a woman in the cab of the truck with him, his hands under
her shirt, her hand down his pants. The light from the lamp in
the car park glinting on his wedding ring had brought him to
awareness.

Alannah had walked into the kitchen, interrupting his
thoughts. He'd slammed the fridge shut and looked at her, his
self-loathing congealing into rage at her. He'd tugged the wedding ring off his finger and told her he was moving in with Aidan
until the divorce was finalized. Sweeping away her objections,
he'd showered and gone to work. An hour later he received a
call – Alannah was in the emergency ward after a car accident.

His gaze caught on the journal. He lifted the small notebook.
He'd always known about it. After their wedding, Alannah had
gone on a spending spree and the bedroom furniture had been
one of her first buys. He'd been putting away laundry soon after
they married when he noticed the string. He'd pulled it, found
the hidden compartment and seen the journal.

At first he'd thought that someone at the furniture store had
forgotten their keepsake. After opening the first page he'd seen
it was Alannah's and had returned it to the drawer, unread. If
there was anything Alannah wanted him to know, she'd tell him.
He'd forgotten about it until tonight.

He frowned as he remembered the entry Alannah had thrust
at him. What was it she was going to tell him? He rifled through
the pages, smiling as her sentences in large, clear penmanship
jumped out at him. 'I love Evan Stanford.' 'I hate Evan Stanford.'
In the entries at the end of the diary the penmanship had
become more messy. The lettering smaller and less clear.

He glanced at Alannah. She was still sleeping. He flipped the
entries over to when he and Alannah had married, his hands
clenching as he read.

· ❤ · ❤ · ❤ · ❤ · ❤ ·

Lana stirred in bed and felt something pressing into her hip. Turning, she saw Tristan was sitting next to her. He lifted his gaze from the journal and looked at her. Her heart raced at the bloodlust in his eyes.

'Who was it?'

The question was anticlimactic in its matter of factness. She was trying to decide whether to play the amnesia card or not. He must have seen the indecision in her eyes because he snapped. The veneer of calmness disappeared in a second.

He dropped the journal and grabbed her hands. 'Who is it?'

'I don't know,' she screamed as she tried to free herself. 'I don't remember.'

He let her go. She scrambled away from him and crouched against the bedhead, watching him as he stood and paced. 'That's right, because you're suffering from amnesia.'

She flinched at the sarcasm in his voice.

He bent and picked up the journal. 'You know what I find fascinating.' He tapped his finger on the cover. 'For a person who supposedly remembers nothing, you didn't seem to have any trouble remembering where you hid your journal.'

She went from cowering fear to blazing rage in a heartbeat. 'You absolute bastard. You know, you're absolutely right.' She arranged her pillow comfortably behind her back. 'I was faking all along.' She looked down, her voice breaking. 'I just wanted you to stay with me.'

She lifted her hand to her face. 'Because– because.' She paused and took a shuddering breath before flicking her hair behind her ears. 'Because you are such a prince among men that I can't live without you.' Her mocking gaze met his and she lifted her eyebrow. 'I always get turned on when I'm called a liar.'

His hands tightened on the journal and for a minute she feared she'd gone too far. He moved toward her and sat on the bed while she fought not to flinch away.

'You're right.'

She blinked.

'I'm sorry.'

She followed his gaze to the journal. Lana rubbed at the goose pimples on her arms as flashes of what she'd read stabbed at her: tearing clothes, bruised flesh, Alannah's confusion and pain at what happened to her. Feeling his gaze on her she looked up. With anger not blinding her, she saw his guilt.

She cupped his face. 'It's not your fault. She just never could find the words to tell you that she was raped.' She looked down at their joined hands. 'You can't save someone if they don't want to be saved.'

He let go of her hand and stood, stepping away from the bed. 'I would have been there for you, if you'd let me.'

'Then be here for me now,' she whispered to his retreating back. She'd given up hope that her words would reach him, when he turned and sat on the other side of the bed. After taking off his shoes he leant against the bedhead.

She lay down. Taking his hand in hers, she closed her eyes. The writing in the journal appeared behind her closed eyelids. She snapped her eyes open and peeked at Tristan.

He was staring at the wall. If he felt her gaze on him, he gave no indication. She looked down at the flowers on the bedspread, trying not to think, not to remember.

·♥·♥·♥·♥·♥·

Lana watched the window displays as she walked down Newbury Street. She was hunched in Alannah's coat, her hands jammed in the pockets. She avoided meeting the eyes of anyone on the street. At one time, she would have known the shopkeepers by name; her walk would have been filled with cheery hellos and detours to view new merchandise. Now she was just an aimless stranger.

She'd woken this morning alone, feeling chilled. She'd found Tristan's note in the kitchen, propped against the toaster – he'd called work for her and told them she was sick. There'd also been an emergency at his work and he'd be back as soon as he could.

She'd crumpled the note in her hand, knowing the 'emergency' would stretch out all day. She'd tried forcing breakfast down, but stopped when it started rising back up. After calling Tammy, only to be brushed off, the walls had started closing in on her. Before she'd known it, she'd flung on a coat and escaped the apartment.

She looked across the street at the dress store. She'd hoped that Vanessa would be here. Now even that hope was torn from her. In her other life the store was called Vanessa's, but here it was still *Le Chez Boutique*. She remembered the day Vanessa had taken over the store after working as manager for five years. Her brown eyes had sparkled as she moved with hopeful energy preparing for the opening.

Lana and Vanessa had met in Le Chez. Lana had just turned eighteen and was on her own for the first time after leaving her foster family. Her first day on the job, she'd been paired with Vanessa. They were the same age, but as different as night and day. Vanessa had exuded confidence and class. The tailored clothes from the boutique had flattered her lithe body as if made for her. The subdued colors set off her dark hair and eyes, making her even more intimidating.

Lana had felt like a fraud. Every time she approached a client and tried to flatter them into buying an outfit, she came across as forced, unnatural. She tried adopting Vanessa's crisp accent, but instead her tongue felt thick and clumsy.

Their friendship shouldn't have worked, yet somehow they recognized the bond they had in common. Neither had a family to call their own, so they adopted each other. They became the mother, sister, friend, confidante, the other had never had.

Lana quit Le Chez after a week, realizing from the manager's hard gaze that it wasn't long before she would be fired, and found a job in Dave's Steakhouse. She and Vanessa moved in together. Two years later, when Lana met Frank, he'd become another member of their family, and his parents extended members of their small tribe.

A car horn jerked her back to the present. She was halfway across the street. Another car swerved around her, the driver gesticulating as he passed. She was disoriented and panicked as she realized she'd lost her bearings and stepped out into the street. She was trapped in a sea of cars with no way out. She heard the rumbling and looked up. A bus was bearing down on her. She felt the butterfly brooch clutched in her hand and heard Vanessa's warning screaming in her ear.

She froze, unable to move. An arm went around her, urging her across the street. She turned her head and met big, brown eyes looking at her in concern.

'Just a little bit more. That's it, walk with me.' Vanessa's voice calmed her.

When Lana stepped up onto the walkway she felt the eyes of the crowd on her. She heard a woman's voice: 'She just stepped off the curb without looking. Another one with a death wish.'

Lana looked away in embarrassment. She saw Vanessa from the corner of her eye. She was glaring at the woman, who looked at Vanessa warily.

'We'd best be moving on,' Vanessa said.

Lana smiled slightly. Vanessa led her to a café and sat her down. At first, Lana was too emotionally charged to look around. When she looked up, her eyes widened in wonder; it was the café she and Vanessa had adopted as their hangout.

Vanessa disappeared, then returned and placed two mugs on the table. 'Drink it. You've just had a nasty shock.'

As she drank, Lana could imagine that this was the Vanessa of old, her best friend who loved her without reservations.

'So.' Vanessa put her mug down. 'What's new with you, Alannah? Apart from the attempted suicide.'

Lana choked on her coffee, the hot liquid jamming in her throat as she looked at Vanessa in bewilderment. Vanessa reached around to slap her on the back.

'You know me?'

'Well, it's kind of hard to forget a college roommate.' Vanessa mopped up the spilt coffee. 'Even if we did only room for one semester.'

Lana backtracked through Alannah's diary entries. There had been a few entries while Alannah was in college before she took a leave of absence at the start of her second year and never returned. 'You're the Icy Pole,' Lana blurted, before clapping her hand to her mouth.

Vanessa laughed. 'Hello, Stick Figure.'

'Ouch.' Vanessa's questioning gaze made her look down at the table. 'I was in a car accident and can't remember anything before. I read her —' she stumbled, quickly correcting herself — 'my diary and knew your nickname.'

She had to steel herself to look Vanessa in the eye. Habits died hard and even though technically this was the truth, it still felt like she was lying to her best friend.

'I'm so sorry.' Vanessa reached across the table and took her hand.

She smiled. 'Thanks.' She sipped at her coffee. 'So we were roommates. Why only one college semester?'

Vanessa looked away. 'I wasn't cut out for college life.'

She stopped with the coffee cup halfway to her lips. In her other life Vanessa had gone to college only to meet her father's expectations. She'd dropped out after one semester and started working at Le Chez.

Vanessa stirred sugar in her coffee, leaving the spoon in as she sipped it. Recognizing Vanessa's quirky habit, excitement filled her. Vanessa was the same. Remembering Le Chez, Lana realized that she just hadn't moved on in this life the way she had in the other.

'Are you still designing clothes?'

Vanessa frowned, looking at her questioningly. 'Here and there.' She opened her purse and passed her a business card. 'I'm the manager at Le Chez. Next time your mom's in the area, tell her to give me a call.'

Lana took the card without a word. As the manager of Boston's exclusive haute couture fashion boutique, Vanessa had always been looking for ways to get her designs in the fashion pages.

'Thanks.' She tapped the card on the table. She guessed a mayor's wife would be quite a coup. Only trouble was, Vanessa never mixed business and friendship.

Silence descended. Lana fidgeted, twisting her wedding ring as panic hit her. That was it? That was the sum total of what they had to say to each other?

'So what's new with you?' She giggled, trying to soften her clunky question.

'Nothing much.' Vanessa rubbed her neck, showing her discomfort. 'Just working. What about you?' She nodded toward her wedding band.

'Oh.' Lana paused awkwardly weighing up what she should say. In the end, honesty won out. 'I'm married, but it looks like we'll be divorcing soon. Or as soon as I'm feeling better from the accident.'

'I'm sorry.'

'Yeah, well, that's life.' She pushed her hair away from her face. 'The only trouble is I never thought of a life without him. Everything I was, everything I am, is tied up in my marriage. Now I have to find out who I am without it as a crutch.'

A harsh ring interrupted her. She felt her face flush at the look of relief on Vanessa's face as she searched through her handbag. As Vanessa spoke into the handset, Lana subsided into her chair, chastened. She'd been talking to her as if she was her oldest friend, yet to Vanessa, she was a stranger.

'I have to get going.' Vanessa returned the cell phone to her handbag.

'Oh, okay.' Lana cleared her throat. 'Um, do you think we could keep in touch?' She knew her voice was pleading but she didn't care about her pride. All she knew was that she'd never felt so alone in her life, and the loneliness was more than she could bear.

'Oh, okay.' She nodded to the card. 'Well, you have my details.'

'Let me give you my number.' Lana dug into her handbag. Feeling Vanessa's impatience to be on her way, her fingers felt stiff and inept. In frustration she tipped out the contents on the table between them and found a pen and paper.

'Do you know Dr Chaine?' Vanessa's voice was uneven.

Lana looked up to see Vanessa holding the business card Jeremy had given her before she was discharged from hospital.

'Yes, he's my doctor. Do you know him?'

'I thought I did.' Vanessa took the paper Lana had written her contact details on and stood, pushing her chair back so quickly it nearly fell. 'I have to return to work.' She placed some notes on the table and, with a distracted goodbye, left.

A rolling blanket of loneliness pressed down on Lana as she watched Vanessa walk out of the café. She felt like a preschooler left alone on her first day, the only difference being a preschooler would be collected by Mommy after school, while she was on her own for the foreseeable future.

It was too much. She wanted to throw herself on the floor like a child having a temper tantrum and scream and shout so the world would know her heartbreak. The emotional shocks had worn her down, and she didn't know if she could face the prospect of the world outside the café.

'Are you all right?' A waitress peered at her with concern.

She wiped her face and swallowed her tears, the embarrassment of crying in public bringing back some semblance of normality. 'Yes, thank you.' She put on her coat and paid for her coffee. 'It's just one of those days.'

The waitress squeezed her elbow. 'Well, don't you let it get you down.' She tucked the money into her apron and bent to stack the coffee cups. 'There's always tomorrow.'

Lana took her first step toward the door before stopping abruptly to watch the waitress carry the cups to the kitchen. It was like jigsaw pieces had slotted into place, leaving her with the reeling wonder of an epiphany.

Tomorrow. The word was a kaleidoscope of wonder. To-morrow. With its endless possibilities. Tomorrow. A word she hadn't thought about in the five years her life had been ruled by Frank's illness. Each day was precious and to be savored because tomorrow was not a certainty. When Frank had asked her to marry him he'd told her his doctors predicted he would die by his twenty-fifth birthday. She remembered looking into his eyes and feeling the weight of the decision on her shoulders: to love and embrace that love knowing that pain would follow, or to walk away and feel the pain of an unfulfilled love as it withered?

Somehow she'd found the strength and made her decision and each day after that she'd never thought of tomorrow. Re-membering the resolve she had felt, she tasted the bitterness of regret. Where had that girl gone – the girl who believed in love without boundaries and the possibility of the future? The girl to whom giving up had not been an option? It was her love that had tethered Frank to life and it was the strength of this love that had brought her to this world. Yet now she was a woman without purpose, hollowed by doubt and fear. She'd given up on Tristan without even trying.

She left the café and turned away from Le Chez. It was time for a new direction.

Chapter 7

Aidan saw him walk in to the office, but with the familiarity of friendship, took one look at Tristan's face and left him alone. Tristan stared at the paper on his desk; progress reports that needed to be submitted to clients, tenders to complete, phone calls to return. But instead of immersing himself in work, he brooded.

He'd left for work in the morning while Alannah was sleeping. *Call it what it is, Walker, you snuck out like a thief in the night.* He twisted in his chair and turned to look out the window, seeing the bend in the Charles River from his Back Street offices.

When he'd woken from a fitful sleep this morning, Alannah had been in his arms. As she slept, her breath hitched in her throat. He had reached out and smoothed her hair, feeling her incredibly soft skin. Tenderness stuck in his throat.

The diary on the bedside table mocked him, dousing his tenderness as he remembered her betrayal. Who had he been living with for the past two years? He ground his teeth. When they'd married and she didn't respond in bed he'd told himself to be patient. He'd slowed the pace down, revered her, adored her, praised her; loved her.

He'd known something was wrong but whenever he attempted to get her to confide in him, she'd retreated. Every once in a while it seemed he was getting through and he glimpse desire in her eyes. But they were few and far between.

Hearing a knock, he nodded at Aidan to enter.

'There's a problem at the Hartford Street worksite.'

Tristan looked at his desk as he listened to Aidan, tracing the wood grain with his finger, his mind far away from work. He had sometimes got the feeling when he was making love to Alannah that she wasn't really with him. One night the frustration got too much and he'd lashed out, telling her making love to her was like making love to a piece of wood.

A week later he came home from an exhausting day at work to a dimmed apartment. Alannah had approached him wearing a silk negligée and high heels. Placing a finger over his lips, she had led him to the bedroom where they made love with abandon. He had fallen asleep smiling. When he woke a few minutes later, she wasn't in the bed with him. He pushed open the door to the bathroom to find her sitting on the toilet seat, muffling her sobs with a towel.

After that, he didn't approach her. She turned to him in the darkness of night and they pretended that the perfunctory lovemaking was enough for both of them. But each time he climaxed he felt empty and inadequate.

The silence in his office jarred him back to the present.

Aidan was looking at him with concern in his eyes. 'You want to talk about it?'

'No.' He picked up the report Aidan had brought in and started reading. The print blurred in front of his eyes. 'She knows about the divorce.' He continued looking at the report he was holding.

'How?'

'I didn't tell her.' Tristan slapped his hand on the desk and stood. Staring out the window, he ran his hand through his hair. 'She read it in her diary.'

'So what's the problem? Now that she knows, you can leave.'

Tristan frowned at Aidan's careless tone. 'It's not that simple. She was —' The word stuck in his throat.

'What?'

Tristan opened his mouth again, trying to force the word out. Raped. She was raped. But the words in his head couldn't get past his throat. He heard Alannah's voice from last night. I wanted to tell you, but the words wouldn't come.

Is this how she'd felt – the burden of a secret weighing her down, but no words to express it? She'd only been fifteen years old when she was raped, with no way to protect herself and no one to turn to.

He felt ashamed as he realized that since he'd read the diary, his only thought had been about how her rape had affected him. He covered his face with his hands, feeling smaller than an ant.

Tristan felt Aidan touch his shoulder. 'I'll go to Hartford Street, you go home. Your wife needs you.'

He left the office, quietly closing the door after him.

The yoke of responsibility settled around his neck as Tristan realized Aidan was right. His wife did need him. With a sigh, he put his truck keys in his pocket and left.

·♥·♥·♥·♥·♥·

'Alannah,' Tristan called as he entered the apartment. He put his keys on the console opposite the front door. He called her name again, only for the silence to echo back.

He walked through the apartment quickly. A bowl of uneaten cereal was on the kitchen table, the dishes unwashed in the sink. The bed unmade, still showing the imprint of their heads on the pillows.

He'd left her alone after the shock of learning about the rape. What had he been thinking? *You were thinking of yourself, Walker!* He pulled open the closet door and was relieved to find her clothes still on the hangers.

Picking up the phone, he called Tammy. The conversation was punctuated by his curt tone, and her reproachful silence. After reading Alannah's desperate entreaties for help that no one had heard, he couldn't view Tammy in the same way. He understood Alannah's anger at her mother; Tammy had failed Alannah by not reading the signs and realizing she had been raped.

Isn't that the pot calling the kettle black? 'I tried to get her to talk to me,' Tristan said aloud, trying to convince himself. But how hard did he try? He recalled how easily he'd let Alannah deflect him.

He was relieved to hear a key turn in the front door. Alannah entered holding a washing basket. As she awkwardly maneuvered herself through the door, he cleared his throat, not wanting to startle her.

She looked up, her blue eyes lit with joy, until she remembered and the sparkle faded.

'Here, let me help.' He reached for the basket and placed it on the carpet.

She closed the door. 'You're home early.' She took off her coat and threw it on the couch. 'The emergency over?'

He winced, following her into the kitchen. 'Where were you?'

Her shoulders stiffened. 'Why? Did you miss me?' She carried the cereal bowl to the sink.

He sat down and watched her as she bustled around the kitchen. She seemed different. After a few minutes he realized why– Alannah had always been a neat freak. When they were decorating and she started showing him samples, he'd tried to convince her otherwise. But she'd been so happy creating her first home that he didn't put much effort into it. The only thing he'd demanded remain untouched was his study. He'd thought that once she lived in her high-maintenance home she'd realize her error. Instead, he was the one who'd erred. She'd been quite content to spend hours every day ensuring that the white surfaces sparkled in their hygienic beauty. Yet here she was washing the dishes and wiping surfaces with none of her former frantic zeal.

After she finished in the kitchen she picked up the basket and carried it into the bedroom. He followed her.

She stripped the sheets and threw them in the corner of the bedroom, then took cotton sheets covered with a white and yellow floral design from the washing basket.

She tucked in the sheets, then he held the matching duvet as she slipped on its new cover. 'So you did some shopping?' he asked.

'Yes.' She pulled the duvet cover down and snapped closed the buttons. 'I think it's time for a change.'

After they made the bed she reached for the curtain rod. He stepped in behind her and lifted it off the brackets, breathing in her scent. As soon as he handed the rod to her, she moved away. She handed him the rod festooned with new curtains and he hung it up. She moved to the open doorway and looked at the room, her eyes blazing in satisfaction.

He locked around with her. With the addition of the colorful bedding and matching curtains, the room didn't look stark any more; it was bright and cheerful. 'It looks wonderful.'

'Thanks.'

He leant against the wall next to her but she stepped away from him.

'I think I'll have a shower.' She stood beside the door and waited.

He knew how to take a hint. He left, the door missing his back by inches when she closed it. Entering the study, he felt dissatisfaction. 'Walker, you are a piece of work.' He switched on his computer, wryly shaking his head.

First he found her too clingy and couldn't wait to create some distance. Now that he got his wish and Alannah was keeping to the boundaries he'd created, he wasn't happy.

He heard the shower turn on. Glancing at the pillow and blanket on the sofa he realized, he had to get clothes for work the next day. Returning to the bedroom, he opened the closet and pulled out a clean pair of jeans and shirts. Alannah's handbag fell from the top shelf and something caught under his foot. Bending down, he picked up a business card. Who was Vanessa?

Alannah walked into the bedroom, stopping abruptly when she saw him. She pulled the towel tighter around herself, outlining her curves.

He soaked in the sight of her, desire clenching in his gut. Her skin was pink, her legs long and smooth. It had been so long since he'd touched a woman his need left him shaking.

Realizing she was looking at the floor in discomfort at his display of lust, he cleared his throat and held up his clothes. 'I'm getting organized for tomorrow.'

She moved away from the door and he held his breath as he passed by, her proximity making his heart thump. It was only when he was outside that he realized he still clutched the business card in his hand. He rubbed his neck, feeling like a schoolboy with his first crush.

He glanced at his watch and saw it was time for dinner. He set about preparing a meal and when Alannah entered the kitchen, dressed, her dry hair gleaming around her shoulders, he was ready to serve up spaghetti. He'd set the table for two and opened a bottle of wine.

She looked at him warily.

'A peace offering.' Seeing she still hesitated, he wiped his hands on a tea towel and approached her. 'Look, things haven't been too great around here. But we have to live together for the next few weeks, so I thought we'd declare a truce.'

He held out the chair for her. With one last look at him, she sat. Lifting the wine bottle, he flicked the tea towel over his arm. 'Good evening, madam. I am Tristan, and I will be your waiter tonight.' He spoke in an Italian accent. 'Will madam be expecting a companion?' He poured a splash of wine into her glass.

She picked it up and took a discreet sip. 'Yes. I'm waiting for an ogre who claims to be my husband.' She looked at him mischievously. 'Do you by any chance know where he is?'

'Ouch,' he muttered, placing his hand over his heart in an exaggerated gesture. 'If madam wants a more civilized companion, I'm sure I can oblige.' He lifted her hand to his lips, his eyebrows twitching comically.

She laughed and something loosened in him; he'd been afraid he'd pushed her too far away and there was no going back.

He picked up the parmesan and grated it over her plate. 'Say when.'

'When.'

He sat down opposite and watched as she ate with gusto.

'This is great.' She held up the fork. 'Aren't you hungry?'

He belatedly picked up his fork, soon catching up to her. It was only when he'd finished cooking that he'd realized they were eating pasta for the second time this week. Usually he'd have a hard time convincing Alannah to eat anything more substantial than a cracker after five pm. He watched her clean her plate. She didn't seem to worry about calories any longer. The leggings and top she was wearing outlined her bountiful curves. He frowned, remembering the business card. She was acting out of character in other ways.

'I found this on the floor.' Placing the napkin on the table, he reached into his pocket. 'You must have dropped it.'

Alannah glanced at the card. 'Thanks.'

'Is Vanessa a new friend?'

'No, an old one.'

'Oh.' He poured her another glass of wine.

'We were in college together.' As she drank, the wine glistened on her lips.

He shifted in his seat and pulled his gaze away from her mouth. 'I don't think you've mentioned her before.'

She looked away. 'We were only roommates for a semester and didn't keep in touch.'

His eyes narrowed. You didn't live with a person for two years without learning a thing or two about them. And he knew that something didn't ring true with Alannah's story.

'So you looked her up.'

'Actually we sort of ran into each other.'

'And...' He gestured with his hand.

'And nothing.' She put down the glass with a thud. 'Why do you care?'

'I'm concerned about you.' He sat back in his chair. 'You've just had a car accident and have been acting a little strangely.'

'Do you think I'm crazy? That the accident screwed with my brain?'

He knew a loaded question when he heard one. 'No, I just want you to be okay.'

'Well, I'm fine. So don't worry about me any more.' She stood and pushed the chair, scraping it on the linoleum. 'You're not going to be stuck taking care of me. You can leave any time.'

'Wait a minute.' He stood. 'That wasn't what I was trying to do.'

'Really. I just find this interesting.' She gestured at the table. 'After I get out of the hospital you spend every minute making me feel unwanted. And now that I know about the divorce, you're concerned.' She crossed her arms over her chest. 'Let's be honest and admit what this is about. You want out. Well, go.'

His heart thudded in his chest. He'd never heard such finality from his wife. He glanced at the door. He could do it; he could walk out right now and leave all this behind him. He took a step.

And stopped. He wasn't ready. Or rather, she wasn't ready. She was still sick and needed time to recuperate.

'No.' He approached her and took her hands in his. She resisted, trying to pull away. He waited her out. Eventually she stood stiffly, staring somewhere over his shoulder.

'I'm sorry, Alannah. I'm sorry I was a jerk after you got home from the hospital. I'm sorry that you had to find out about the divorce the way you did. And I'm sorry I ruined our dinner together.'

As he was talking, she met his gaze. She glanced at him searchingly, gauging his sincerity. She must have found what she was looking for because the tension eased in her arms.

'No, I'm sorry.'

As they stood facing each other, sexual awareness blindsided him. She was so close. Her breasts were almost brushing his chest. He inhaled, breathing in the fresh scent of rose shampoo. She felt it too– he saw her eyes darkening as awareness dawned on her. Her nipples hardened beneath her top.

'Well.' She cleared her throat and finished in a near whisper. 'I'm glad we got that sorted out.'

'Me too.'

He waited for her to retreat like she always did. Instead she stood on her tippy toes. He held himself in check. She pressed a kiss on his cheek, her smooth skin brushing his.

He turned his head and met her gaze. With her eyes wide open, she placed her lips over his. She put her hands on his shoulders. He kept his movements slow and easy as he gently placed his hands on her waist, supporting her.

They kissed chastely, as if they were innocent high school kids learning their way around the opposite sex. He pressed against her, his hands tightening on her waist as he pulled her closer. Her hands tightened on his shoulders. He pulled back and saw longing instead of the fear he had come to expect.

'You're a great kisser,' she murmured, her voice raspy with yearning.

His eyes widened in surprise. It had been so long since he inspired desire in a woman, he'd forgotten the heady feeling of being a man. Alannah's constant rejection had made him question his manliness – if a guy can't turn on his own wife, there had to be something wrong with him. It was that feeling of rejection and the inadequacy that it had spawned that had led to him nearly making the biggest mistake of his life.

She laughed with delight. 'But I think.' She stopped and rubbed her cheek against his, arching her back like a cat. 'That we need to stop now.'

He loosened his hold on her and she put her arms around him. He looked down at her head burrowed into his chest and drew her closer, pressing a kiss to her temple. Closing his eyes, he heard their hearts beating in unison as they each drew comfort from the other. He was sinking, sinking deep into her.

She shifted, and he let go of her, feeling regret and relief at the same time.

'I better get to bed. I've got the early shift tomorrow.'

'Are you sure —'

She put her finger on his lips. 'No more. I'm a big girl and can take care of myself.'

There was a strength he'd never seen in her before. He nodded. The burden he'd carried since meeting her melted away.

'Good night.' She squeezed his hand.

As he watched her walk away he trembled for a different reason. He squeezed his hands into fists, wanting to follow her. Wanting to just... be with her.

You're in big trouble, Walker. 'Yeah, I know.'

He wrenched his gaze away from the swell of her hips and took a deep breath.

Chapter 8

Lana was scooping condiments from the industrial-sized plastic tubs into serving portions when Holly rushed into the kitchen, tugging Joshua behind her. Her skin was flushed and shiny. She dropped Joshua's hand and wrestled a stool to the corner of the kitchen. After lifting him on to it, she quickly pulled a coloring book and crayons from his backpack.

'Okay, kiddo, you just draw for a little while and we'll be off to school in no time.' She smoothed down the cowlick in his otherwise straight brown hair.

'But Mom,' Josh whined, 'it's story time today and Grandma was gonna come and read for us.' Josh's bottom lip trembled and his eyes filled with tears.

'Okay, okay. Don't start the waterworks, honey. I'll give your dad a call and see if he can do it.' She kissed him on the cheek and grabbed her handbag, hotfooting to the office.

Lana followed and watched as she flipped the contents of her handbag onto the table. 'What happened to your mother?'

'She fell off her bed and hurt her leg,' Holly muttered. 'Where is my address book? This is the day from hell.' She ran her hands through her already messy hair. 'I had a really hot date last night and we ended up at my place. Aha.' She pulled out her address book triumphantly.

'At seven this morning my dad burst in on us and left Joshua on my doorstep on the way to taking my mom to the hospital.' She lifted the handset and dialed. 'My hot date took one look at Joshua's crying face and ran out the door. Aidan Meagher, please,' she said into the handset. 'I don't even have his phone number. And now to top it all off, I have to ask Aidan to do story time. We have the Cooper Waterhouse function today and I have to be here. Aidan,' Holly said, her voice taking on a sugary tone.

Lana returned to the kitchen, closing the door behind her. Joshua was watching Shirley put the desserts in the fridge.

'Did you have breakfast yet, Josh?' Lana asked.

He shook his head.

'Why don't we get you a glass of milk and make some toast?'

Lana was slathering peanut butter on Josh's second slice of toast when Holly slammed the office door open. 'Lana!' she shouted impatiently. Seeing Joshua looking at her, she gave him a tight smile before disappearing back behind the door.

When Lana closed the office door behind her, Holly started her tirade. 'The bastard. You'd think I was asking him to give me a kidney instead of take care of his own kid.'

The office phone rang. Holly continued pacing, biting her nails. Lana looked at her questioningly. Holly shrugged. With a sigh, Lana answered it.

'Holly, I did not say that I don't care for my own son, but that you need to start taking care of your responsibilities. You can't keep using your mom as a nanny and me as a babysitter while you live it up.' Aidan stopped and waited for a response.

Lana had taken deep breaths during his monologue, trying to interrupt but the staccato sentences made her gulp and wait him out. 'Um, it's Lana.' She gestured at Holly, who wouldn't look at her.

'Hi Lana,' Aidan said. 'Sorry about that.'

'That's okay.' Lana waved at Holly, but she wouldn't take the phone.

'Please tell Holly that I'll pick Josh up after school.'

After she hung up, Holly rushed to her. 'So will he do it?'

'He said he'd pick Josh up after school.'

Holly threw up her hands. 'That man is a robot. Nothing affects him.' She took a deep breath. 'I guess there's only one thing for it.'

She walked over to Josh and picked up his backpack. 'Okay, let's get going.'

Josh wiped his hands on a napkin. 'Are you going to do story time?'

Holly took the napkin and wiped his cheeks. 'Well, honey, it's complicated. I asked your daddy but —'

'Daddy did the race last week.'

Holly paused before crumpling the napkin. 'Well, Mommy's busy.' She handed him the backpack.

Josh's face crumpled. 'It's not fair. It's not fair!' He threw his backpack onto the floor. 'No one's going to come and do my story time. Every other kid has someone.'

'Josh, I'm sorry. Both your daddy and I have to work.' Holly put her hands on his shoulders and tried pulling him into a hug.

Josh threw her hands off, his face scrunching up in rage. 'You always have to work.'

Looking at his heaving chest and red face, Lana's stomach tightened in sympathy. She knelt down in front of him. 'Listen, Joshua, I'm not your mom or your dad, or even your grandma, but if you want, I'll come do your story time.' Joshua stopped crying. At least she had his attention. 'You can tell everyone that I'm your aunt.'

His face was slowly brightening and he smiled. 'Yeah, you're married to Uncle Tristan.'

'Sure,' Lana agreed. She turned to Holly only to be engulfed in a bear hug.

'Thank you,' Holly said against her shoulder.

Lana jolted as her legs were embraced. Looking down, she saw Joshua's head pressed against her hip. 'Thank you, thank you,' he said too, his voice high with excitement.

'Shit.' Holly abruptly pulled away. 'What about your shift?'

'I'm on top of it.' Lana disentangled herself from Joshua. 'I'll call Siobhan and ask her to take my shift. She's desperate for the work.'

Ten minutes later, Lana was walking out of the café holding Joshua's hand. Siobhan had been more than happy to rush in to work. She walked to the museum car park and opened the passenger side of Holly's red Corolla. After closing the door behind Joshua, she walked to the driver's side and opened the crumpled invoice Holly had scrawled directions on. She made a mental note to return the invoice to Holly to be paid.

She buckled her seatbelt and smiled at Joshua. 'Here we go, bucko.' She gingerly turned the key in the ignition.

The school grounds were bustling with other children when they arrived. Apart from missing the turn onto Tremont Street and having to double back, she hadn't had much trouble with the route. Within fifteen minutes she and Josh were walking into Condon Elementary School. Lana followed Josh through the maze of corridors and into the classroom.

He reached into his backpack and handed her a book. 'I want you to read this.'

Lana quickly glanced at the cover. *The Adventures of Captain Underpants.* Under the title was an illustration of a giant baby in white briefs.

'You go speak to my teacher.' He nodded to the woman at the head of the class before sitting down.

With a soft sigh, Lana approached the teacher. 'I'm here to do story time.'

'Oh, you're Josh's mother. How are you, Mrs Meagher? I'm Jenny Clarence.'

'Oh, no, I'm Holly's —' Lana stopped remembering that Josh wanted her to call herself his aunt. She gulped. 'I'm Josh's Aunt

Lana. His grandmother hurt herself and had to go to the emergency so I'm here to help out.'

'Is Mrs Keneally going to be all right?'

'She should be fine. She hurt her leg.'

Jenny winced sympathetically. 'Please pass on my best wishes for her recovery.'

Lana nodded. 'Will do.'

'What are you going to read this morning?' She looked at the book Lana was holding.

'Is this going to be okay?'

Jenny smiled. 'That's fine.' She clapped her hands. The chattering hushed then died out. There were squeaks of chairs being moved as the kids settled.

As Jenny introduced her, Lana looked at the children's faces. Her stomach was slowly tightening in nervousness. She hadn't done story time in a while. In her other life, she had volunteered at the local library and read at story time once a week. She'd loved working with kids; loved the feeling of always being on her toes and of every day being a surprise as they discovered something new about the world.

She'd had to stop after six months, when Frank developed an infection and she had to take care of him. By the time he was better, her slot had been filled and she never went back.

Lana sat down on the reading chair. 'Hi, everyone. As Jenny said my name is Lana and I'm Josh's aunt. I will be reading *The Adventures of Captain Underpants*.' She held up the cover and heard some giggling as two heads leant together to whisper to each other. One look from Jenny and the heads pulled apart guiltily and looked at the front of the classroom.

Lana flipped to the first page and began to read. The kids giggled in all the right places and cheered at the end.

When she closed the last page, the kids were wriggling on their seats and giggling as they relived the story.

'How did Captain Underpants defeat Dr Diaper?' she asked.

Hands shot up. Lana picked a little girl with a ribbon tied ponytail.

'Captain Underwear shot his underwear at Dr Diaper,' the little girl answered, twirling her ribbon.

The kids cheered.

'Was that your favorite part?' Lana asked.

The little girl nodded, her ribbon fluttering with the movement.

'Who else has a favorite part?'

Lana picked a little boy in a Spiderman T-shirt. 'I liked it when they shot the fake doodoo.'

The kids erupted into high-pitched giggles.

Lana stood. 'I think you guys need to do some work now.'

'Aaw,' the kids complained in unison.

Lana laughed and stepped back.

'Okay, everyone.' Jenny stepped to the front of the classroom. 'Open your coloring books to page six please.' She called Joshua. 'Did you want to say goodbye to your aunt?'

Joshua jumped up from his seat and ran to Lana, giving her a hard hug around her waist. 'Thanks, Aunt Lana.' He just as quickly slipped back in his seat and continued coloring.

'There's a topic kids love,' Jenny said wryly as the odd 'doodoo' broke out, followed by giggling.

'I hope I haven't made it too hard for you to get back to work.'

Jenny smiled. 'The good thing about kids is their short attention span. You were great.' She walked Lana into the corridor. 'The kids were really involved in the discussion.'

Lana felt a goofy smile spreading across her face. 'Thanks.'

'Have you taught before?'

'Oh, no. I did some volunteering at my local library a few years ago so that gave me some practice.'

Hearing the kids stirring, Jenny glanced behind her. 'I'd better be getting back. But thank you again.'

Lana walked out of the school and into the car park. A glow of achievement surrounded her like a bubble. When she'd volunteered at the library she'd checked out the courses at her community college to be a primary school teacher. It would have taken her eight years on a part-time basis, but she'd seriously considered enrolling. She'd been intending to speak to Frank when he'd gotten sick. After that, she'd put the course information in the bin and forgotten her dream – Frank and his health were her priority.

She rifled through her handbag searching for her car keys. Seeing the cell phone, she pulled it out and turned it on. Her fingertips touched the rough edges of the keys at the bottom of her bag. As she wiggled them out, the cell phone beeped. She read the screen– she had a voicemail message.

She opened the car door, tossed in her handbag and dialed the number. Her stomach tightened as she recognized Tristan's voice.

'Hi Alannah. Just called to check in. Holly told me you were with Josh. Hope everything's fine.' There was the sound of him clearing his throat. 'Well, I guess I'll see you at home.'

She deleted the message, her hands trembling slightly. He'd called her. She sat in the driver's seat and looked blankly at the phone in her hand. Last night had meant something.

A smile spread across her face as she squeezed the phone. Maybe it was going to be okay. She felt a stirring of arousal as she remembered their kiss. He'd let her set the pace and she'd been bold. Instead of flashes of fear, she'd felt as if she was with Frank – secure and cherished.

She lifted the phone and scrolled through her address book then pressed the button to call Tristan. She held her breath as the phone rang. He answered on the second ring, his voice distracted.

'Hi, it's Lana.'

'Oh, hi.'

An awkward silence stretched out. She rushed in to fill it, the words spilling quickly. 'It went really well. Josh was so happy. It was great.'

She heard the shuffling of papers. 'Good.' He paused. 'What was great?'

Her pleasure deflated like a pricked balloon. 'Story time.' She tried to keep the dejection from her voice.

'Sorry, I've had a crazy morning.' His voice faded as if he was moving around. 'I'm glad everything was great. Dammit,' he muttered. She heard a thud as if he'd dropped something. 'I'm going be home late tonight so don't hold dinner for me.'

'Okay.' She deliberately kept her voice upbeat. 'I'll see you later.' She hung up before she revealed her disappointment.

She returned the phone to her handbag feeling tired. The brief optimism washed away as if it had never been. She was tired of hoping, only to be disappointed over and over. Maybe it would be better if it all just —

The phone rang.

'That didn't go the way I planned,' Tristan said when she answered. 'You called at a bad time but that's no excuse for blowing you off. I'm glad you had a great morning. I'll pick dinner up on my way home and you can tell me all about it tonight.'

She smiled. 'I'd like that.'

'Great, I'll be home at six. See you then.'

After he hung up, she put the key in the ignition and the car sputtered to life. As she checked the rear-view mirror and carefully pulled out into the street, a glimmer of her good mood returned.

At a traffic light she looked across and saw a couple kissing playfully, wrapped in their own world of love. As the light changed and she sped up, she realized that's what was missing between her and Tristan; they had flashes of connection hinting at the love she and Frank shared, only to have it swept away by a crisis. Should love be this hard? When she and Frank had met, they'd clicked like two old souls rediscovering each other, but with Tristan it was so different – there was an undercurrent of danger with every step she took toward him.

She realized she was rubbing at her lip and driving one handed. As she pulled into the museum car park she shook her head, trying to dispel the doubts circling like a dark cloud.

Of course it was hard. With Tristan, she had none of the simplicity she'd had with Frank. Tristan was her husband, but

Lana felt like she was just starting a relationship with him. She remembered Alannah's diary. Tristan asked me for a divorce. For her the relationship might be just beginning, but for Tristan, it was long over.

'Yes, but he wanted to divorce Alannah, not me.' She slammed the car door shut.

Turning around, she smiled weakly at Charlie's frowning face. 'Hi.' She jiggled the keys in her hand. 'Just thinking out loud.'

Charlie shook his head and continued his rounds.

She slouched into the museum. 'If I do that too often, Tristan won't have to divorce me. I'll be committed to an asylum.' Realizing she'd done it again, she looked around to see if anyone had heard her. She was in the clear.

There was a tearing in her chest as she thought of the divorce. Yeah, well, it ain't over till it's over.

When she entered the kitchen, Siobhan was bouncing in and out the door, carrying platters of food. She smiled at Lana and quickly ducked back out into the eating area.

Holly was standing in front of the stove stirring a pot. As Lana approached, she breathed in the aroma of creamy corn soup. Sometime during the morning, Holly had found the time to repair her make-up, but she still looked frazzled and on edge.

She looked up and met Lana's eyes. 'How did it go?'

'Great.' Lana started describing the kid's reactions to the book and Joshua's joy. Seeing Holly's preoccupied face she stopped. 'Anyway, it was a good morning. I'll see you tomorrow.'

Noticing the silence, Holly glanced up. 'Oh sorry, yeah, I'll see you tomorrow.' She moved to the bench and started slicing tomatoes.

Lana quietly let herself out of the kitchen. She exited the museum and stepped onto the pavement, before stopping abruptly. Where was she going? Home?

Picturing the pristine apartment in her mind she felt her stomach lurch. She looked around the car park. Where else could she go? She lifted her head and felt the weak sun on her face.

She started walking, with no destination in mind. As she strolled, she remembered her past life. Her days had revolved around her part-time job and spending time with Frank. But here, there was nothing to keep her grounded. Her life with Tristan was uncertain. She had no friends. Tammy was her only family, but when she'd called her the other day, Tammy had been abrupt and ended the conversation after a few minutes.

Lana came to a stop on the sidewalk. She had no one. She was completely on her own with an empty future stretching out before her. There was a fluttering in her stomach and she pressed her hand against it.

She realized it was up to her. Was she going to wait around for something to happen or was she going to decide on a destination?

Chapter 9

Lana entered the apartment and dropped the plastic bags she was carrying before pulling the key out of the lock. She looked at her watch. Tristan was due home in half an hour.

After she showered, she stared blankly at the closet. Her skin tingled with urgency. She had to get dressed, but she felt paralyzed by indecision. She didn't feel like putting on real clothes; she wanted nothing more than to lounge around in her pajamas, winding down.

She remembered last night's kiss and flushed. Real clothes it was. She reached for the jeans she'd bought on her last shopping spree and started pulling them on. After she did up the zip, she looked at herself in the mirror. The pants hugged her hips and thighs, making her feel squashed in and uncomfortable.

She looked at the bag containing her new purchases. After avoiding Alannah's silken PJs and sleeping in Tristan's old T-shirt for a week, Lana had been more than ready for a change of sleepwear. She pulled out the purple flannel PJs. When she'd seen the cute pussycats covering them she'd known they were the ones for her.

She glanced from the mirror to the PJs in her hand. 'Screw it,' she muttered, stepping out of the jeans. 'He'll just have to take me as I am.'

Tristan walked through the apartment door as she was entering the living room, her damp hair hanging around her shoulders. They stopped and looked at each other. She rubbed her bare foot on the carpet, feeling awkward and out of place.

'Cute PJs.' He passed her the bags he was carrying.

She smiled, standing straighter. 'Thanks.' She sniffed appreciatively at the aroma emanating from the bags. 'Chinese. Yum.'

An awkward pause followed.

'Well.' He ran a hand through his hair. 'I'll have a shower.'

'I'll serve.' She backed into the kitchen.

She dished the food onto plates and prepared drinks, before setting it all on the dining table. Stepping back to view it, she realized she couldn't sit down. She pictured them sitting opposite each other, the stilted conversation and awkward pauses bouncing between them, and cringed. She was leaning against the bench when Tristan returned from the shower.

He sized up the situation quickly. 'Why don't we eat in the living room?' He took a plate and glass and stood by the doorway, waiting for her.

She nodded, walking past him into the living room. They sat on the floor, placing the plates on the coffee table. As she ate, she glanced at him surreptitiously. He was wearing old, faded jeans that moulded to his hips and emphasized... everything. An old white T-shirt with a hole in the armpit stretched across his chest.

He caught her looking at him. 'I don't own any PJs.'

She remembered the few times she'd caught him in the morning before work. He'd had on tracksuit pants and a T-shirt.

After he'd picked through the noodles, dim sims and spring rolls, Tristan looked up. 'So how did you end up doing story time?'

She told him about Holly's fiasco. 'It was so amazing to be among children again.' She dipped her spring roll into the sweet and sour sauce. 'They're so responsive and open. There's no artifice.'

Tristan put his chopsticks down. 'Again?'

Lana glanced at him blankly.

'You said it was nice to be among children again.'

'I used to do story time voluntarily at the local library.'

Tristan frowned. Her stomach clenched in tension. She'd put on a CD while he was in the shower and music filled the silence between them.

'It seems I find out something new about you each day,' he murmured.

Her hands clenched on the chopsticks. 'Maybe you don't know me at all.'

There was a beat of silence. 'Perhaps you're right.' He smiled tightly. 'Why don't you enlighten me?'

She stopped and blinked at him. 'Okay.' She put the chopsticks down and wiped her hands on her thighs. 'Well, I love tulips. My favorite color is blue.' Taking a deep breath she girded herself for her announcement. 'And, and —' The words stuck in her throat. She dared herself to say it, to articulate her dream.

Tristan's gaze narrowed as he waited.

She looked away, forcing the words out. 'I'm going to study to be a primary school teacher.'

After leaving the museum she'd gone to Boston University. The college counsellor, Rena, had given her the application forms for elementary education at Boston University. She had a month to submit her application for September admission or she would have to wait another six months. To make the deadline, she had three days to find Alannah's certificates and prepare her application.

At Rena's insistence, she'd made an appointment for Monday to discuss her application, but wasn't sure if she'd keep it. She had to think through the logistics of applying. Was it fraud to apply with Alannah's credentials since she wasn't really Alannah? This whole being in another body was a pain in the —

'A teacher?'

She looked at her bare feet. 'I always had a secret dream to be a teacher. But life got in the way.' She smiled wryly, thinking of the obstacles she'd faced in her other life. She looked at Tristan. And now even though things were put to right and she and Frank were reunited – in spirit if not in body – there was an even bigger obstacle. She and Tristan didn't share the love she and Frank had.

'You're right.' He met her gaze and she saw his bitterness. 'I don't know you at all.'

She bit her lip in guilt. Reaching out, she took hold of his arm. 'No, no. It's not your fault. I mean, I didn't let you know who I was. It's my fault.'

He looked down at his arm and cupped her hand with his own.

'I'm sorry. I didn't listen to you enough.' His voice was rough with emotion.

She felt her eyes tearing up. 'I'm sorry too. I didn't let you in.'

He met her gaze. Her eyes took in every part of his face. The cut in his eyebrow. The sun-browned skin. The small lines that fanned from the corner of his eyes. Her eyes widened as the realization smacked her between the eyes: this was the first time she was seeing him as a man she was attracted to. She'd refused to see anything about Tristan that didn't fit what Frank had been.

He felt her retreat. 'What is it?'

'I'm sorry,' she muttered.

He waited.

'I'm sorry for not seeing you either.'

He brushed her hair away from her face. 'How about we start again?'

She looked at him blankly.

'I'm Tristan.' He put his hand out.

Catching on, she hesitantly put her hand in his. 'I'm Lana.'

He shook her hand. 'Nice to meet you, Lana.'

After they finished eating, they carried their plates into the kitchen.

'There's just one thing I'm confused about.' Tristan finished scraping the plates and put them on the sink.

Lana tensed, holding a plate under the soapy water.

'If blue is your favorite color, why are we living in an igloo?'

She turned and seeing the twinkle in his eyes, she laughed. The tension eased and they continued washing up in silence.

Tristan dried the plate. 'Whatever you want to do, I'll support you.'

She smiled at him. 'Thank you,' she whispered.

He didn't look at her. 'When we divorce, I'll pay alimony so you can study.'

Her hands tightened on the glass she was holding. She turned her face away from him. 'Good.' She wiped her hands on a tea towel. 'I'm going to bed.' She threw the cloth onto the dining table.

Tristan grabbed her arm, pulling her to a stop. 'I didn't mean that the way it sounded.'

She didn't look at him.

His hand eased on her arm, and he took her hand instead. 'I wasn't there for you before. I want to be there for you now.'

He turned her to face him. Their bare toes were touching. Her breasts were loose under her PJs, swaying with her every motion. Her nipples stiffened as they rubbed against the soft fabric.

His chest expanded as he breathed in deeply. She saw the awareness in his gaze. She waited for him to kiss her. He watched her patiently, still holding her hand, and she realized he was waiting for her to make the first move. She put her hands on his shoulders and stood on her tippy toes, her breasts pressing into his chest.

A heady sense of power flowed through her and she gently placed her lips on his, before moving away and pressing soft kisses along his jaw.

His hand gripped hers tightly, making her aware of the control he was exerting to hold himself in check. She pulled his arms around her, placing them on her hips. Winding her hands around his shoulders, she met his gaze as she pressed her lips on his again.

Their breath melded. He kissed her chastely, his hands resting gently on her. She thrust her tongue into his mouth, testing the waters. His hands tightened on her hips as he kissed her deeply, taking her breath away.

She lost herself, floating in bliss. Her foot hit something. She pulled away. Looking around dazedly, she realized they were on the sofa. She was draped across Tristan's lap, the hard ridge of his arousal under her buttocks. She shifted.

He quickly took hold of her hips and held her in place. 'We can stop whenever you want.'

He took her hand and kissed his way from her wrist up her arm. Soon she was limp with arousal, her body pliant against his. They were lying on their sides, her chest against his, legs entwined. Looking into her eyes, he reached under her top. His callused hand cupped her breast and his thumb flicked her nipple. Dampness spread between her thighs. His hand caressed her stomach and headed under her PJ pants. She stopped him, turning away from his searching gaze.

He tilted her face to look at him. 'It's okay.' He pressed a kiss on her brow.

As he shifted she bit her lip in disappointment at ending their closeness. 'I'm sorry —'

'Shhh.' He cut her off. 'We have all the time in the world.'

He lifted her and lay back on the sofa, pulling her to lie with her head pillowed in the curve of his shoulder. One arm curled around his chest and her leg draped over his, she listened as his heartbeat slowed. His hand stroked her back, gentling her as their arousal dissipated. Her tension loosened and she sank deeper into him.

She closed her eyes and enjoyed the moment. Tonight she was secure and cherished. She pressed a kiss over his heart and closed her eyes, drifting into sleep.

·♥·♥·♥·♥·♥·

Lana walked through the apartment door from work the next day and smiled in delight as she caught sight of Tristan.

'Are we going somewhere?' She looked at his black fitted jeans and white T-shirt.

He looked at her with consternation, his mouth snapping shut as the knock on the door forestalled his answer. She opened it and looked quizzically at Aidan. Her smile faded as she noticed in his recently pressed jeans.

'Sorry, Aidan. There's been a change of plans.' Tristan reached her side. 'I'm staying in tonight.'

She moved away as they spoke. What did you think, one night of tenderness was going to magically repair everything?

Last night, they'd fallen asleep in each other's arms. Sometime during the night, Tristan had carried her to the bedroom and joined her. They'd woken facing each other, their hands clasped on the pillow. While getting ready for work they'd operated in harmony, not needing words as they found excuses to exchange gentle touches.

She'd spent all day watching the clock, her body tingling as she anticipated coming home to Tristan. Holly had noticed, teasing her by asking her to stay an extra hour. When Lana had blanched, she'd laughed in delight before shooing her out.

Hearing the door close, she turned around. 'Where's Aidan?'

'He's gone.' He dropped his keys on the coffee table. 'So what did you want to do tonight?'

She hesitated and saw uneasiness in his eyes.

'Actually I've got plans.' She picked up the keys and handed them to him. 'And so do you.' She nodded to the door. 'You better hurry to catch up to Aidan.'

He opened his mouth to argue.

She smiled brighter and made her voice light. 'Holly invited me for a girl's night and I really want to go.'

He eyed her. She reached out and pushed him gently. 'Go, I've got to get ready.' Seeing how her pushes nudged him to the door, she was relieved at her quick thinking. He only wanted to stay with her out of duty.

'Hurry up!' She laughed, her relief adding sincerity to her voice. 'You're going to make me late.'

She was closing the door when he pushed it back open. He swept her against him and kissed her on the lips. She was careful not to linger when he ended the kiss. She smiled softly and kept smiling as he walked to the elevator. As the elevator doors closed she saw his tension ease.

With a shuddering sigh she closed the door and flicked the bolt. She turned to look at the empty apartment. What was she going to do with herself now?

·♥·♥·♥·♥·♥·

Lana twisted in front of the mirror examining her bare thighs above the knee-high boots.

There was a pounding on the door. 'Are you ready?' Holly asked.

'Coming.' Lana tugged at the hem of the A-line skirt she was wearing.

After Tristan left, she'd called Holly and asked if her offer of a girl's night out was still open. When Holly had arrived to pick her up half an hour later, she'd taken one look at Lana's carefully chosen outfit before calling her friends to tell them they'd be late.

'If you don't come out, I'm coming in.' Holly shook the wooden partitions of the changing rooms in the clothes shop she'd dragged Lana to.

Taking a deep breath, Lana smoothed the see-through chiffon shirt over her stomach and opened the door. Holly looked her over critically before twirling her hand. Having been through the routine for three outfit changes, Lana shook her head and performed a little twirl. She'd learnt not to argue when Holly was in her imperious mood.

'Hmm, something's missing.' She looked at Lana's cleavage.

She disappeared down the stairs into the main store, return-ing with a pendant necklace. Lana bent her knees slightly as Holly hooked the chain behind her neck. Holly had forced her into four-inch high boots.

'Perfect.' Holly adjusted the stones between Lana's breasts.

'Okay, nearly ready.' She put her hands on Lana's shoulders and pushed her to sit down on the chair in the corner of the changing room. 'Now we just have to fix your make-up.' She pulled an eyeliner pencil from her handbag and leant into Lana's face.

'Keep your eyes open,' she ordered as Lana automatically squinted.

A few minutes later she held up a hand mirror. Lana blinked. Her blue eyes looked smoky and mysterious. The shiny pink lipstick glistened on her lips, giving her a pout.

'Okay, now we're ready.' Holly stepped back with a wicked smile.

As Lana stood and tugged at her hem she tried to console herself that she was still modestly dressed compared to Holly's fitted hipster red silk pants, which looked like they could slip off. The matching halter top left her midriff bare and showed off her taut stomach. She followed Holly to the checkout and tapped her fingers on the counter as her purchases were to-taled. Holly moved to look at herself in the mirror, flicking her wavy blond hair down her back. The light twinkled off her navel ring.

Seeing Lana looking at her, she smiled gently. 'You look beau-tiful.'

'Credit card or cash?' the checkout girl asked.

Reading the receipt total her eyes widened and her mouth gaped.

'I think we'll put this on the credit card.' Holly took Lana's purse.

As the credit card was swiped through the ATM, Lana fought a wince.

'Don't worry, it gets easier every time,' Holly said as Lana signed the receipt.

Twenty minutes later, Lana followed Holly to the club entrance. Feeling the hard stares of those standing in line as they walked past them, she hunched deeper into her coat.

'Hey, Rocky.' Holly hugged the burly bouncer manning the front door. 'How's Lisa?'

As Holly and Rocky chatted, a man with slicked back hair standing next to Lana gave her a once-over. He winked at her when he saw her looking at him. She shifted to Holly's other side.

Rocky unclipped the red rope and waved them through. Lana walked stiffly, feeling the weight of the stranger's stare until they turned the corner.

The loud music thrummed through her. It was crowded and as they walked past the dance floor to the back of the club, Holly waved and air-kissed what seemed like every second person they passed.

Holly approached a table of girls and was swallowed into a hug while Lana stood on the side clutching her purse. Extracting herself, Holly introduced her, yelling names out as she pointed. Lana nodded, smiling vaguely as she heard, 'Rachel, Anna, Michelle and Karen.'

'What do you want to drink?' Holly shouted in her ear when the waitress approached to take their order.

'Orange juice,' Lana shouted back.

Holly ordered for her. Taking a sip when the drinks arrived, Lana jerked back.

Holly smiled wickedly, clinking their glasses together. 'Enjoy.'

Lana tentatively sipped, tasting the heat of rum on her tongue. She settled into a conversation with Michelle, who worked with Holly at the cocktail bar she was moonlighting in.

In between snatches of conversation, Lana watched as Holly expertly fended off the attentions of men who approached their table yet somehow still left them with a smile. Holly bent and took a sip from her straw. She wiped the corner of her mouth with her fingers, licking them when she was finished, before looking discreetly across the room.

Following her gaze, Lana saw a man with a lithe dancer's build who was mesmerized by Holly's performance.

Holly leant over to her. 'Do you need to go to the bathroom?' she shouted, not looking away from the man.

They weaved their way through the crowd and past the man, before heading down the corridor where the bathroom sign pointed.

'Not bad,' Lana said when they walked into the bathroom.

Holly flicked her hair as she looked in the mirror. 'I love a man with a good set of shoulders.'

Watching her as she primped, Lana was struck by Holly's vivacious energy. She felt like she was orbiting a pulsing sun with its rays of warmth giving her life.

'How do you do it?' Lana asked.

Holly looked at her questioningly as she re-applied her lipstick.

'How do you have so much energy for life?'

Holly's smile faded as she met Lana's gaze in the mirror. 'I thought I'd met the man of my dreams and based my whole existence around him.' She smiled sadly as she looked at herself again. 'I was wrong. There's a whole life out there I have yet to experience.'

She returned her lipstick to her purse, her hair hiding her face momentarily. When she looked up, the melancholy was gone and party Holly had returned.

'Are you coming?' She held the door open.

'I'll be out in a minute.' Lana looked at herself in the mirror.

The truth in Holly's words chimed through her, setting off a warning bell. Wasn't that what she was doing, again? She smiled wryly. She should have learnt her lesson in her other life – Frank's illness had narrowed her life choices and here she was doing the same thing again.

She flicked her hair over her shoulders and opened the door. It was time this girl did some living.

Chapter 10

Lana stumbled out of the elevator and headed up the corridor, humming her own version of 'Foxy Lady' under her breath. She swayed her hips to the rhythm in her head.

She and Holly had lived it up. Her body felt loose and limber from a night of dancing and booze. At one point they'd been lifted onto the bar and had enticed the crowd with their own Coyote Ugly moves.

Alannah's body obviously didn't have much of a tolerance for alcohol. She'd had two mojitos and a daiquiri and instead of her usual pleasant buzz, she was giddy. She searched for her keys, smiling to herself as she remembered her conquests: men asking for her number, offering to buy her a drink, peering down her top.

Finding her keys, she clutched them and bent to unlock the door. On the third try she got the key in the lock and with a twist of her wrist, she was in. Entering the apartment she stretched her hand out and searched for the light switch. The light came on, blinding her. By the time she'd blinked the glare out, Tristan was in front of her.

'Where the hell have you been? It's two am.'

She looked at his open shirt and undone jeans, and dropped her handbag to the floor. She glided toward him, lust coursing through her. The music had primed her for a different kind of action.

She ran her hands up his chest and gently kissed his shoulder. 'Did you miss me?' She licked her way up his neck before kissing the corner of his mouth.

'Alannah,' he said her name on a sigh.

'Call me Lana,' she said, nipping his shoulder.

'Lana,' he whispered. 'You'd better stop.' He stood still, clenching his hands and not touching her.

'Why?' She took his hand and popped his fingers into her mouth, sucking and licking them. 'Don't you like it?' She nibbled his knuckle.

She remembered Holly's words after they'd had a few drinks: 'Sex is like a game of chess. You manipulate the other opponent with a series of lightning-fast moves.' Holly had sipped her margarita before smiling and lifting her eyebrows cheekily.

Lana put her hands on Tristan's firm butt and pulled him against her. Oh yeah, she was manipulating this opponent. She rotated her hips, grinding herself against him. A few more moves like this and she'd have checkmate.

Tristan bent and pulled her into a firm embrace. The alcohol had relaxed her and fear was the furthest thing from her mind. She was pressed against him, her hollows softened into his hardness. Her already rum-heated body almost sent off sparks as he devoured her with deep, soul-stirring kisses.

His large hands enveloped her butt, lifting her. She wrapped her legs around him and closed her eyes, lulled by the motion of his body as he carried her to the bedroom. She was consumed by the heady confidence of a desired woman. 'Checkmate,' she murmured, her lips brushing his.

He dropped her onto the bed and was about to follow her down.

She pressed her boot-clad foot against his chest. 'Not yet.' She propped herself up on her elbows. 'Take'em off, cowboy.'

He smiled at her as he unzipped her boot. 'Nice outfit.'

She lay back and laughed as he removed both boots. 'I went shopping.' She felt kind of floaty, as though she was in a wonderful dream. Tristan put his hand on her bare calves and rubbed her thighs under her skirt. She moaned as his work-roughened hands caressed her.

He lay down over her, pulling her top off and undoing her bra. His lips grasped her nipple, licking and nibbling as the heat built inside her. She squeezed her thighs around him, his jeans creating delicious friction between her legs. He lifted himself and eased off her panties before pulling down his zipper. She put her hand over his on the zipper, and he looked up at her, his face taking on a painful expression.

'Me first.' She hooked her foot behind his head and pulled it between her thighs.

Her hips bucked at the first thrust of his tongue against her clit. The wet, rough edge teased her and she bit into her knuckle, panting her pleasure. His pushed a finger into her slowly, thrusting in and out, matching its rhythm to the caress of his tongue. She felt a second finger stretching her and the friction was almost to much to bear. Her hips rose as she pushed herself against his stubbled jaw. She went over the edge, coming with a shuddering moan.

He kept thrusting his fingers and tongue, forcing her delicious pleasure on and on. Then he replaced his tongue with his lips, his fingers withdrawing with gentle thrusts. She sighed and fell back against the bed.

After a moment, she thrust her hands in his hair and lifted him up. 'Your turn.'

She kept her eyes closed as he pulled down his zipper, the rasp of the tab making her shiver in anticipation. He positioned himself and pushed all the way in with one firm thrust, making her moan as her aftershocks continued.

She opened her eyes and gasped. His face was above hers, his surprised eyes staring deep into hers. She watched the pleasure spreading over his face. He lost himself, the flush of passion climbing higher on his face as he thrust harder and faster. She held onto him, thighs tight against his skin, matching her rhythm with his. He came with a deep moan.

She caressed his back as he lay against her breasts, their sweat-slicked bodies pressed against each other.

Tristan lifted his head and looked at her with dazed eyes. 'What was that?'

She laughed, ruffling her fingers through his thick, wavy hair. 'That was two mojitos and a daiquiri, one bar-top dance and two weeks of abstinence.'

He lifted himself off her and they lay on their sides facing each other. 'More like two months of abstinence.'

'You have to be kidding.' She lifted her head and looked at his serious face. 'You're not kidding.' She pressed a kiss on his shoulder. 'I guess we have a long night ahead of us.'

She threw a leg over his hips and straddled side of him, then pressed a kiss to his neck. His chest brushed against hers as he laughed.

·♥·♥·♥·♥·♥·

Lana sat in Jeremy's waiting room, turning the magazine pages aimlessly. She looked at her watch and sighed.

The receptionist looked at her with sympathy. 'He won't be long.'

Lana smiled at her. The receptionist nodded before turning her attention back to the computer monitor.

The fax machine rang, and the noise hit her with a force of a sledgehammer. She whimpered and rubbed at her temple. She'd woken this morning to the ringing of the telephone; Jeremy's receptionist calling because of her missed appointment. She'd had an hour to get to his offices to make the next vacant slot.

It was only as the shower pulsed over her, clearing the fogginess of a hangover, that she'd remembered why she'd made the appointment.

After she'd seen Vanessa at Newbury Street and recovered from her bout of self-pity, she'd remembered Vanessa's face as she held Jeremy's business card and knew that somehow they had connected in this life. So she'd made an appointment with Jeremy to investigate further and promptly forgot about it with everything else that had happened.

She licked her dry lips. Seeing the water cooler, she stood and her sore thigh muscles complained. She bent to pour herself a glass of water and felt a twinge in her back. Snatches of the night before replayed in her mind: she and Tristan entwined, their sweaty bodies pressed up against each other, his wide-eyed gaze as he watched her lick her way down his body. She felt her nipples harden and heat pulse between her legs as she remembered their passion. She sighed softly.

Feeling eyes on her she looked up to see the receptionist looking quizzically at her. She flushed in embarrassment and quickly sat down. She sipped her water. All she needed was a cigarette holder with smoke curling to the ceiling to complete the picture of sexually sated femme fatale.

She laughed as she realized she'd taken Holly's words literally and tried to experience all life had to offer in one night. She uncrossed her legs and winced as her thigh muscle twitched uncomfortably. Now she was paying the price for that excessive living. She looked into her empty cup and wondered what Tristan was doing.

Jeremy Chaine entered the waiting room with a rush of energy. 'This way, Mrs Walker.'

Lana stood and followed him down the corridor.

When they sat down in his office, he opened her chart. 'So, how have you been feeling?'

'Good.' Her hands tightened on her handbag in her lap. Seeing he was waiting for more, she cleared her throat. 'Well, I've remembered some things.'

While he was writing in her chart she examined him, comparing him to the Jeremy of her memories. His red hair was cropped short and his face was clean-shaven. The Jeremy of her memories had been relaxed and carefree and his personal appearance had reflected that. His hair had curled around his nape and a scruffy beard covered his face.

Jeremy looked up. Catching her gaze on him, he smiled, his brown eyes remaining wary and guarded. What had changed him into this reserved stranger?

His smile faded. 'Something wrong?'

She shook her head, returning to the present. 'Does everything look okay?'

He nodded, a frown still on his face. 'It seems you're recovering well. I just want to check one more thing.' He stood and walked to the scale. 'Do you mind?'

Leaving her purse on the chair, she stood on the scale and held her breath as the numbers spun before settling. Looking down, she smiled in relief. She had put on three pounds.

She took hold of Jeremy's hand above the wrist. 'I did it.'

He smiled without reservation for the first time, his brown eyes softening as genuine amusement filled them. 'I think you're the first patient to smile after putting on weight.'

She laughed as she stepped off the scale. 'I think I was the only patient who was impersonating a scarecrow. Look at this.' She lifted her top and showed him the bruises on her ribs.

He touched them gently then sat down, motioning for Lana to take a seat too. 'I'll prescribe some multivitamins to get your immune system back up.'

As he wrote the prescription, Lana rubbed at her lip, trying to think of a way to bring the conversation to Vanessa. Her brain was sluggish and incapable of forming probing yet discreet questions. Taking a deep breath, she plunged in anyway.

'Why did you pretend you didn't know Vanessa Diaz?'

He froze, his pen stopping in mid-motion. 'Mrs Walker, I'd really prefer not to discuss my personal life.'

'So you and Vanessa did date?'

He twisted the pen between his hands before meeting her gaze. 'Vanessa and I had a brief fling that we both decided to end.' He returned the pen to his pocket. 'Did Vanessa put you up to this?'

'No!' Fear clutched her stomach as she thought of the potential mess she was creating. 'We were roommates for a very short time in college but Vanessa and I are strangers to each other now.' She felt a sting of hurt as she spoke.

'I know. After you awoke, I spoke to your mother and husband. They both said you didn't have any contact with Vanessa after college.'

She nodded, clutching her handbag in her lap.

'Why do you think you created this fantasy about me and Vanessa?'

She gulped, her mouth drying as her brain finally kicked into gear. 'Well, the thing is ...'

She cobbled together a story that her unresolved feelings about her and Vanessa's friendship had contributed to the fantasy of Vanessa and Jeremy being married. Her lie-a-thon left her drained and she wasn't even sure if he bought it.

He frowned and closed her file. She took a deep breath, wincing as she prepared herself to be exposed.

'Your recovery is on track and I don't think I'll need to see you again.' Jeremy stood and shepherded her to the door.

'Okay, thanks.' She awkwardly reached to shake his hand.

He returned her handshake without meeting her eyes. The door closed behind her and she sighed in relief. It seemed lying got easier with practice.

·❤·❤·❤·❤·❤·

Tristan parked his truck in the car park of his company's office and roughly tugged at his tie. After throwing it onto the passenger seat, he slammed his hand on the steering wheel. He'd been so close, so close, and it was all going to fall apart.

He opened his briefcase and gently ran his fingertips over the raised print of the contract. These forty pages of paper represented his dreams, everything he had worked toward for the past ten years, and it was all going to come to nothing. He picked up the envelope that had been on his desk this morning. Pasted to the paper inside it were three words, cut out of newspaper headlines:*Blood will tell.*

He sighed and laid his head against the headrest, looking at the Walker and Co sign. The company was a means to an end—his life's ambition was not building car parks and office buildings. He'd wanted to be an architect. As a young boy, he'd filled numerous sketchbooks with jottings of houses he was going to build. As a nineteen-year-old he'd been studying architecture and on the way to achieving his dream when his world came to an end. Out of necessity, he'd turned to work in the building industry and almost by accident came to own his company. But no matter how many successes he achieved, or how much money he made, it never filled the empty space inside.

Glancing at his watch, he snapped his briefcase shut and got out of the car. Once his company was well established, he'd become a corporate sponsor of Rebuilding Together Boston, a non-profit organization working with the community to assist disabled or elderly homeowners in repairing their homes. At first he was involved strictly as a donor of money or leftover building materials. But when a skilled builder had been needed, he'd volunteered on the odd worksite on his weekends and eventually became a project supervisor.

Now RTB had raised funds to build a housing project in Roxbury and he was to be the developer. All he had to do was sign on the dotted line and his dreams would come true. He would finally have the chance to create something with his own two hands that he could take pride in. It seemed so easy.

He pushed open the glass door to his office and heard a woman's laugh. His stride slowed as he recognized Lana's voice. Reaching his office, he looked through the door, and stopped in his tracks.

She was sitting on his desk with Aidan was standing opposite her. Jealousy cut through his gut when he saw she was glowing, her smile lighting up the room. For a man who used sentences as if each word cost a dollar, Aidan seemed to have found deep pockets and was tickling Lana's funny bone.

Aidan saw him, and abruptly finished his tale. 'I'll catch you later, Lana,' he said, and walked out of the office past Tristan.

Lana stood as he entered. 'Hi, lover boy.'

Her come-hither smile had the effect of an electric shock on his body. He took a deep breath, breathing in her scent as the memories of the night before drew a lust-filled veil over his eyes. She took a step toward him and his hands started reaching for her before the blood pooling in his groin seeped back to his brain. Shrugging off his coat, he walked past her and hung it on his chair. He sat and turned on his computer before looking at her.

Seeing her bewilderment he felt like slime, but self-preservation kept him firmly glued to his seat. Two years of being sexually rejected by his wife had made him doubt himself as a man. Learning that her fear of sex was because she was raped should have evened out past wrongs, but instead, when he remembered her passionate lovemaking last night, an overwhelming sense of unfairness returned. It didn't seem right that a woman, who had two weeks ago flinched at his every touch and looked at him with suspicion, had been reborn as a sexually confident woman who saw him as her Prince Charming.

When he'd woken this morning with Lana draped across him, her breath on his neck, a thought had clunked into his head with the force of a crashing ball: I brought another woman home from the hospital. He'd peered at her face as she slept, looking for some evidence to explain his feeling. On the surface she was the same woman, down to the freckle above her top lip, yet his gut told him not to trust what he was seeing.

'Tristan ...'

Lana's voice brought him back to the present. He realized he'd been staring at her, searching for a clue to explain his feeling. She was standing awkwardly in front of him, her face puckered in worry as she twisted her wedding ring.

He smiled softly. 'So what are you doing here?' He gestured her toward a chair.

She smiled her relief and sat down. 'I thought we'd go out to lunch.'

He was irritated at his own weakness. He should have remained distant and hurried her on her way to give himself time to think about everything that had happened.

'So this is your secret lair.' She gestured at the room around her. 'I see you've even got a hidden bat suit.' She pointed to his jacket and tie. 'I tried calling you but I kept getting voicemail, so I thought I'd just pop in.'

Chagrined, he reached for his in-tray, spreading paper across his desk as he lifted a pen. 'Sorry, I can't take a lunch break, I'm banked up.' He looked down and started writing.

'Are you avoiding me?'

His hand tightened on the pen as he steeled himself to look at her. He felt like he'd kicked a puppy. He quickly looked away before he weakened again. 'I had a meeting with clients.'

'I didn't see any appointments in your diary.'

He threw his pen down. 'What do you want from me?'

'I want you to be honest.' Her eyes pleaded with him and she leant across the desk. 'I want you to tell me how you feel.'

He stood abruptly, pushing his chair into the wall. 'You want to know how I feel?' he shouted.

Her eyes remained calm, stopping his tantrum in its tracks.

He ran his hands through his hair and breathed in deeply. 'Okay, Lana. I'm freaking out.' He kept the desk between them as he met her eyes. 'I feel like I brought a stranger home from the hospital.'

She looked away and twisted her engagement ring in what looked like an admission of guilt. 'Oh.' She stilled her hands. 'You're right.' She met his gaze. 'You did take home a stranger from the hospital.'

He sat down in shock.

'I am not the person you married.'

The ring of truth in her words caught him unaware, until she breathed in dramatically and started reciting some drivel about realizing the value of life after the accident. He concealed a yawn, deciding to wait her out then push for the truth.

As he watched her, he was reminded of their first meeting at a fundraiser for RTB; she'd had the same spark of vitality she was exuding now. He'd noticed her when she walked in with her family but quickly looked away, judging her as the mayor's demure daughter. Driven out onto the balcony by the need for fresh air an hour later, the aroma of cigarette smoke told him he wasn't alone. Turning around, he'd seen Lana watching him with amusement in her eyes and recognized a kindred spirit.

He caught the tail end of her sentence. 'So you see, the accident made me realize that I only had one life, and I had to make the most of it.'

He nodded, restraining the urge to clap his hands at her performance. Anyone else would have been taken in by the sincerity in her eyes. But he knew Lana in all her guises: the demure daughter; the underhanded rebel; the cringing victim. Although the sexual vamp of the night before had been an eye opener. He would have thought it was a performance but there were some things a woman couldn't fake and undisguised enthusiasm was one of them.

He returned to the business at hand. 'Well, that's very illumi-nating.' He stood and circled the desk, sitting on the edge next to her shoulder. She looked at up him, shifting uneasily at his proximity.

He picked up the pen and twirled it in his hands, letting the silence stretch out. 'How did you know about my father?'

Her eyes widened. She opened her mouth to answer, but stuttered into silence instead. She smiled sadly, her eyes gently caressing his face. 'You wouldn't believe me if I told you.'

She reached for his hand and kissed it, and with that one gesture, all the confidence he'd felt sputtered and died. Feeling the smoothness of her skin as she held his hand cupped against her cheek, her head leaning against his knee, he couldn't hide from the truth any more: she scared him. When he'd left the apartment this morning he'd been running scared from the emotions she stirred in him. Emotions he'd thought were long dead and buried. He didn't want to feel this, this —

He pulled his hand away and returned back to his chair. 'Okay, I'll see you at home later.' He stared at the desk, his voice choked with emotion.

He watched from the corner of his eye as she stood and walked to the door. He breathed out in relief as the door slammed shut, only to jerk his head up when he heard her speak.

'I'm not leaving until we talk about last night.' She stood with her back against the door, her gaze unflinching.

He stared at her in amazement, starting to doubt his sanity. Who was this woman watching him with rock-hard purpose in her eyes? This was certainly not the woman he'd known for the past two years. He slammed his hand on his desk.

'Christ, Lana. What the hell do you want from me? My heart, my soul?' He leant back in his chair. 'We're getting divorced.'

'So what was last night about?'

Her insistence for the truth cooled his bluster. He fought to maintain eye contact as a curdle of shame opened up in his gut. He'd been trying to convince himself that last night had been for old times' sake. It had started out as sex, but sometime in the morning, they had made love, their eyes wide open as they caressed each other. The lies he'd been trying to hide behind disappeared when he saw the love and trust shining in her eyes.

'I'm sorry, but last night changes nothing.'

'Sorry,' she whispered. She was looking at her clenched hands, her hair shielding her face so he couldn't see her expression.

'It's all my fault. Please don't cry,' he begged, seeing her chest rise with a deep breath. He held out a box of tissues, feeling inept in the face of her distress.

'You conceited asshole.' She lifted her head, meeting his gaze head on. Her eyes were sharp as glass. 'You just used me for a fuck.'

For a minute he was stunned, then her words slashed through his befuddlement, and anger kickstarted his brain into action. 'There were two of us in that bed.' He dropped the tissues back on the desk. 'What did you think? One night of great sex would magically heal our marriage?'

Seeing her blank face he regretted his honesty. He should have been gentler with her. She turned again to the door. He lifted his hand to reach for her before quickly dropping it back to his side, biting back the words of apology and regret rising to his lips. It was best this way. A sharp, quick cut would set them both free.

She stopped with her hand on the doorknob. He frowned, waiting for her to walk out. Instead he heard the click as she locked the door.

She turned around slowly and ran her hands down her thighs as she gazed at the floor. She was wearing a skirt with slits on each side and when she bent her leg, a white garter appeared. His heart started pounding at the blatant eroticism of her gesture.

'Lana.' His voice broke. He cleared his throat and tried again. 'We should talk about this at home.'

His gaze was glued to her skirt as she walked toward him, stopping so close he felt her warm breath on his forehead. Her hands moved to the buttons of her shirt. She undid the first button and her cleavage appeared.

A small part of his brain was still working, despite all the blood having rushed out. He knew that she was manipulating him. She sat on the edge of his desk, her legs against his torso. He clenched his hands on the armrest as he smelt her familiar vanilla scent surrounding him. He decided he didn't care that her manipulations were working. She leant forward, her lips a hair's breadth from his, and he didn't think any more. Urgency and impatience burned in him. He was inflamed with lust for her and reached out for her.

She whispered in his ear, 'Now you know what it's like to be used,' and hopped off his desk, sashaying to the door before he could process what happened.

She looked over her shoulder and met his eyes. His hands tightened on the armrest when he saw the satisfaction in her eyes.

'We could have had something.' She opened the door, 'If you had let me in.'

She closed the door quietly behind her, leaving him stripped bare in all his weakness.

Chapter 11

Lana wiped the already clean kitchen counter as she listened for Tristan to step out of the shower. By the time he'd arrived home from work, she was dressed for Tammy's anniversary party and was angrily pacing the bedroom.

Fury cramped in her stomach as she remembered his face as he told her last night meant nothing. She squeezed the sponge in her hand forcefully, the water spilling on the floor and splashing her shoes. With a muttered oath, she bent and wiped them with a paper towel. Her ears twitched as she heard the bathroom door open. She froze and held her breath, not ready to face Tristan yet. Please go to the bedroom, please go to the bedroom. She breathed out a sigh of relief as her prayers were answered.

Since Tristan had returned from work she'd managed to avoid him by moving around the rooms in the apartment. She knew her time was coming to an end and they would have to face each other on the drive to Tammy's party, but somehow she kept hoping for a miracle.

She had desperately wanted to cancel tonight and had been holding the phone in her lap to do just that when Tammy rang. She'd apologized for blowing Lana off, which seemed a lifetime ago, and asked her if she and Tristan were still coming. Lana had been all set to fake an excuse but the need in Tammy's voice stopped her. Lana wasn't going to make the same mistakes in this life by letting her grudges fester. So here she was, all dolled up and waiting for her date to get dressed.

The atmosphere in the kitchen changed and she knew he'd entered. She turned slowly, her eyes moving no further than his neck. She smoothed her hand over her coat. She saw his Adam's apple bob as he swallowed and knew he was about to speak.

She rushed past him and picked up her purse off the kitchen table. 'We'd better go or we'll be late.' She wrenched open the apartment door and burst out into the hallway.

By the time he caught up with her, she was stepping into the elevator, making sure to stand in the corner furthest from him. She counted the floor numbers, urging the elevator to speed up. They stopped at the second floor and another couple entered and stood between her and Tristan.

When the elevator stopped in the basement, Tristan didn't wait for her but stalked to the truck. He barely waited for her to close her door before taking off, his sharp tug of the steering wheel revealing his frustration.

She turned on the radio and looked away from him, the tension in the cabin building as they drove through the streets of Boston toward Tammy and Michael's brownstone on Louisburg Square. When Tristan parked the car, she was wound tighter than a Jack-in-the-box and her hand was clasped the door handle ready for a quick escape.

He placed his hand on her arm. 'We need to talk.'

'Can't it wait?' She inched away from him.

The dull thunk of the door locks being activated stopped her in her tracks. She kept her gaze on the door handle, feeling like she was suffocating beneath the oppressive silence filling the darkness of the cab. Her skin prickled as if ants were walking on her as the desperate need to move overwhelmed her.

Tristan spoke. 'We're not leaving this car until we talk about what happened in the office.'

With a sigh she sat back against her seat and looked through the windshield. 'What do you want to talk about?'

She heard him take a deep breath. She looked at him but could only see the outline of his face from the street lamp. She relaxed and leant back in her seat, feeling more comfortable with the darkness hiding them from each other. Still, she hunched deeper into her coat, desperately wanting to hide.

'Lana, I —'

She reached out and put her finger over his lips, not wanting to hear what he had to say. 'Don't,' she pleaded, shaking her head. 'Let's just chalk it up to the petty desire for revenge and leave it at that.'

He hesitated, before nodding. When he unlocked the car doors, she jumped out, breathing in the crisp air and feeling like she'd had a lucky escape. She didn't know what had possessed her to attempt to seduce him in his office. All she knew was that when he rejected her, all her love, anger, fear and frustration had converged into the dark need to make him pay.

She looked at him from the corner of her eye as he waited for her on the pavement. Since she'd woken in this new world, all she'd done was waiting for him to recognize in her the woman he loved. And when last night it had seemed he saw her – truly saw her – and still rejected her, the pain had been too much. She'd wanted him to feel some of her confusion and hurt. It looked like she'd succeeded.

Looking at the brownstone Tristan was standing in front of, Lana realized Tammy had made the big time. While the townhouse was modest in size, any Bostonian worth their salt knew that in Beacon Hill, Boston's most exclusive and expensive neighborhood, property was spoken of in terms of square footage only, rather than the number of bedrooms or bathrooms.

Her heel caught on the sidewalk and she stumbled. Tristan caught her. Feeling his arms around her she looked up, her heart racing as she saw Frank's face. Tristan moved, nudging her toward the stairs leading to the front door and stepping further into the streetlight. The shadows faded from his face and Frank disappeared.

They stood in front of the brownstone's door and she blinked as he asked if she was all right. She nodded, not trusting her voice as she stepped away from him, needing some time to recover. She bent her head and touched the clasp of her handbag while Tristan knocked.

Tammy opened the door, spilling light onto Tristan's face, highlighting every craggy feature. All this time, Lana had been behaving as if Tristan was Frank, the husband she loved and who adored her. She'd been waiting for him to realize the truth of their love and all her anger and frustration had been in reaction to his distance. But Tristan wasn't Frank and he never would be, no matter how much she wished it.

'Hello,' Tammy said, her smile illuminating her face when she saw them.

Tristan looked at Lana in concern. 'Lana, are you all right?'

She nodded. Seeing Tammy peering at her, she quickly pulled her into a hug. 'Hi Mom.' She hid her face as she regained control.

Frank was dead and nothing she did would bring him back. She blinked at the tears burning her eyes as the truth stripped her bare. All this time she'd been living a make-believe life, trying to transform this world into one she was comfortable with.

She pulled away from Tammy, who tenderly brushed her hair behind her ear. This world and these people were real, and she was the one who had to make the change and accept that.

She smiled at Tammy. 'Happy Anniversary.'

Tammy smiled, her eyes sparkling and giving a hint of the vibrant woman she'd once been. 'Thanks, baby,' she whispered, giving Lana a kiss on the cheek. 'Thank you too, Tristan.' Tammy stood on her tippy toes as Tristan bent down awkwardly and accepted her kiss without returning her embrace. Tammy looked nonplussed at his lack of affection.

He met Lana's gaze and she saw the discomfort in his eyes before he walked past Tammy into the house. Since he had read Alannah's diary entries and saw the rage she felt toward Tammy for not recognizing she was in trouble, he'd become uneasy in his mother-in-law's presence. Lana squeezed Tammy's arm as she entered the foyer.

After she'd read the diary, she'd felt betrayed again, but the feeling had quickly passed. She'd realized that if she truly wanted to heal the estrangement from Tammy and learn from the past, then she had to stop passing judgement before she had all the facts.

Lana looked around as she took off her coat. They were in a hallway that was oppressive in its opulence: grey marble floor tiles and walls covered in burgundy wallpaper. There was a round mahogany lamp table with a vase of red roses, their scent almost overpowering, set beside a mahogany staircase. Tristan helped her with her coat. She breathed in his aftershave and met his gaze. He was giving her the once-over.

Lana wore Alannah's soft pink dress. On Alannah it was probably loose and feminine, hinting at the curves underneath, but Lana's weight gain stretched the dress taut over her curves, dipping into her waist and draping around her hips. She'd known it was tight when she put it on, but hadn't realized how tight until she caught Tristan's gaze zeroing in on her breasts as they swelled over the lace insert cowl neck. She wanted to snatch back her coat and hide in it.

Tristan smiled, his teeth gleaming against his tanned face. 'Wow,' he mouthed quietly.

Her self-consciousness faded and she basked in his admiration. He shrugged off his coat and it was her turn to stare. He was wearing a charcoal suit with a red tie. The suit was fitted, highlighting a body molded by hard work. She flushed under his heated gaze, but couldn't look away. Butterflies fluttered in her stomach as an overpowering surge of attraction swept over her. Her breath shortened as she realized this was the first time she was truly seeing him as a man in his own right. Up until now, all he had been to her was a reminder of Frank.

After handing their coats to the hovering waiter, Tristan placed his hand on her back and led her into the lounge room after Tammy. She looked at him discreetly and saw he was feeling the same spine-tingling awareness– it was in the way he watched her, as if he wanted to devour her. They sat together on the sofa, a gap between them, but she was as aware of him as if they were glued to each other.

She looked around the lounge room as Tammy sat on the sofa opposite them. The walls were covered with dark blue wallpaper and the sofas were upholstered in blue velvet with matching armchairs grouped around the mahogany fireplace. The house was like a museum, opulent, and with no warmth. Something in the way each room was perfectly accessorized and color-coordinated removed any hint of life.

Realizing that this was Alannah's childhood home, Lana finally understood her choice of décor. Their apartment was a modern oasis compared to the outdated showpiece they were in.

'Michael won't be long. He just had an urgent phone call,' Tammy said.

Lana nodded. A tense silence stretched out. Tammy bit her lip and smoothed her grey silk skirt. Tammy looked almost unrecognizable from the woman Lana had known in her other life; the Tammy of vibrant clothes, puffed-up hair and loud laugh had been replaced by a matronly woman who nearly faded into the background.

'You look nice, Mom,' she said.

Tammy's face brightened and Lana saw the glimmer of the woman she'd known. She opened her mouth as if to say something but, looking over Lana's shoulder, her face changed once again. She stood.

'Michael, Tristan and Alannah have arrived.'

Lana looked over her shoulder at the man heading toward them. He'd once been a handsome man and was still fighting the ravages of time, his blond hair carefully styled to conceal the fact it was thinning, his jacket slightly loose around the waist to disguise the paunch. Lana and Tristan stood and Michael air-kissed Lana then shook hands with Tristan.

'Glad you could make it,' Michael said. He put his arm around Tammy.

The waiter who'd taken their coats entered holding a tray of drinks.

Taking a glass, Michael sipped before continuing, 'It's wonderful you feel comfortable enough to be,' he paused as he looked at Lana, as if searching for the correct adjective, 'casual.'

Lana glanced at Tammy, who was playing with her pearl earring and biting her lip. She looked up and smiled weakly at Lana. Her whole demeanor sent the message that this was something she'd heard many times before and had learnt to tune out.

Tristan put his arm around her waist and pulled her against him. 'I agree.' He smiled at Lana. 'She looks beautiful.'

Lana smiled in Tristan in gratitude, before shifting away imperceptibly. She didn't need him to fight her battles.

She gave Michael the same once over. 'And you look,' she paused, staring at his thinning hair, 'handsome?' She stretched out the word and looked back to his face. His eyes had narrowed, his lips stretched into an insincere smile.

'Thank you, my dear,' he murmured, sounding anything but grateful.

Lana smiled coolly. She looked over Michael's shoulder, refusing to give in first and break the silence.

'Well, it's lovely to have you here,' Tammy said, her eyes shifting from one to the other. 'Sit down and make yourselves comfortable.' Her hands fluttered in the direction of the sofas.

Lana waited a beat before sitting down.

Michael sat, unbuttoning his jacket so it didn't bunch around his waist. 'So I hear you're branching out to build houses?' he asked.

Tristan stiffened beside her. Glancing at him, she saw his face was immobile, but she could feel his displeasure.

'That's right.'

Michael laughed, the jagged edge rubbing her nerves raw. 'Who would have thought, from car parks to houses. Is this a considered career plan? You know that those people won't pay.'

'That's why the consortia came together to build the houses for free.' Tristan's voice was firm, not inviting further discussion. He touched Lana's elbow gently. 'Remember, darling? I told you about the project a few weeks before your accident. We're building an independent housing development in Roxbury to create affordable housing.'

She met his gaze, gauging the sincerity in his eyes. He didn't look away.

'You should let the government deal with those issues,' Michael said.

'The government won't deal with the issues,' Tristan replied, keeping his gaze on Lana.

She covered her hand with his and nodded. She saw in his eyes the glimmer of Frank's passion to make a difference in the world however he could; it was Frank's compassion that drew her to him in the first place. They had met when Frank came to Dave's Steakhouse, where she worked as a waitress, to seek food donations for the homeless shelter he'd volunteered at.

She smiled at Tristan. He turned her hand over and clasped it.

Michael's snide voice interrupted them. 'So Alannah, I hear you're going to be a crusader in the classroom.' He sipped. 'You know there's not much pay in that.'

Lana held his gaze. 'I don't care about the pay.'

Michael smiled, seemingly happy at the anger she was exhibiting. He sat back against the sofa and draped his arm around Tammy. 'I'll call the principal of your high school on Monday and organize for you to work as a teacher's assistant.' He looked at Tammy, who smiled at him in gratitude.

'That's not necessary,' Lana said firmly. Tammy's smile faded and she looked at her lap. She softened her voice and spoke to Tammy. 'I'm fine on my own.'

'Just like you're fine in that café you insist on working in.' Michael removed his arm from around Tammy and sat on the edge of the seat, his face genuinely perplexed. 'I don't understand why, with all the opportunities I can offer you, you have to keep doing it the hard way?'

'I don't need anyone to take care of me.' Lana turned to look at Tristan. He held her gaze as she realized the implications of what she'd said. She didn't need anyone. All this time she'd behaved as if she was a drowning woman and Tristan was the only one who could save her. From the time she'd remembered her other life, she'd been convinced that her arrival in this world was a second chance for her and Frank to be together again. But what if she and Frank had had their time and this life was for her to try *her* life again? Some people had a lifetime to be together, she and Frank had five wonderful years; maybe that was all they were supposed to have.

Loud voices at the front door brought her back to the present.

'Hi, sis,' said the young man bouncing into the room.

Lana blinked as she looked at a younger version of Michael. He had the same blond hair and icy blue eyes. His eyes were glassy and red-rimmed and his face was flushed. She tensed, recognizing all the signs of drug addict.

'Evan, you're late.' Michael's voice was full of displeasure.

Evan ignored his father as he looked down at Lana, his gaze firmly focused on her cleavage. 'Well, haven't you filled out in all the right places.'

Lana shifted uncomfortably. Tristan stood and stepped toward Evan, forcing him to move away from her.

Evan met Tristan's gaze. 'Walker.'

'Stanford,' Tristan replied.

Testosterone charged the atmosphere before Michael put his arm around Evan and drew him away. With a last look at Tristan, Evan turned to Michael and hugged him. Michael held himself stiff in Evan's embrace.

'Congratulations, guys.' He bent and kissed Tammy on the cheek. 'Ten years. Wow. Who would have thought after the Boston Globe broke the news about your affair you would end up here, still married? It's a true testament to the power of the media.'

Tammy flushed and looked away.

'I told you not to come to the house in this state,' Michael said.

'Daddy-o, I wouldn't miss the party for the world.' A waiter approached him and Evan plucked a glass from the tray he was holding. 'I propose a toast to the loving couple.' He laughed raucously, his hand shaking. The glass dropped and spilled over Tammy.

'Oops' Evan covered his mouth, his eyes glittering maliciously above his hand. 'But I guess better out than in, huh, Mom?'

Tammy gasped and looked at the spreading stain on her shirt. Her eyes teared up and she ran from the room.

'You need to apologize to your stepmother right now!' Michael's face turned red.

'Don't be such a fuddy-duddy.' Evan sipped from his glass. 'I did her a favor by giving her a much needed break to tipple.' He mimed a bottle going to the lips.

Lana threw her martini into Evan's face. He plucked out the red silk handkerchief from the front pocket of his suit and wiped his face while looking at her.

He put his wet finger in his mouth and licked it. 'Just the way I like it. Shaken, not stirred.'

Michael's hands formed into fists. 'Get out.' He approached Evan as if to hit him.

Evan smiled at Lana, before turning to Michael. They stood toe to toe. 'I wouldn't recommend it, old man.' His voice was quiet and controlled.

Michael blinked, his face blanching. His bluster disappeared and he looked shaken. He moved out of Evan's way.

Reaching the doorway, Evan stopped and turned with a smile. 'It's been a pleasure that I hope to repeat soon.' He held Lana's gaze before disappearing from sight.

Michael ran a trembling hand through his hair. 'Well, that was quite a display, Alannah. But I'd appreciate if you behaved in a civilized fashion in my house.' He walked out before she could retort, his confident stride replaced with a slow and precise gait.

Lana smoothed her damp palms on her thighs, feeling shaky in the aftermath.

Tristan helped her sit on the sofa and handed her another drink. He pushed her hair behind her ears. 'Are you okay?'

She nodded before taking a sip of the drink.

'You did good.'

She laughed. 'So, what's between you and Evan?'

He sighed and sat next to her. 'He asked me to build a residential development he was financing. I found out that the ground was contaminated and notified the state authorities. He lost his outlay and to say he blames me is an understatement.'

She leant against his shoulder. 'A great family I have.'

He laughed. 'You're still doing better than me.'

Lana lifted her head, something in his voice ringing alarm bells.

He stood and offered her his hand. 'What do you say we blow this joint and have a real party?'

She hesitated, a question about his family on the tip of her tongue. With a smile, she pushed it aside and took his hand. They headed to the door when she remembered Tammy.

She stopped. 'I should say goodbye to Tammy.'

Tristan took her coat from the waiter and helped her into it. 'I'll wait.'

'No, it's okay. You go ahead and start the truck.' She headed up the stairs. 'I'll only be a minute.'

When she reached the top of the stairs, she hesitated before calling out Tammy's name. When there was no answer, she walked further into the hallway, stopping outside an ajar door. She heard raised voices. Recognizing Tammy's voice, she pushed the door open.

Tammy was on the floor. She'd changed her blouse but hadn't had a chance to finish buttoning it up. Michael stood over her, his hand raised. Seeing Lana at the door, he hesitated.

Suddenly she was eight years old again, watching as Tammy's boyfriend punched her. While her mother lay on the floor, he lifted his leg to kick. Lana rushed in, only to be flung against the wall. She watched helplessly as his foot connected with Tammy, the sickening thud too much for her eight-year-old self to bear.

Returning to the present, Lana rushed in and pushed Michael away from Tammy. 'Don't you touch her!' she shouted.

Michael lost his balance and grabbed the bed to stop his fall so she pushed him again and he hit the wall.

'Lana, enough.' Tammy's voice stopped her.

Lana reached down and helped her mother stand. Tammy straightened slowly and buttoned her blouse. 'You should go downstairs and greet our guests,' she said to Michael.

He hesitated before leaving the room in brisk strides, slamming the door shut behind him.

Tammy sat on the stool before the vanity and lifted her hands to her head to redo her bun. She winced, touching her ribs before getting on with fixing her hair.

'Is that it?' Lana looked at her with disbelief. 'He hits you and now you're going to go downstairs and greet your guests.'

'Yes.' Tammy didn't meet her gaze.

'You haven't changed at all,' Lana said. 'All that matters are the perks: the house, the car, the bank balance. Never mind if you earn each cent by being a punching bag.'

Tammy put the brush down. 'There are some things you don't understand.'

'No, Tammy. I understand perfectly.' Lana reached the door and turned the handle before stopping. 'Happy tenth anniversary.'

When she reached the foyer, Michael was greeting guests. Seeing her alone, he smiled in triumph.

'Tammy will be along,' she said. 'She just has to —'

'Thank you, Lana,' Tammy's voice interrupted. She was at the top of the stairs, the impeccable mayor's wife once again, and descended with the grace of a debutante. Only someone looking closely would notice the tightness at the corner of her mouth. When she reached the front door, Michael pulled her into a possessive embrace, causing her to wince. Lana walked past the embracing couple and out the door.

'Lana!' Tammy called.

'Let her go, darling. You can call her tomorrow.'

Reaching the truck, Lana turned and looked behind her. Tammy and Michael stood in the open doorway, Tammy's face was distressed as Michael whispered in her ear, the composure she'd carried around her like a cloak disappearing. Lana took a step back to the house but Michael closed the door.

'What happened?' Tristan asked as she got into the truck.

'Just drive.' She tiredly laid her head against the headrest.

With one last searching glance at her, he started the engine and drove.

She rubbed her eyes as she thought of the family she'd landed into. Seeing the smudged make-up on her hands, she swore and searched for a tissue in the glove compartment. Flipping the visor down, she looked into the mirror as she wiped away her smudged make-up and thought about Alannah's diary. There had been no mention of Michael's real side; Alannah had been enrolled at a private girl's boarding school and had only visited home once a month at weekends.

Lana frowned as she remembered what Alannah wrote about Evan. He'd been her schoolgirl crush, but Lana had had no idea he was Alannah's stepbrother. After Tammy had put her in boarding school, all entries about him had ceased.

'So you want to tell me about it?' Tristan interrupted her musings.

'Did you know?' She shredded the tissue. She glanced at Tristan. 'Did you know Michael beat Tammy?'

Tristan's hands tightened on the steering wheel. 'I suspected.' He hit the indicator and carefully turned. 'But there was never any proof.'

Lana laughed bitterly. 'What's a few bruises compared to the million in the bank?'

Not hearing him jump to Tammy's defense she looked at him sideways. 'What, nothing to say?'

He pulled up into the car park of their building and turned off the ignition. With his elbow on the steering wheel, he leant toward her. 'No. I think you know your mother better than I do.'

She was speechless. He leant into her. She quickly moved away and opened the truck door. In her rush to jump out her skirt got tangled in the seat belt, leaving her thighs exposed. She swore as she tugged on it.

Tristan came to her side of the truck. His arm brushed against her as he pulled the skirt free, his hand caressing her thigh before he helped her out. She sucked in her breath as they stood pressed against each other. His hand reached behind her head and she felt the thrill of anticipation as she waited to be pulled against him. But he slammed the door shut and put his arm around her waist, leading her to the elevator. Inside, she leant against the wall limply.

After pressing their floor, he put his arms on each side of her head. 'I believe we have some unfinished business.'

Heat spread through her body as she imagined him pleasuring her. She licked her lips. His iris enlarged as he watched her tongue. He started leaning in, his gaze locked on her lips.

'But.'

She put her hand on his chest and stopped him. He dragged his gaze away from her lips and met her eyes.

'If I can't have your love, then I don't want anything from you.'

He leant back, letting her pass by him when the elevator doors opened on their floor.

She felt his gaze on her, burning her skin as she walked. She pulled out the keys to the apartment. Looking over her shoulder, she saw the elevator doors closing, Tristan still on it.

In the split second before they closed she saw pain in his eyes. She looked back at the apartment door, her eyes blurry with tears as she unlocked it and stepped inside.

She leant against the door, closing her eyes as the tears seeped out. She walked to the coffee table and pulled a tissue from the box, wiping her face. The framed photo of Alannah and Tristan on the TV cabinet caught her eye. She walked over to it and looked closer at Tristan. The feeling of déjà vu returned. She felt a certain sense of recognition when she looked at him, the recognition of the love she'd felt for Frank. But that was all. She wasn't in love with Tristan.

If only he'd given her something of himself, allowed her to truly see him, she might have loved him, but he'd always pulled back and after a while so had she. She and Tristan had had a window of opportunity to be together but their past hurts and betrayals had kept them cautiously circling each other, and their time had passed.

She looked around the apartment, saying goodbye to her life in it. She sighed and headed for the bedroom. Tomorrow morning she would find her own apartment and move out. As she wiped her cheeks, she realized she felt aching regret but it was tempered with the feeling of hope. This life was a blank canvas on which she could paint whatever story she wanted. She smiled as she stepped out of her shoes. It was time to plan for her new life.

Chapter 12

Their eyes met just before the elevator door closed. He read the finality in hers and knew in his gut that if he didn't step out of the elevator now, he'd lose her. His hand reached for the gap in the door. Then he hesitated and the door closed.

It was for the best. What they had was just a flash of attraction– that's all they'd ever had. He had been foolish to confuse it with something more meaningful.

Walking through the basement to his truck, foreboding crept over him as he saw the white envelope trapped under the windshield wiper. He lifted the envelope, looking around to see who could've left it. The basement was empty.

Opening it, he pulled out the sheet of paper. It was the same note he'd received before, this time featuring an article headlined Walters found guilty of manslaughter. There was a photo of a broad-shouldered man in handcuffs being led by police. He turned the sheet over, searching for a message. Nothing.

In frustration he punched the truck hood, leaving a dint on the spotless surface. He wanted to keep going, to keep pounding his frustration until he was spent, but reason asserted itself and paranoia crept over him. The first message had been mailed to his office, and now this one had been left at home. The bastard knew where he worked, where he lived– everything about him – and was taunting him with his past. He was at their mercy, his whole life and everything he'd achieved vulnerable to some nameless person. What the hell was he going to do?

He got in the truck and started it, before realizing he had nowhere to go. He wasn't in the mood to be among people, so his regular bar was out of the question. He'd worked hard to keep any potential friends at a distance, the need to not reveal anything about his past making him cold to any overtures.

The only one who'd gotten past his guard was Aidan, but they had been working together for ten years and still maintained their careful distance, thanks to Aidan's natural reticence and Tristan's well-kept boundaries. It was only in the past three months, since Holly and Alannah had started working together, that the personal and professional began to blur.

He turned the wheel and left the garage, realizing he'd already made his decision. This blackmail thing was bigger than him, and he needed help. Fifteen minutes later he was pulling into Aidan's driveway.

Aidan appeared on the front porch. Recognizing the truck, he approached the driver's side with a worried frown.

'Is everything okay?'

Tristan handed him the article and opened the truck door so Aidan could read it by the light of the cab.

Aidan looked up from the paper. 'You'd better come in.' He headed back into the house and held the front door open for Tristan, who jumped out of the truck and followed. He noticed the messy living room, toys littering the floor.

'Is the little tyke asleep?'

'Yeah.' Aidan smiled as he ran his hand through his hair. 'He finally zonked out on the couch an hour ago.' Reaching for the liquor cabinet in the corner of the room, he took out a bottle of Jack Daniels and poured two drinks. 'I just carried him to his bedroom before you arrived.' He handed Tristan a glass, before taking a swallow from his own. Taking a seat across from Tristan, he waited.

Tristan gulped his Jack Daniels, the fiery scotch burning its way down his throat as he tried to find a way to start. Twisting the empty glass between his hands, he slowly found the words and told Aidan his story, or as much as he could tell.

'My real name is Frank Tristan Walters.' He cut a quick glance at Aidan and saw that his friend immediately connected his name to the biggest scandal to hit the Boston building industry in twenty years.

'Well, if you know the name Walters, then you know the story.' Tristan stared at his glass. 'After it happened I had to change my name to get work in the building industry.' He smiled bitterly. 'It's all I was qualified to do. And now someone knows who I really am.' He finally looked at Aidan.

'I don't see the problem. This —' Aidan held up the article '— is in the past. It has nothing to do with who you are now.'

Tristan jumped to his feet and paced the living room floor. 'It's not that simple,' he began. Remembering Joshua was sleeping he lowered his voice, his restrained frustration making it slightly hoarse. 'You don't know how it ruined my life. Once the news hit, we lost everything: our home, our reputation, our friends. We had nothing.' He punched his fist into his hand. 'We were nothing.'

Aidan stood and clasped his shoulder. 'Then they weren't the right kind of friends.' He took Tristan's glass and poured him another drink.

Tristan stared at the full glass Aidan was offering him. There was a lump in his throat and no matter how hard he swallowed, it wouldn't go away. Taking the glass, he quickly grasped Aidan's hand. He forced himself to meet his eyes. It was the first time since he'd left Frank Walters behind that fateful day ten years ago that someone truly saw him and didn't look away.

Aidan nodded, acknowledging all that Tristan couldn't say. 'Does Alannah know?'

Tristan shook his head without looking up.

'Don't you think you should tell her before someone else does?'

'It's not that easy.' Tristan rubbed his face. 'I think she knows already.'

Aidan paused. 'You think she's behind this note?'

Tristan didn't answer, but the suspicion had been festering since she'd called him by his birth name.

'My track record in the relationship department speaks for itself.' Aidan gave a wry smile, his eyes on the wedding photo on the wall. 'But I know from personal experience that if you don't talk to Lana about this, you will regret it for the rest of your life.'

Tristan nodded, knowing things had come too far for him to back away now. But what if he found out his suspicions were right? He gulped the rest of his scotch, the slow burn of alcohol distracting him from the ache in his gut.

·♥·♥·♥·♥·♥·

He entered the apartment. The lamp was on but Lana wasn't in the living room. He and Aidan hadn't had a chance to talk after Joshua woke from a nightmare, but their brief conversation had given him food for thought.

He realized that he'd gotten burnt as an idealistic nineteen-year-old after the news broke and his supposed friends disappeared. He'd become wary of letting anyone close to him, because then he'd have to tell them who he really was.

Aidan was the first person Tristan had told about his past and Aidan had accepted him without judgement; his actions over the past ten years spoke louder than something that had happened in the past. Wasn't that what he was doing to Alannah? Judging her by past mistakes rather than her actions now?

As he rubbed the back of his neck, something on the coffee table caught his eye: the manila file he and Lana kept their documents in. As he sorted through them, he saw Lana had separated all her school and college transcripts. There was an application checklist downloaded from the net and she'd ticked on it all the documents she'd collected.

He frowned as he saw she'd also printed out a list of apartments for rent. Looking closer, he saw that the apartments that were open for viewing tomorrow were circled. He was too late. He'd pushed her too far and she was walking away.

Lana entered, stopping abruptly when she caught sight of him. She quirked her eyebrow. 'Back already?' Without waiting for a response, she started collecting her papers from the coffee table. 'I'll take those too.' She put out her hand to take the apartment advertisements from him.

He took hold of her arm to stop her leaving the living room. He opened his mouth to speak, but the words caught in his throat, choking him. He swallowed, and tried again.

She frowned in concern. 'What is it Tristan?'

'Don't—' His voice cut out.

She placed the papers on the coffee table. 'Are you okay?'

'I know that you've made your decision to leave.' He gestured to the ads in her hand. 'And I don't blame you.' He smiled ruefully. 'I've certainly given you enough reasons.' Seeing she was about to interrupt he put his fingers to her lips. 'I'm not asking you to change your mind. I just want you to let me tell you my side of the story.'

She watched him uncertainly, but she breathed in and sat on the sofa.

He clenched his fists and paced as he tried to find the words. What he'd told Aidan was only one part of the story.

'After my father...' He looked at the cream carpet and started again. 'After my father died we lost everything because he'd made some bad business decisions.'

He sat on the sofa beside her. 'My mom got sick.' He stopped and breathed deeply. 'Our medical insurance ran out so I left university and got a job on a building site through my dad's friend.'

He swallowed hard, having to force himself to remember all the things he'd worked so hard to forget. 'No matter how hard I worked or what I tried, it wasn't enough.' He cleared his throat. 'She died alone six months later.' Hearing Lana's gasp, he met her gaze and explained. 'The hospital tried calling me, but I was on site and the message didn't reach me.'

He still remembered the bone-numbing cold that had descended on him as he listened to the message. It had been at the end of his work day. He'd been so tired after twelve hours of wheeling bricks up make-shift ramps that he'd had to listen to the message twice before his tired brain understood it. Speeding like a maniac to Massachusetts General Hospital, he'd prayed that he wasn't too late.

He held his fists against his eyes and his breathing became ragged. 'My mother died alone.' He tried to block out the image of his mother on his last visit to the hospital, the day before she died. She'd been lying in the hospital bed, her eyes on the door as she waited for him. When he'd walked through the door she'd smiled, the lines of pain easing to reveal the mother he remembered. He'd visit in every day after work, freshly showered with his hair still damp, he'd just sit beside her and hold her hand. He'd been too tired to talk, and she'd been too ill to listen. All she'd wanted was the comfort of his presence.

He felt Lana's arms around him, holding him tightly, her vanilla perfume surrounding him. Her hold didn't ease until he won his battle with the pain and his breathing evened.

He pulled away and met her eyes. A tear slipped onto her cheek. He caught it with his fingertip and licked it. Tasting the faint saltiness, he realized he'd never allowed himself to cry. Life had been an unending grind of work and survival and he'd tamped down all his emotions and fought just to get through each day.

He lifted her arm off his shoulders and walked to the window. He turned around. 'Then I met you. I remember the first thing you ever said to me.' He smiled and looked at her. Seeing her blank look, his smile faded. "Can you butt out please and stop polluting my air.' Do you remember what you said?'

She shook her head.

He looked away from her. After the crush of people and their never-ending chatter, he'd been itching for privacy and went onto the balcony in the cool night. After he'd snapped he'd turned and been stunned to see the mayor's daughter, who snapped back, 'Why don't you stop polluting my balcony?'

Catching Lana's smile, he continued. 'There was a spark in your eyes. You looked like a woman who'd fought a few battles and won.' He turned back to the window. 'But after we married, the spark faded. I thought I was the one draining the life out of you.' He shook his head. 'After my mother died, I'd promised myself I would never be responsible for another human being in that way, and then I met you.'

'What were you studying?' Lana asked.

He looked out the window and caught sight of the city, remembering the buildings he'd worked on. 'Architecture. At first I thought I'd save money and go back to finish my degree. But when I'd reached my goal, the company I was working for was about to go under, so I invested my money and became partner. And a few years after that, I bought the whole company.'

'Is that why you want to do the development in Roxbury, to get back your dream?'

He nodded, looking away so she wouldn't see his expression. Remembering the blackmailer, he felt a familiar rage and bitterness.

He stilled as she put her hands on his waist and leant into him– he hadn't heard her coming toward him. 'I'm so sorry, Tristan.' She took hold of his hand and turned him toward her. 'But you're not alone any more.' She lifted his hand to her lips and kissed it. 'I'm here, and I'm not going anywhere.' She pulled him to her and, standing on her tippy toes, hugged him.

He tried to contain the raging emotions inside. She gently caressed his neck and it broke him. He embraced her hard, trying to pull her into his skin. He dropped to his knees and held her hips, pressing his face into her navel. She hugged him tightly, holding him as if she'd never let him go. Her hands stroked his back, soothing him.

He breathed in her scent. She'd changed into her PJs and the soft cotton curved around her body. As he breathed out, his cool breath blew on her breast. Her nipple hardened, pressing into his cheek. The mood changed. He rubbed against her like a cat. As he watched, her eyes changed from melancholy to desire and she lifted her hand to unbutton her top.

His hands firmly gripped her buttocks, slowly lowering her so she knelt before him, his mouth working its way up her stomach, onto her breasts and her neck. Her face was flushed with passion, and she looked at him with hunger. He kissed her deeply, breathing in her shuddering sigh. She held his face in her hands and dropped light kisses on his cheeks and his mouth.

He closed his eyes as the tenderness of her touch took his breath away. The raw passion consuming him gentled and he wanted to treasure her, to show her what she meant to him.

He lifted her hand to his lips as he kissed his way up the inside of her arm. She trembled at the sensation his kisses produced on the delicate skin. When he reached her neck and then her mouth, she insistently returned his kiss. He broke away to pull her top off, dropping it to the ground before taking her breasts in his callused hands. He stroked his thumbs across her silky skin then bent down to suck first one nipple, then the other.

She pulled his head back up and kissed him as her hands worked their way under his shirt. She pulled it off and pressed against him, gasping as his hairy chest chaffed her nipples.

Their kisses became heated, their caresses more urgent. He stood her up and pulled off her PJ pants, kissing her navel while he worked a hand between her thighs. Moving one hand to her lower back to support her, he caressed her with his hand. He kissed his way down her stomach and replaced his fingers with his tongue, but she pulled away, and made him stand in front of her.

She undid his jeans and pulled his jeans off, kneeling to help him step out of them. He was standing in white briefs and she ran her hands up his thighs then let one stray under the fabric, teasing him by stroking him, before she eased the briefs down and took them off. Sitting back on her heels, she hesitated, glancing up at his face before leaning forward and licking the length of him. She pursed her lips and slipped them over his tip, then took him into her mouth before slowly moving her head back and forth. He closed his eyes and fisted his hands in her hair at the pleasure.

Breathing heavily, he pulled away from her mouth then knelt and eased her onto the carpet. In the dim light from the lamp, her pale skin was golden. Lifting her legs over his shoulders, he dipped his head and tongued her. She jerked and he changed his strokes, lengthening them to caress her gently. Her thighs tightened around his neck as she lost herself in the pleasure he gave.

He inserted one finger, then another, slowly, then began thrusting as her muscles tightened around him, and she orgasmed. His tongue returned to gently massage her as her legs splayed apart in the aftermath.

Pulling a sofa cushion onto the floor, he turned her over, and arranged her on her front, legs wide. He knelt between her thighs and entered her from behind. He felt her stretch around him, her muscles still pulsing and reached his hand under her to press his thumb gently on her. He thrust into her slowly, moving his thumb in rhythm with his thrusts. She gasped and began to writhe under him. He bent over her and bit her neck, making her moan.

She reached back with her hand and grasped his butt, trying to pull him into her. 'Harder,' she murmured.

He slowed his pace.

She groaned. 'Oh god, you're tormenting me.'

He smiled grimly, his hand tightening on her hip as he forced himself to go even slower. He pulled out so his tip sat at her entrance and paused before pushing evening more slowly into her slick heat. Her muscles tensed as she spasmed around him again. He bit hard on his lip, continuing his slow thrusts as he prolonged her orgasm. She collapsed onto her stomach.

He pulled out and turned her over onto her back. She was like a limp doll, her thighs spread wantonly. She was slippery and swollen, her body soft and pliant. He entered her, hard.

Placing his hands under head he rained kisses on her face. 'Look at me,' he demanded.

Her eyes fluttered open.

He thrust harder, giving her what she'd asked for, pushing her deep into the carpet. Her eyes fluttered closed.

He bit her neck. 'No.' He kissed her deeply, as if he was trying to absorb her very soul.

They stared into each other's eyes and knew they were one in every sense of the word.

He felt her shuddering once again and closed his eyes as he began to shudder in response, giving one last great thrust and spilling inside her. He collapsed on top of her, his head pillowed on her breast. He was saved and reborn.

·♥·♥·♥·♥·♥·

Lana lay under Tristan's weight, their sweat-slicked bodies pressed against each other. Her racing heartbeat slowed. He stirred and lifted his head to meet her gaze. In the aftermath of their passion his hazel irises were almost golden.

He kissed her gently on the cheek. 'Okay?'

She nodded.

He hesitated. Then smiled, his white teeth glinting in the shadowed room.

She smiled, her heart slightly bruised. Her face must have shown something because he bent his head and pressed his lips on the curve of her breast, just over her heart. The hurt faded under the tenderness of his caress. He pulled her to him and they held each other. She shut her eyes in contentment.

She was settling into sleep when Tristan stood, lifting her in his arms. She nuzzled deeper in the curve between his shoulder and neck, pressing her nose and lips into the soft skin. He laid her on the bed and fitted himself behind her, curving his arm over her ribs so that his hand cupped her breast.

She lifted his hand and pressed a kiss to his palm. She opened her eyes and noticed his wedding band, making her frown. It was the same as Frank's except Tristan's band still had the sheen of new gold. Disquiet filled her as she tried to picture Frank in her mind. Her heart sped up. She couldn't picture his face any more. The only image she conjured was of Tristan's guarded gaze.

She bit her lip as she realized she hadn't thought of Frank much recently. It was as if her other life was a dream that had felt real upon waking, yet as each day passed it faded more. When she thought of her other life, she could only remember faint impressions of emotions. Remembering Frank now, only brought an echo of sweetness and love.

Tristan shifted behind her, returning her to the present. She became aware of his callused fingers on her skin.

Tonight, as he'd made love to her while gazing into her eyes, she'd seen his vulnerability. He was finally letting her in and not allowing his memories of how Alannah was before the accident hold him back. She tensed as realization hit her square between the eyes: Isn't that what she'd been doing? Keeping Tristan at a distance because Frank's ghost was in her heart? Tristan shifted. She unclenched her muscles and gently stroked his hand.

She realized that the pain of Frank's loss had become a faint sting rather than a burning agony. She'd done her grieving for Frank long before he passed away. It was time to lay the ghost down and face the uncertain future with an open heart.

Tristan turned her onto her back. 'Everything all right?'

She met his gaze and found a softness she'd never seen before. He was with her and not holding back.

She smiled tremulously. 'Everything's great.' She kissed him, putting all her love, hope and passion into the kiss. He lifted himself over her and she saw the promise of love in his eyes. He kissed her, his lips almost harsh as his tongue probed her mouth.

She wrapped her legs around his waist and took him inside, watching his face as he thrust into her. She knew that she was opening herself to hurt, but she was opening herself up to love too.

After they made love, he pulled her into his embrace so that she lay with her head on his shoulder, their legs and arms entangled. His breathing deepened as he drifted off to sleep.

She thought about his vulnerability as he told the truth about his life. She finally understood his reserve when she'd been released from hospital: Alannah's anorexia and his inability to help reminded him of his mother's death. Her throat tightened as she thought of Lillian losing her husband and her life.

Tristan hadn't told her about Kevin's death but she assumed the same tragedy had happened as in his other life: money was embezzled from his father's company, leaving the family destitute. In Frank's life the tragedy had united the family after his heart condition became known, but here it had destroyed them.

Tristan's life had been different than Frank's and that's why he'd become so guarded. She knew from her own experience that when you got hurt so badly and were left on your own at a young age, you developed barriers and could never trust in the same way. She'd spent the first three years of her marriage to Frank expecting him to wake up and realize she wasn't the one for him before his steadfast love and loyalty made her believe.

She watched Tristan as he slept; he looked at peace in a way she'd never seen before. Now that he'd unburdened himself they could move forward without the past holding them back. She frowned as she guiltily realized she hadn't repaid his openness by telling him the truth about herself.

She lay back and started at the ceiling. How do you tell someone that you were from another world? She sighed, burrowing deeper into his embrace. She'd worry about that later.

She pressed a kiss above his heart. 'I love you Frank Tristan Walter,' she murmured.

His breathing jerked. She tensed, waiting to see if he was awake and had heard her. He nuzzled her head and his breathing evened out again. She sighed in disappointment. Tonight she'd felt his love for her with every caress and kiss. She just had to be patient and one of these days, she'd hear the words.

·♥·♥·♥·♥·♥·

As Lana fell asleep, Tristan opened his eyes and looked at the ceiling. She loved him. He pulled her tighter and kissed her head. One day soon he would return the words.

Guilt nudged him as he realized he hadn't told her the whole truth about his father. Her hair tickled his face. He pushed it behind her ear and yawned. Maybe it was best to leave sleeping dogs lie.

Chapter 13

Lana woke in Tristan's arms filled with contentment and peace. After making love again, tenderly and sweetly, the weak morning sunshine drifting through the curtains and lighting up the room, she was full of hope and excitement at the future awaiting them.

While she made breakfast, Tristan disappeared into his study. He reappeared as she was serving freshly squeezed orange juice and stood by the door, watching her with a smile.

'What?' She met his gaze.

'Do you want to spend the day with me?'

Laughing, she nodded.

Two hours later, they were sitting together at TD Garden. The crowd roared as the Celtics scored. Tristan stood and lifted her, embracing her exuberantly. She laughed with joy, her arms wrapped tight around his neck; he smelt of sweat and hot dogs. When he looked down at her, her breath caught in her chest. Desire gleamed in his eyes. He bent down, his lips a hair's breadth from hers when Joshua threw his arm up in the air.

'High five!' he demanded.

With a rueful smile at Lana, Tristan put her down to oblige. Aidan looked at them sympathetically. They returned to their seats to continue watching the game. She snuggled up to Tristan's side, her arm wrapped around his. He turned to her, smiled slightly and kissed her knuckle. Desire fluttered in her stomach. She leant her head back against his shoulder and watched as the two teams battled it out on the hardwood court below them.

Tristan's bicep tensed under her cheek as he cheered the Celtics on. She remembered the power of those arms and the way he'd caressed her body when they made love. Her breathing sped up as she remembered the passion they'd shared.

This was everything she'd wanted: having her husband back; being madly in love with the promise of forever stretching out before her. Leaning over, she put her head against his chest and listened to his steady heartbeat. She never had to worry he'd leave her again. She kissed him gently on the lips.

Tristan put his hand on her cheek. 'You okay, babe?'

'I'm perfect,' she murmured, tucking her head back against his shoulder.

The siren sounded, marking half-time. The audience shuffled in their seats.

Feeling the pressing of her bladder she stood and passed by Tristan. 'I'm going to the ladies'.'

'Just one more hot dog, please, Dad. Just one more,' she heard Joshua beg.

Lana ruffled Joshua's hair. 'I can take him if you like.'

Aidan shot her a look of gratitude.

Taking hold of Joshua's hand, Lana walked up the stairs. Joshua chattered excitedly, gesturing with his hands the way Holly did. After buying a hot dog with chili and cheese, they walked to the ladies' bathroom. Taking hold of his face, Lana bent over.

'You wait for me right here. Okay?'

Joshua nodded, biting into the hot dog, chili smeared on his face as he chewed. She brushed his hair away from his face and walked to the bathroom. She looked at herself in the mirror as she waited for the line to move forward. Her cheeks were flushed and her blue eyes sparkling with happiness.

When she exited the bathroom, Joshua was finishing his hot dog. 'Can I have an ice-cream?' he asked.

'No,' Lana said firmly. His lips formed a pout but he took her hand when she held it out. She smiled. Boys and their appetites. They just didn't know when to call it quits.

A man in a denim jacket and cap was in their way. 'Excuse me,' Lana murmured. The man shifted, turning his head in her direction briefly.

Her breath stopped, her heartbeat speeding up. 'Kevin,' she whispered.

She was looking into Kevin's blue eyes. His face looked older than she remembered. There were creases around his mouth and he had a nose that hadn't existed in her other life. The man met her gaze, looking at her without recognition.

'Kevin Walter,' she said his full name.

His eyes filled with fear at being recognized. He pulled the cap further down his face and hurried away.

Lana dropped Joshua's hand and tried to follow him, but by the time she'd taken a few steps, the man had blended into the crowd. She stared after him. Feeling a tugging on her arm, she looked down at Joshua's concerned face.

'I'm okay.' She put her hand on his head. 'Let's get back.'

She looked across the stadium to where Kevin had been staring: Tristan and Aidan were standing as they talked to each other. Tristan threw his head back and laughed.

She stared at him in bemusement. Her husband, her lover, the man who had her heart. The man who'd lied to her.

·♥·♥·♥·♥·♥·

Lana sat in the car next to Tristan as they drove home. She was frozen. She didn't know what to feel, what to think. The husband she'd been madly in love with an hour ago was a stranger again.

Tristan unlocked the apartment door and let her in first. He followed her in and closed the door behind him. 'Okay, what the hell's going on? Why are you giving me the silent treatment?'

His words flicked a switch, bringing to life all the anger and pain she'd felt since seeing Kevin. She stood in front of him. 'I saw your father at the game, Tristan. He looked pretty good for a dead man.'

She watched his face carefully. There was no surprise in his eyes.

He took of his cap and ruffled his hair while looking at the floor. 'He didn't say anything to you, did he?'

She strode the length of the room, trying to get a hold of her anger. 'Like what?'Hello, I'm your husband's dead father'?'

He flinched. At least she was getting to him.

'No, that's not what I meant.'

She made an effort to calm her anger. 'Why did you lie to me?' Her eyes stung with tears. She wasn't going to lose it in front of him. She wasn't. She turned her back to him as she formed her hands into fists, the nails biting into her skin.

He put his hand on her shoulder. 'I didn't lie to you.'

She turned and looked at him, an ache in her chest. 'What would you call it?'

He caressed her arm. 'I told you the truth. My father is dead to me.'

She shook him off. 'What the hell is wrong with you? He's your father!' She gazed into his face. Who was this cold-hearted stranger in front of her?

'Not any more, he isn't.' His tone was final.

Goose pimples broke out on her skin. She rubbed her arms, trying to warm herself. How could he turn away from his own flesh and blood so easily?

Father and son had been so close in her other life. Kevin worked for the state and had gotten Frank a job as a 911 emergency operator on a part-time basis. On the days Frank worked, his father picked him up and dropped him off. They had the same build and looked almost like brothers.

Her anger gone, she looked at Tristan with clear eyes. He was rigid and tense, fighting hard to contain his emotions. But she knew this man. The veneer might be different, but the heart of a man never changed. This wasn't easy for him.

She put her hand on his arm. 'What happened between you two?'

He shrugged her arm off. 'I don't want to talk about it.'

She exhaled, feeling like he'd punched her in the stomach with his rejection. *Get a grip, Lana. This isn't about you.* Fighting her urge to curl up into a ball and hide from the world, she pursued him.

'We're married. You can't keep things like this from me.' *Let me in, Tristan, please let me in.* She couldn't take his rejection, not now after she'd opened her heart to him.

'I'm not keeping anything from you. I just don't want to talk about it.' He headed for the door, the keys jangling in his hand. 'I'm going for a drive. Don't stay up for me.'

As the door closed behind him, pain ate her as if she'd swallowed acid. *Oh God, not again.* She couldn't stand to lose him again. All her dreams and hopes disappeared in a heartbeat. She stared at the empty apartment in disbelief. How did it come to this? She'd been flung from blissful happiness to heart-wrenching despair.

Dammit. She wasn't going to let him do this. She was not going to be passive and hope for the best.

He was getting into the elevator when she burst into the hallway.

'Tristan, we have to talk,' she demanded.

He didn't respond, just looked at the floor. She caught up with him and he met her gaze, his hazel eyes glistening with unshed tears, as the doors began to close.

She reached out, but her palm met the elevator door. *Tristan, come back.*

She waited by the elevator but when it returned empty, she walked back to the apartment and sat on the sofa to wait for him. He wouldn't be long. She'd seen his vulnerability and pain –

he needed her as much as she needed him. She shifted to lie on the sofa and stare at the ceiling. When he came back they'd talk. He'd tell her what had happened with his father and everything would be okay again.

She must have fallen asleep but when the door opened she quickly sat up, rubbing the tiredness from her eyes. He looked dangerous and on edge as he came through the door.

'Tristan, we need to talk.' She stood,

He put his keys on the console and approached her. Putting his hands under her armpits he lifted her to his eye level. 'Later,' he said, locking his lips on hers.

She kissed him back timidly, feeling vulnerable as she hung in air. He growled, nipping her bottom lip. She put her hands on each side of his head and kissed him back, returning his passion, then wound her legs around his hips. His hands were on her butt, grasping, stroking, while desire made her grind herself against him.

When she came up for air, they were in the bedroom. Tristan laid her down on the bed and pulled off her T-shirt and bra. He filled his hands with her breasts, squeezing and caressing as he pressed his mouth to them and sucked hard on her nipples. His hands roamed her skin, rubbing, embracing, soothing as she writhed on the bed beneath him. He undid her jeans and pulled them off, his hot gaze keeping her pinned in place.

She pulled him to her, his jeans rasping against her thighs as she pushed herself against his hardness. With a rapid movement he undid his jeans, released himself and pushed roughly inside her. Her body responded to his abandon, moving in a frenzied rhythm to keep up with him. There was no careful restraint between them, no tender touches, just tempestuous passion.

She watched his face. He was lost, his face straining as his pleasure overwhelmed him. It was as if he was trying to escape inside her and leave the world behind.

She felt his rhythm increasing. Her breath hitched as her body responded, and she gasped as her muscles spasmed and she was pushed over the edge into an orgasm. Still he pushed inside her, prolonging her pleasure, seeking his own.

He tensed, his hands on her butt as he lifted her harder against him. His eyes met hers as he spent himself inside her with a shuddering groan. He lay against her, trembling as he regained his breath.

She soothed his back, rubbing and stroking as he subsided.

'Tristan, we need to —'

His lips pressed to hers, stopping her words. His hands stroked over every inch of her body, leaving a trail for his lips to follow. She lost herself in the pleasure, the need to talk fading.

Later in the night she lay against his chest, the covers pulled tight around them. She felt his alertness. Glancing at his face, she saw he was staring at the ceiling.

He ran his hands through her hair. 'Go to sleep, Lana,' he murmured, kissing forehead.

She burrowed under his chin. They could talk tomorrow. She kissed his neck and closed her eyes.

·♥·♥·♥·♥·♥·

Lana carefully walked up the mud path to Tristan's work site, her boots sinking into the thick mud. After waking alone this morning, a note on the empty pillow beside her, reality had once again knocked her over.

She felt like hiding in bed, but she'd called work to tell Holly she'd be late, before calling Tristan's office. Tristan's assistant, Julie, had given her directions to the site. She checked the piece of paper clutched in her hand and mentally thanked Julie again for warning her to rug up.

A sharp whistle pierced the air. She jerked in surprise and looked at the platform above her. A man in a hard hat winked cheekily at her. She smiled despite herself.

Cupping her hand to her mouth, she shouted, 'I'm looking for Tristan Walker.'

She watched as the man shuttled down using a pulley. 'You're looking for the boss?' he asked.

She nodded.

Hearing her name, she turned. Aidan was striding toward her. The man nodded at her and returned to the worksite.

'What are you doing here?' Aidan asked when he reached her.

'I need to see Tristan.' She twisted her hair around her finger.

He looked at her in concern. 'Is everything all right?'

She hesitated, trying to decide what to say. 'I saw his father.'

Aidan looked at the ground.

'Do you know what happened between them?' she asked.

'Some of it, but I think it's best if Tristan tell you.' He put his hand on her back and led her to the elevator. 'He's on the twentieth floor checking the bearings.'

She looked suspiciously at the mesh lift.

'It's perfectly safe,' Aidan said reassuringly. 'Tristan wouldn't ever allow substandard equipment on a work site.' He took a hard hat off a hook by the lift and put it over her head. 'Now you're ready to go.'

Taking a deep breath, she followed Aidan onto the platform. He pressed a button and her stomach dropped as the lift lurched. She gripped the steel fence tightly and closed her eyes, which just made her more aware that she was hanging in thin air. She snapped them open and exhaled shakily. The world below looked far away, and the cars on the street seemed like toys. She slowly turned around and watched the concrete floors as they passed instead.

The lift stopped, the cage rocking slightly in the wind. Aidan helped her out. Feeling the solid concrete under her feet she felt a wave of relief. She stepped away from the lift, wanting as much distance as possible between her and the edge of the concrete that jutted into the air.

Tristan was standing among a group of men, his hands moving as he talked to them. When he spotted her, his body went rigid and he walked away from the men toward her.

Seeing his scowl, doubt crept over her. Why had she thought this would be a good idea? The squeak of the elevator made her look over her shoulder. Just before Aidan disappeared from view, he winked at her.

By the time Tristan had reached her she'd squared her shoulders. She was the wronged one, dammit. He wasn't turning this around onto her. He looked tired – there were dark smudges under his eyes. Sympathy clutched at her as she remembered him staring at the ceiling as she fell asleep. His jeans and shirt were marked with dirt and his hair under the hard hat was damp.

He was waiting for her to speak. She let the silence stretch out.

He sighed, rubbing his hand over his sweat streaked brow. 'Let me show you around the site.'

Lana smiled, the anger and anxiousness in her chest easing a little. He smiled back, his eyes wrinkling in the corners.

'Aren't you going to kiss your wife?' she asked teasingly, feeling the eyes of the men on them.

He smiled wryly and pulled her into his embrace. She gasped, breathing in his musky scent. He took off his hard hat and kissed her deeply. She hesitated, her body clenching in embarrassment. He started to lift his head, but she wasn't going to let him off that easily. She drew his head down, giving herself up to the kiss.

The wolf whistles brought them back to earth. Seeing his reddened cheeks, she laughed delightedly and dipped into a curtsy for their watching public. Holding her hand, Tristan bowed.

'Okay, the show's over. Get back to work.'

The crew drifted off as Tristan said, 'Let me start the tour.' He put his hard hat back on.

Annoyance swept over her; he was still being evasive. Meeting his gaze, she saw the plea in his eyes and softened. Their conversation could wait until they got home. This was a chance for her to learn more about him. He was beginning to let her into his world.

'I'd love a tour.'

He squeezed her hand and led her through the building. As they walked they were occasionally interrupted by his crew asking for instructions. Seeing his calm authority and rapport with the men, she realized he really took pride in his work. The way he'd talked about not completing his degree in architecture and having to work in construction, she'd got the feeling that he hated his job and his company. But now she wondered if he'd been so busy focusing on all that he'd lost after his mother died that he hadn't paid attention to all he'd gained.

'Walker and Co has been building car parks and office buildings for five years now. On our first job we had a crew of thirty. Now I have a crew of eighty working for me.' He spoke matter-of-factly, but there was pride coloring his voice.

Tristan walked to the side of the building. Pulling Lana to his chest as they stood one meter from the edge, he pointed out the car parks he'd built. The blue sky stretched out over the city. She forgot their future and their past, and lost herself in the moment. He pulled her tighter against him and kissed her on the forehead.

'Excuse me, boss.' They stepped apart at the interruption. She glanced at her watch.

'I'd better get to work.'

'I'll show you out.' Taking her hand, he turned to the worker who'd interrupted them. 'I won't be long.'

The man nodded.

Tristan walked her to the lift. They went down silently, standing apart. When they reached the ground level, he kissed her on the cheek.

Seeing a bus approaching, she ran to the bus stop. She turned on the stairs of the bus to wave at Tristan. He looked lonely and in pain. She was torn and her hands loosened their grip on the steel rails. She wanted to jump off the bus and run back to him. With a short wave, he turned and entered the lift.

She found a seat and sat down heavily, watching as the work-site disappeared from view. Lana regretted not pushing him for the truth about his father. She squared her shoulders. Tonight she wouldn't be swayed – he'd tell her the truth if she had to sit on him to get him to talk.

Chapter 14

Lana exited the T and crossed Chapel Street. The apartment block loomed in the dark above her. After work she'd gone for a drink with Holly, needing time to put things with Tristan into perspective.

She'd decided she had to tell him the whole truth and demand the same from him. She'd had enough of trying to hide from who she really was and bend reality to her own fantasy. It was time to grow up.

She looked up at the sky. The moon was full and the stars sparkled. A surge of hope filled her; she had a feeling everything would be okay. She and Tristan would find a way back to each other. She didn't doubt he cared for her.

As she walked to the entrance she felt a prickle on her neck, as though she were being followed. She increased her pace and found her keys. She slipped the keyring around her finger and made a fist around the keys as she lengthened her strides, ensuring she walked smoothly and didn't give away her panic.

A man stepped out in front of her, his face in shadow. She reacted instantly, stabbing her keys into his face while her knee rose and hit him between the legs. The man crumpled with a scream of pain. Lana ran for the front door without looking back.

'Oh God! Jesus, Mary and Joseph.'

Lana stopped. She knew that voice. She turned slowly. The man was trying to rise from the ground but his legs weren't cooperating.

Lana walked back to him. 'Kevin?' she called out when she was closer.

The man lifted his head. 'Yes.'

'I'm so sorry.' Lana tried to help him rise. He flinched away from her touch. 'I didn't see it was you.'

She helped him stand and they walked together to the light. Seeing his bleeding face, she winced. 'I hurt your face.'

'It's what I deserve for skulking in the shadows.' He gave her a weary version Tristan's wry smile.

She got her handkerchief from her pocket book and dabbed at the cut. Kevin tolerated her ministrations.

'You're my son's wife?'

Lana stopped dabbing his face. Oh, boy. Alannah and Kevin had never met. She held out her hand. 'Yes, I'm Lana.'

Kevin wrapped his hand around hers. 'How do you know who I am? Did my boy tell you about me?'

Lana twisted the handkerchief in her hands. 'Not exactly. I recognized the resemblance at the basketball game.' She tensed, waiting for his reaction.

Kevin touched his nose and mouth. 'Aye, well the boy got his mother's coloring, but my face.'

'You'd better come inside so I can tend to that cut.'

He looked to the lit-up windows of the apartment block, his face full of yearning. 'No, I think it's better if I left.'

Lana put her hand on his arm. 'Please, let me bandage it. I feel guilty about hurting you.' She tugged his arm and led him to the elevator.

Lana unlocked the apartment and stepped in to turn on the light. 'Come in.' She headed for the bathroom. Not hearing him follow, she turned to see him standing in the doorway, staring around the apartment. She walked back and pulled him in.

'So this is where my boy lives.' He stared at the white interior. 'He used to love color.'

Lana disappeared into the bathroom and came back with the first aid kit. 'Well, the apartment was decorated by the people who lived here before us.' She pushed away a pang of guilt— it was technically the truth. She gestured for him to sit on the sofa and dabbed the cut with antiseptic.

'He was studying to be an architect, you know, when I was put in prison.'

Lana froze, her fingers tingling from the cold antiseptic on the cotton ball. 'Prison,' she repeated.

Kevin met her eyes. 'Didn't he tell you?'

Taking a deep breath, she got a Band-Aid and taped it over the cut. 'No.'

Kevin looked down at his hands. 'I've tried seeing him in the two years since I've been released.' He swallowed, his eyes moist with emotion. 'But my boy's stubborn.' He smiled ruefully.

Lana sat down on the couch next to him. 'What happened?'

'I was taking risks. Lost in the thrill of big business.' He rubbed his neck, reminding her of Tristan when he was tense.

It all made sense now. Tristan's silences about his parents and his bitterness. The reason Kevin's face was much older than in her previous life; the years of incarceration had left their mark and the man who was in front of her now bore only a passing resemblance to the man she'd known in her other life, the one with blue eyes full of happiness and love.

After Frank's diagnosis at eight, Kevin had lived for his family. She realized that because Tristan had had the heart operation, this Kevin must have lost his way and drifted from his family and into work.

He stood. 'Well, I guess you want me to leave now.'

Lana stood in front of him. 'No, I want you to stay.' She put her hand on his arm. 'You're Tristan's father and he needs you. Until he learns to accept his past he won't be able to move forward.'

Kevin smiled. 'You sound exactly like Lillian. That's what she said the last time I saw her.' He leant down and kissed her on the cheek. 'I'm glad my boy's got you.' He put his cap on his head. 'Just the same, I think I'd better leave.'

She heard keys in the lock and watched as the apartment door was pushed open. Tristan's smile when he saw her faded to bitterness when he spotted his father. They all froze, then Tristan pulled the door closed and left without a word.

Lana let out a pent-up breath and sprang into action, running after him. The elevator doors were closing when she arrived.

'Dammit.' She pounded the steel door in frustration. What was she going to do now? She turned to find Kevin behind her, twisting his cap between his hands.

'I'm sorry for causing you trouble.'

Lana forced a smile to her lips. 'No, it's not your fault.'

Kevin pressed the button for the elevator. They stood in awkward silence.

'Can I have your number, please? I'll talk to Tristan and see what I can do.'

Kevin got a piece of paper from his wallet and scrawled a number on the back of it. He didn't say anything but his skepticism about Tristan changing his mind was apparent.

When the elevator arrived, Kevin offered his hand. 'I'm glad we met.' He smiled Tristan's smile. 'You're good for my boy.' He stepped into the elevator. 'Don't let me get between the two of you.' His mouth opened as if he wanted to say more but he only nodded as the elevator door closed.

Lana walked back to the apartment. Closing the door behind her, she sat on the couch to wait. She carefully smoothed out the piece of paper with Kevin's number on it and put it in her purse. She didn't know what she was going to say to Tristan when she saw him. Remembering the brief flash of pain on his face when he'd looked at his father, she wondered if she'd have the courage to reopen the wound.

·❤·❤·❤·❤·❤·

Lana shifted on the couch and glanced at her watch. Three hours had passed. Her stomach clenched in fear as she thought about what might have happened to Tristan. What if he was in a car accident? She stood and started pacing, running her hands through her hair. Damn him. How could he be so inconsiderate and leave her worrying? She'd been calling his mobile for hours and had left numerous messages.

She reached for the phone and rang Aidan's mobile. After the fourth ring he answered. She fought to keep her voice even. 'Hi Aidan. It's Lana. Look, I'm calling to see if you know where Tristan is?'

Aidan sighed, as if he was coming to a decision. 'I'll come pick you up and take you to the office. That's where he hides out.'

Lana blinked back tears. 'Thanks.'

They pulled up at the office building and Lana sighed in relief, seeing Tristan's truck and the light in the office window. She followed Aidan to the front door.

He unlocked the door and held it open for her. 'Make sure you yell out his name otherwise he'll think you're an intruder.'

He started to close the door but she held it. 'Wait, aren't you coming?

He looked at her with sympathy. 'Just tread lightly and you'll be fine.' He closed the glass door and re-locked it. With a quick salute, he walked back to his truck.

Lana carefully walked up the stairs. The light from the corridor at the top lit her way. Even though she'd been at the office the other day, the darkness made everything look sinister. Her skin prickled as the silence surrounded her. When she got to the top of the stairs she hesitated, trying to decide where to go.

To her right was the reception area and behind that Aidan's and Tristan's offices but they were empty. To the left was a door with light around the edges. She walked slowly toward it, each creak and sigh of the building bringing to mind every horror movie she'd ever watched. The door squeaked loudly as she pushed it open. Behind it were stairs leading to the basement.

She walked down and bent, peering at the floor below. The basement was well lit by a bare bulb hanging from the ceiling. There was a water heater in the corner and pipes hanging from the walls and ceiling, but otherwise it was clean, with archive boxes stacked neatly against a wall.

'Tristan,' she called.

A door she hadn't noticed opened and Tristan walked to the bottom of the stairs and leant against the rail, a bottle in his hands.

She walked down the stairs quickly. Her steps slowed as she realized he was drunk by the deliberate way he sipped from the bottle. He met her eyes again and she felt like she was looking at a stranger. Gone was the tenderness she'd seen the night before and instead his gaze was predatory as he looked her over.

She crossed her arms over her chest. 'Are you all right?'

'I could use some comforting.' He reached out and pulled her harshly against his body, his hand latching onto her butt as he nuzzled her ear.

Feeling his rough touch and the smell of alcohol on his breath she panicked, and jerked out of his arms.

'Go home.' He turned and went back to the room, closing the door behind him.

She sat on the bottom step, her body shaking in the aftermath of her panic. Why had he touched her like that? Since he'd known about the rape he'd been careful in the way he touched her, until now. Feeling bruised, she started walking up the stairs.

Remembering the look in his eyes when he'd seen his father in the apartment she stopped. He was trying to push her away. Taking a deep breath, she stomped back down the stairs. Well, it wasn't going to work. They were in this together.

She pushed the door open. He was sitting in the middle of the windowless room with his back to her. In front of him was an easel. Each wall was papered with pictures. She entered and looked closer at the walls. All the sketches were of houses. She recognized the sketches as the oil paintings in the apartment that had inspired her déjà vu.

But while Frank had painted people and life around him, Tristan's sketches and paintings were of the dream houses he wanted to build. She put her hands on his shoulder. He accepted her touch for a moment, then lurched to his feet and moved away from her.

'So did you get to hear the whole sad sob story about how Daddy-O fucked up little Frankie's life?' He swayed slightly.

She put her hand on his arm. 'He's sorry he hurt you.'

He laughed, and gulped from the bottle again. 'Is he sorry for his murders?'

She felt his words like a slap.

He must have seen the bewilderment on her face. 'I see he didn't tell you the full story.'

She shook her head.

·♥·♥·♥·♥·♥·

Tristan breathed in. He'd fought so hard never to tell this story again. He gestured to the couch and waited for her to sit next to him.

He cleared his throat and began, smiling softly. 'My father had his own building company.' He paused, trying to find the words.

'Like you.'

'Yeah, like me.' He nodded, clearing his throat. 'But unlike me, it wasn't enough for him. No matter how much he achieved, he was always pushing for more. Over time, he crossed a line. At first he replaced some inferior building materials and pocketed the difference and then he slowly went further until he stopped seeing right from wrong.'

He swallowed, trying to finish the story he'd started, but his mind kept flinching away from the image that had haunted his nightmares. 'Ten years ago I was at college, studying architecture. On summer break I worked at my father's building site to earn money for a trip to Europe.' He rubbed his neck. 'My friend Taylor from college was working with me.' He stopped, remembering Taylor's smile the last time he saw him. 'Paris here we come,' Taylor had shouted as the scaffold rose, his fist lifted in the air.

'He was on a scaffold with another worker, Jose, putting up drywall. They should have been in harnesses and wearing helmets but Daddy dearest was in a hurry to keep on schedule.'

He clenched his fists and Lana wrapped her hands around them. She held him tightly as he continued.

'The scaffold broke. Taylor and Jose fell twenty feet. Taylor died from internal injuries on his way to the hospital, while Jose ended up a paraplegic.'

He remembered Taylor's funeral. The glances as people recognized him; Taylor's mother not being able to look at him when he passed on his condolences.

'My father was charged with involuntary manslaughter. The publicity surrounding the scandal ruined his company. Hundreds were out of work. They lost their entitlements and weren't paid out. The projects he'd been contracted to build stalled and the clients sued him.'

He stood, the memories overwhelming him. 'We lost everything.' He went to stand by the window. 'My mother got sick–the stress and shock affected her heart. I quit college and had to get a job to pay her medical bills. By this time, any friends we had were thin on the ground. The only thing I was qualified for was building so I put pressure on a friend of the family. He said he'd take me on but only if I changed my name.' He turned and smiled wryly. 'So that's how Tristan Walker was born.'

He started drawing circles on the glass pane. 'As you know, in the end my efforts were futile. No matter how hard I worked, there was never enough money. Six months later, my mother died.'

Silence descended. He heard her ragged breathing and knew without looking at her that she was crying.

'And your father?' Her voice was choked.

'He was sentenced to ten years jail.'

·♥·♥·♥·♥·♥·

Lana remembered Frank telling her about the kind of man his father was before he got sick: distant, obsessed with ambition. Only when he and Lillian had nearly lost Frank did he change and become a family man. In his adulthood, Frank had learnt that his father had been pushing the limit on his building site and it was only fate's intervention in the form of Frank's illness that made Kevin realize what was truly important in life.

Tristan kneeled in front of her. 'I don't ever want to see him. He ruined my life and he's not going to get the chance to do it again.' He took her hand and kissed it. 'He's dead to me.'

He put his head in her lap. She bent and embraced him. Now she understood what Kevin had meant when he said that she shouldn't let him come between her and Tristan. She had to choose whether or not to push Tristan to speak to his father. Right now, his bitterness was so overwhelming he'd see it as a betrayal.

'Okay,' she murmured. There would be time to deal with his past; for now they had to focus on their future.

He helped her stand. 'I think we'd better get home.'

She drove them home through the dark Boston streets. When she parked in the apartment building's basement she took his hand and led him to their apartment. He was like a lost boy and followed her without resistance. The only thing she could do for him was show him her love and hope that it healed the wounds stirred up by his father

In the bedroom she made him sit on the edge of the bed. She pulled off his boots and his shirt. before removing her top and bra. She felt his need as he watched her intently.

She pushed him to lie on the bed, then removed his jeans. She took off her own pants and lay over him, pressing butterfly kisses on his face, infusing each kiss with her love. She moved so she was straddling him, her hands caressing his body.

Slowly she felt him come to life, each stroke and kiss bringing him back from the past. He returned her kisses, breathing her in like she was his reason for living. They moved slowly and tenderly, as though they were discovering each other for the first time; every touch to be savored and revered.

She reached between them to guide him into her and as his hardness filled her, she felt tears in her eyes. She felt he was truly seeing her for the first time. As they made love, he pulled her toward him and kissed her tears away. She increased her tempo, drawing him with her to the very edge. As they climaxed together their eyes were wide open and watching the other.

·❤·❤·❤·❤·❤·

Lana woke slowly. She was lying on her side with Tristan's arms around her. As she shifted, he kissed her shoulder.

'Good morning,' he murmured against her skin.

She turned onto her back. 'Good morning.'

He lay watching her with a smile on his face. She gently traced his eyebrows and then the lines of his face.

He shook his head and smiled. 'You know, sometimes I could swear that you're a different woman.'

She stilled in his embrace. 'Maybe I am,' she answered hesitantly. 'Maybe I —'

The phone rang, interrupting her. Tristan looked at her intently, before picking up the handset from the nightstand. He listened for a few minutes before covering the mouthpiece. 'It's your mom. Do you want to speak to her?'

When Lana nodded, he looked at her, puzzled. She could read his unspoken question: why did she want to speak to Tammy after what happened last time she saw her? She couldn't really answer his question, she just knew that she had to deal with the past, rather than trying to ignore it. She shrugged, kissing him on the lips as she took the phone from him.

'Hi Tammy,' she said and, watched his naked butt as he walked to the bathroom.

'Hi baby,' Tammy said. 'How are you?'

'Good. What about you?'

'Oh, I'm the same as usual.'

Silence stretched out on the line as Lana tried to think of something to say. 'Is something wrong?' she eventually asked.

'I was wondering if we could get together today— there's something I want to give you.'

Lana frowned, remembering the appointment with the student counsellor at Boston University. 'Actually I have an appointment—'

'Oh, never mind if you're busy—' Tammy interrupted, her voice jerky.

'No, no, I wasn't going to say that,' Lana rushed in. 'I was just going to say it would have to be after one pm.'

'Oh.' Tammy paused. 'That's great. I have a fundraising committee meeting this morning but it should finish about that time. Why don't you come to the townhouse after your meeting?'

Lana tried to think of an excuse.

'Michael will be at Town Hall all day,' Tammy continued.

'Okay,' Lana said.

When Tristan returned she was lying on her back staring blankly at the ceiling.

'Everything okay?' He dropped his towel and opened the closet door.

'Yeah.' Lana sat up. 'She wants to get together to give me something. I'm going to meet her at her house after my meeting with the student counsellor.'

Tristan looked at her with a frown. His look darkened.

'She's my mother.'

He turned away from her.

She bit her lip as she realized she'd struck a nerve. She stood and put her hand on his arm. 'Tristan, I didn't mean to —'

His lips on hers stopped her. 'I know,' he whispered against her lips. 'I have about ten minutes before I have to leave for work.'

She laughed as he tossed her on the bed. 'Mmm, I don't know if ten minutes is —' She stopped talking as he burrowed between her legs and started stroking her with his tongue.

Fifteen minutes later, Lana walked out of the shower and into the living room, a smile stretching her lips as she felt the pleasant aches from a night of love making. She entered the kitchen and started the coffee maker, realizing that this was the first time she felt content since her arrival.

She and Tristan were progressing toward a future. She sighed as she remembered his reaction to Tammy's phone call. While things weren't perfect, she had every hope they could be. As she sipped her coffee and waited for Tristan to finish his shower, she remembered what else Tammy's phone call had disrupted: she'd had the opportunity to admit her past. She sighed as she walked into the living room and sat on the sofa. They had time.

Noticing a piece of paper on the floor by the front door, she put her cup on the coffee table and stood to pick it up. It was a newspaper article: Walters found guilty of involuntary manslaughter. She frowned. Turning it over, she froze. *I know your secret* was scrawled in red pen across the back.

Tristan walked in. Seeing her face, he hurried over. She handed him the article and took her cup to the kitchen.

She felt him standing behind her as she rinsed out her cup. 'Something else you forgot to tell me.'

He put his hand on her shoulder. 'I'm sorry, Lana. I wasn't deliberately keeping it from you.'

She shrugged his hand off her and dried the cup with a tea towel. 'I'd like to believe you, Tristan.' She opened the cupboard and returned the cup, holding onto the door for support. 'But you have lied to me every step of the way.' She slammed the cupboard door closed and turned to face him. 'I don't know if I can believe anything you have to say any more.'

She started walking out of the kitchen, but he pulled her back. 'Please, Lana. We have to talk.'

She took a deep breath, forcing her hurt away, and turned to him. 'I have an appointment with my student counsellor.' She glanced at his watch. 'In a little over an hour. I can't afford to be late.' She forced herself to meet his gaze. 'We can talk about this later.'

He took hold of the door on each side of her. 'I'll leave work early and meet you here.'

She shook her head and looked down. 'I'm meeting with Tammy after that.'

He put his hand under her chin and lifted her head. 'Lana, I am so sorry. Please baby ...'

Seeing the entreaty in his eyes she nodded. 'Okay, pick me up from Tammy's.'

He leant in to kiss her. She moved her head and his kiss landed on her cheek. He sighed, his warm breath caressing her face before he stepped back.

'I'll see you later.'

She returned to the bedroom and closed the door gently, listening to his footsteps as he walked away. She had to believe that he was telling her the truth and he'd just forgotten to tell her, but it was getting harder and harder to believe that his omissions weren't on purpose. She couldn't think about it any more. She opened the closet. What did one wear to an interview with a student counsellor anyway?

Chapter 15

Lana stepped out of the cab in front of Tammy's brownstone on Louisburg Square. Her meeting with the student counsellor, Rena, had finished sooner than she'd expected. She still felt a flush of disbelief as she remembered the counsellor's words. After reading Alannah's straight-A transcripts Rena's eyebrows had lifted and she'd smiled at Lana. 'You're certainly an exemplary applicant.'

Lana had flushed. She knew that Rena's praise was just as much about Alannah graduating from one of Boston's exclusive private schools. The only thing that kept Lana from sliding her eyes away from Rena's was the knowledge that when she'd graduated with her community college high school diploma, it had been with straight As.

Before she left, Rena had shaken her hand. 'I'm sure I'll see you around soon.'

Butterflies fluttered in her stomach as she realized that in as little as three months her new future would start when admissions were mailed. After all her wishing and dreaming, she was finally on her way to achieving her dream of being a teacher. She couldn't wait to tell Tristan.

Her elation faded as she remembered their fight. After he left, sheer will had propelled her out the apartment and to her appointment. The shocks she'd experienced since waking in hospital after her accident would be enough to send a lesser person into a mental institute. But somehow she'd rallied, getting stronger each time, until fighting back became second nature.

This was who she'd been before meeting Frank. Living with a foster family who only saw her as a source of income for two years had hardened her, but the five years fighting Frank's condition had taken all her strength and determination. Focusing exclusively on his needs had exhausted her, but her hard-won strength kept her going and now she felt stronger than ever

She rang the doorbell, but no one answered. As she waited on the stoop, a wet drop landed on her cheek. She lifted her face to the sky and poked her tongue out, catching a raindrop. She laughed softly, glancing around to see if anyone had seen her. The street was empty. She shivered in her coat and stomped her feet, trying to get her circulation moving.

She stilled, her ears pricking as she heard a shattering noise from inside Tammy's house. She put her hand on the doorknob and the front door opened. Poking her head in, she called out Tammy's name.

Her vision swam as she was grabbed and thrown through the air, landing on her side. She heard the door slam behind her and then footsteps approaching her side.

Two feet appeared in her line of vision. 'Sorry, sis, hope you didn't land too hard.'

She sat up slowly and turned to face Evan. 'Not hard at all.' She rubbed her stinging knees. Her gloved hands and voluminous coat had cushioned her fall.

Noticing the trashed living room and his dilated pupils, she realized the danger she was in. She nodded at the backpack by his feet. 'Doing some shopping?'

He laughed jaggedly, then snorted to a stop. 'You were always a clever one.' He wagged his finger at her and crouched down beside her. Zeroing in on her handbag he picked it up, rifling through the contents until he found her purse. 'Are you judging me, little sis?' Before she could reply he continued. 'But then again you're not exactly in a position to judge anyone. We both know your mother and Jack Daniels are on good terms.'

While he was occupied she stood slowly, careful not to make any quick movements he would misinterpret.

He removed the cash from her purse and threw it on the floor. 'If only that were my weakness.' He walked to the living room, laughing again. Seeing she was still standing by the front door he stopped abruptly. 'I wouldn't if I were you.' He nodded to the front door and held up the key. 'After you.' He motioned to the living room.

Taking a deep breath Lana walked past him. She knew how unpredictable junkies were and while she was trying to portray a calm demeanor she was on edge, assessing her options. As she walked past Evan she looked at her watch. Tammy and Tristan were due to arrive at any moment. Until then her best hope was to stay calm and try not to aggravate him. Hopefully he'd found what he was looking for and would be on his way soon.

'Sit,' he ordered. 'Walters parking the truck, is he? Be joining us soon?'

She shook her head. 'Tristan's at work.' Picking up on his slip up, she stilled, reminded of the notes Tristan had received. 'You're the blackmailer.'

He smiled enigmatically 'See how clever you are? I got Walters in on the deal of a lifetime, but Mr Righteous had to contact the EPA over a little pollution. But no matter, Walters will pay.'

Lana looked around the shattered living room, trying to find somewhere to sit Every breakable object was shattered on the floor, the sofas were slashed and other pieces of furniture over-turned.

Evan looked around with her. 'I see I've been too thorough in my task.' He walked toward her, carelessly kicking the objects littering the floor out of his way.

She held herself stiffly but instead of approaching her he went to the windowsill where there was a mirror with two lines of white powder on it. He picked up the straw and inhaled both lines.

Straightening, he rubbed his nose as his eyes glittered. 'Father thought that his attempt at tough love would curtail my vice. Instead of helping smooth the hand of justice at my last arrest for a DUI, he left me hanging in the breeze. Either I go to rehab or I go to jail. Silly Father.' He shrugged his shoulders negligently. 'He has to be taught a lesson.' He looked at her sharply. 'You understand don't you, Lana?'

She nodded.

His eyes took on a faraway look as his attention wandered. 'This can be our little secret. No one has to know. We share many secrets, don't we, Alannah?' He crossed the room and stood so close his breath ruffled her hair. He reached out and lifted a strand before caressing her face with his index finger. 'We know about Father's little predilection for discipline.' His voice softened. 'And we know why little sis was so sick.'

Lana pulled back her head and met his eyes. 'You know Alannah was raped,' she whispered.

He pushed her away from him. 'I didn't know,' he screamed, his face turning red and spittle flying from his mouth. 'I didn't know!' He started crying, hugging himself and covering his mouth with a fist. He whispered, 'I was with my friend Johnny – we were doing lines when you appeared in my bedroom door. I offered you some. You stared at me with your big blue eyes, then you did a line.'

'I didn't know. I didn't know!' he shouted as he rubbed at his face with shaking hands. 'I passed out and when I woke up, Johnny was hurting little sister. Little sister was calling for me.' He beat his chest. 'You were calling for me.' He briefly met her eyes, the guilt a black stain in his iris. 'But I couldn't move. I passed out again and when I woke up you were gone.'

She flinched as he punched the wall in a frenzy, eventually stopping from exhaustion. He stood with his back to her, breathing heavily.

'I told myself it was a dream,' he said quietly. 'Just a bad dream, but then you wanted to go to the police and I said —' He gulped as he tried to force out the words. 'I told you —'

'You told her it didn't happen.' Lana pieced together Alannah's diary entries. Her rage and betrayal were clear in the way she'd crossed out Evan's name on the pages, the ink smeared by her tears on the page.

He nodded jerkily.

'It's okay,' she soothed.

'It's not my fault. It's not my fault!' he shouted. 'It's his fault.' He waved at the house. 'He ruined my life.'

The pain in his voice gave her pause as she remembered hearing those same words from Tristan.

He leant against the wall. 'If he hadn't remarried, none of it would have happened,' he muttered as he headed back to the windowsill and the white powder.

'Evan, no.' She automatically reached out to stop him. She could see his body was overheating. A sheen of sweat coated his body. The tremors in his hands had increased since he did the last two lines. She took hold of his arm. He pushed her away, his shove catching her unaware. She fell awkwardly on her side, her head hitting a lamp base he'd overturned.

She watched helplessly from the floor as Evan tipped out more powder onto the mirror. He used a razor to chop up the powder, and did four more lines.

'Evan.' She called out to him but her voice was barely above a whisper. She tried to get up. Dizziness overcame her and she fell back on the floor, hitting her head again and knocking herself out.

·♥·♥·♥·♥·♥·

Someone was shaking her awake, the pain in her head echoing like a bell through her body.

'Little sister, little sister, wake up,' Evan shouted, as he shook her again.

She moaned and pushed him away.

'I'm sorry, I'm sorry ...' he whispered as he held her hand.

She opened her eyes. Evan was crouching above her, his eyes feverishly bright, tears coursing down his face. She winced at the pain in her head, but contained her moan when she saw Evan's distraught face. Feeling something wet on her ear she touched it, her fingers coming away with blood.

'It's okay. I'm fine.' She forced herself to sit up.

He smiled at her, revealing the sweet boy he might once have been. He opened his mouth to say something, then his eyes rolled and he fell to the floor, his body convulsing.

The suddenness of his collapse shocked her into action. She scrambled to his side, her every movement frustratingly slow as dizziness affected her coordination. She forced back nausea and took a deep breath, trying to get her thoughts in order.

She needed to get help. Seeing the phone she stood; her legs were shaky and she could barely hold herself up. Moving as if she was underwater, she held onto the wall for balance. She knelt by the phone, her head feeling like a marble that was about to roll off her neck and shatter. Picking up the headset she heard silence instead of a dial tone. Lifting the cord she saw that Evan had ripped it out of the wall in his rage.

She didn't realize she was crying until the tears fell onto her hands. She heard thumping behind her as Evan writhed on the floor. Lifting her head, she looked at the foyer where Evan had emptied her handbag. Her cell phone lay next to the front door.

She tried to stand but her vision swam and her legs buckled. Her phone was only ten feet away but it seemed the foyer was the size of a baseball field. With slow shuffling steps she covered the distance, the edges of her vision black and narrowing with each step. When she was near the phone, she fell to the floor and dragged herself the last few feet. Picking it up, she dialed 911.

·♥·♥·♥·♥·♥·

When she opened her eyes again a feeling of déjà vu overwhelmed her. She was lying in a hospital bed and her head was throbbing with pain. She lifted her hand to her temple and felt a bandage. Returning her hand to her side, she touched something. Looking down, she saw Tristan's head by her hip.

He woke immediately at her touch, his eyes full of concern. 'Are you okay?' He caressed her face.

'Evan,' she whispered.

'We'll talk about this later —'

'How is Evan?'

His eyes filled with regret. 'He's in a coma. The doctors are hoping he'll recover.'

Her hands fisted in the quilt. 'I... I tried helping.' She broke down.

'You did your best, Lana.' Tristan pulled her into his embrace and caressed her hair as she cried against his shoulder. 'The paramedics came as quickly as they could after your call.'

After she finished crying he wiped her face with a tissue and gave her some water. 'All right now?'

She nodded, wincing at the faint pain in her head.

He looked at their hands. 'I was so scared.' He lifted her hand and kissed it. 'When I came to pick you up the police had cordoned off the house.' He looked at her, for once not hiding the emotion in his eyes. letting all his pain and fear be visible. 'I love you, Lana. I'm sorry for not realizing it sooner.'

Lana looked at the tears on Tristan's face. The events of the past day had drained her of emotion. While she felt a loosening in her heart at Tristan's confession, she was in emotional overload and couldn't react. When she opened her mouth to try to explain, he pressed a finger to her lips.

'Shh, it's okay. I know it's been a tough day. We'll talk about this later.' He leant over and kissed her gently, the sweetness of his touch confirming his feelings. 'Sleep now. You need your rest.' He pulled the covers over her. 'We have our whole life to talk about this.'

She lay back and closed her eyes, seeing Evan's face again when he told her about Alannah's rape. 'It was Evan,' she murmured.

'I know,' Tristan said. 'Evan was the blackmailer.'

She shook her head without opening her eyes. 'Yes, and he knew that Alannah was raped.'

She fell asleep. In her dream she was walking up the stairwell leading to the apartment she'd shared with Tammy in her other life. She'd run away from the foster home while the family slept.

She wiped a tear from her face. A week ago she'd returned home from school, only to be greeted with her packed bags and a child protection officer waiting for her. Tammy had told her a neighbor reported her to the authorities for neglect and promised that within a few days everything would be sorted out. It was only tonight she'd learnt that Tammy had put her in foster care voluntarily.

Lana reached Tammy's apartment door and knocked on it loudly. When there was no answer she started kicking it. She knew why Tammy had given her up. The door opened abruptly and she nearly fell.

'Where's Tammy?' she demanded, meeting Billy's eyes.

Billy was Tammy's new boyfriend and the reason Tammy got rid of her. A sixteen-year-old interfered with her love life and so she'd sent her away.

'Well, well, well.' Billy drawled out the words. 'Little Lana Madden decided to pay me a visit.' He pulled the door open wider and stood aside for her to enter. In the room behind him sat a biker friend and there were beer bottles scattered on the floor.

She walked past him, wrinkling her nose at the smell of alcohol fumes on his breath. 'Tammy!' she called out.

Silence echoed back. She walked through to the bedroom and frowned when she saw the empty closet. The room was a mess with beer bottles littering the floor and cigarette ash on the bed. While Tammy wasn't Martha Stewart, she'd never let the apartment get to such a state.

Lana turned and met Billy's eyes. 'Where's my mother?'

He stood in the doorway, leaning his tattooed arms on each side of the doorframe. 'The bitch split.' Moving into the bedroom, he took a sip from the bottle he was holding. 'I came home from work and she was gone.' He shrugged his shoulders. 'So I guess now this is my home.' He sat on the couch and picked up a tequila bottle, swallowing half its contents in a gulp.

Lana looked at the floor with a frown. Since she'd been in the foster home Tammy had called her every day, assuring her that soon they would be together. She hadn't mentioned anything about moving. She looked up and saw Billy's eyes were closing as he passed out. She felt a chill on her skin and turned to his friend, who was watching her with hungry eyes.

'I guess I'll get going.' She was walking toward the door when she heard the chair fall to the ground behind her.

Billy's friend grabbed hold of her arms. 'Hey, what's your hurry?' His oily smile made Lana queasy. 'I'm Rob. Stay for one dance.' He held her with one arm and turned on the radio with the other, turning the volume up loud.

'No, I have to go.' Lana tried to free herself.

Rob held her tighter.

'You're hurting me,' she said, meeting his eyes.

There was a smile of satisfaction on his face. He lifted her up by the arms so that she was on her tippy toes, his fingers biting into her flesh. 'I want to have fun, baby doll.' He threw her onto the bed.

Lana turned toward Billy and screamed his name, begging for help. His eyes briefly flickered open, before closing again. As the music played, Lana screamed again. She realized she was on her own. Her foot was dangling off the bed and she felt something hit her heel. She was lying on her mother's bed and Tammy always kept a baseball bat under it, her protection against intruders. Rob reached for his zip and Lana held herself in check as he pushed his jeans down his thighs.

When the jeans reached his knees, she sprang up and yanked the bat out. Rob tried reaching for her but he was hobbled and fell to the floor. She hit him on the head, feeling the reverberation of the wood across her palms.

She held the bat in the air, but he wasn't moving. She turned to walk away when he reached for her again.

Lana jerked awake and screamed as a man's hand touched her leg. She scrunched into a ball against the headboard.

'Lana, baby, it's me. Please, baby, look at me.'

Hearing Tristan's pleading voice she looked up.

He was standing at the end of the bed, looking at her with pain in his eyes. 'Lana, I'd never hurt you.' He held out his hands to her.

She looked around the hospital room in a daze. The dream had been so real she almost expected Rob to leap at her from the shadows. 'I was dreaming.'

'I know, baby.' Tristan slowly made his way to her side. 'But I'm here and no one's going to hurt you.' He gently touched her arms.

As he caressed her, soothing away the memory of Rob's brutality, she came back to full awareness. She remembered that after hitting Rob for the second time he was finally unconscious and she ran away. Kneeling, she wrapped herself around Tristan. 'Don't let me go,' she murmured against his neck, wrapping her legs around his waist as she tried to fuse herself into his skin.

He rubbed her back as he sat on the edge of the bed. 'I won't. I won't let you go. I'm here,' he crooned.

She knew that no one could harm her while she was in Tristan's embrace. She nuzzled into his shoulder and drifted off to sleep.

·♥·♥·♥·♥·♥·

Lana shuffled from the bathroom back to the bed. She was suffering from concussion but would be discharged this morning. When she entered the bedroom she saw Tristan waiting for her. She stopped, discomfited. Had he seen the police officer leaving her room?

His face lit up with a smile. 'Are you feeling better?' He leant down to give her a kiss.

She sighed and kissed him back, pressing her closed mouth to his. He hadn't realized her deception.

He lifted his head with a frown. 'Is something wrong?'

She shook her head without meeting his eyes. She sat on the edge of the bed and watched as he unpacked the bag he'd brought from home. 'Tristan, I'd like to visit Evan.'

He slowly lifted out her jeans and a jumper. 'I don't think that's a good idea.'

'It's something I need to do.'

'Lana, the man assaulted you.' He pointed to her bandaged head. 'He broke into your parents' house and if he wakes up, he'll be arrested and thrown into jail.' He was fighting to keep his voice controlled but his frustration seeped through. Seeing her set face, he softened his voice. 'Why, Lana? Tell me so I can understand?'

She looked down at the floor and took a deep breath, trying to find the words to tell him. Her other life and current life had collided and now she had to fit the pieces together and make sense of it all.

'I can't.' Seeing his hurt, she quickly added, 'Not now.' She stood and put her hand on his arm. 'I just need some time to figure things out. Please help me.'

He sighed. 'Get dressed. I'll talk to the doctor.'

Ten minutes later, Tristan walked her down the corridor to the intensive care unit. When she saw Evan lying on the hospital bed, his skin bleached of all color and machines monitoring his heart, her trepidation faded.

Tristan pulled up a chair next to the bed. He crouched in front of her. 'Do you want me to stay with you?'

She shook her head. 'This is something I have to do alone.'

She didn't watch as he left the room. She knew that he was hurt by her inability to confide in him but for now she could only focus on one thing at time.

'Hi Evan.' Her voice was too loud in the room. 'I bet you're surprised I'm here.'

She watched his immobile face for a reaction. Seeing no movement she took a deep breath and her tense muscles loosened. 'I'm going to be okay. I just hurt my head a little when I fell but it's not serious.'

She almost felt like she was in a confessional box where a priest was going to listen to her sins and absolve her.

'I wanted to talk to you about what happened between you and Al— and me.' She kept her eyes on the fold of the sheet as it curved around the mattress. 'I don't blame you. Evan. I know it's not your fault.' She took a deep breath and felt her eyes sting. 'I should have trusted that my mother loved me and was doing what was best for me by sending me away, but I was so angry at her, so angry at everything that happened —' Lana breathed in, remembering the rage of her abandonment. She'd carried this rage for so many years, but now it was time to put it to rest. It was time to forgive and heal.

She took his hand in hers. 'I wanted you to know I forgive you, Evan. You were young and scared. You made the wrong decision in letting Alannah take drugs and putting her in a situation where she was hurt, but it's time you stop beating yourself up over it.'

His fingers moved like the softest butterfly under her hand. She looked up and saw his eyes were open.

His chapped lips moved. 'Water,' he murmured.

She passed him the plastic cup from the bedside table and he sipped from the straw.

'I'll call for a doctor.' She reached for the button beside the bed.

He reached out and took hold of her hand. 'No.' He returned the cup back. 'You don't remember, do you?'

She met his eyes and shook her head.

'While I appreciate your forgiveness,' he emphasized the word, 'I think you need to hear the full story before you hand it out.'

He moved his hand away from hers. 'I was home from college break with Johnny. There was no one home so we did a few lines. You caught us in the act.' He threw a hard look her way. 'I knew the only way to keep you quiet was to get you to take some. You did. I passed out. You came to me the next day, saying that Johnny raped you and you wanted to go to the police. I told you that if you told anyone I'd call you a liar and tell them that you wanted to have sex with Johnny.'

Lana shook her head, remembering his despair when he's spoken about the rape at Tammy and Michael's house. 'You were scared,' Lana said. 'You knew that if the truth came out they'd find out about your drug taking – and your father had a way of exacting his own punishment.'

His hands were formed into fists as he fought to keep his face impassive.

'It's okay.' Lana took his hand.

'What do you want from me?' His eyes were red as he fought to hold back tears. 'I'm a fuck-up. You were my little sister.' He pulled away his hand. 'I was supposed to protect you and instead I destroyed you.'

She took his fisted hands in hers. 'I want you to forgive yourself, Evan. I want you to realize that yes, you did make a terrible mistake, but it was just that, a mistake. I want you to stop punishing yourself and trying to kill yourself because you can't deal with the guilt.'

As she spoke she realized it was herself she was speaking to. For the past eight years, she'd been so angry about what happened to her. She'd blamed Tammy for putting her in that situation by not telling her the truth about breaking up with Billy, and didn't want to accept that she should have trusted her mother had her best interests at heart when she put her into foster care.

He gripped her hand tightly, lifting his other hand to his face. She squeezed his hand. 'Let it go, Evan. Leave it in the past where it belongs.'

He nodded. 'It doesn't matter anyway,' he said. 'The judge gave me a suspended sentence and rehab instead of going to jail for my DUI, but I fucked that up too.'

'How?'

'Are you obtuse?' He turned back to look at her. 'Look at you.'

'I guess you don't remember.' She stood up and walked toward the door. 'I found you unconscious when I came to the house and was attacked by the burglar you'd interrupted.' She turned to look at him. 'And that's exactly what I told the police officer that interviewed me this morning.' She smiled at him. 'I'll visit you in rehab.'

'What about Tristan?'

'I trust you to do the right thing.'

He looked at her in surprise and she saw the glimmer of the man he could be, before he hunched his shoulders and shrugged. 'Whatever.'

When she walked out, Tristan rushed to her, taking hold of her arm like she was a helpless fawn. 'Why didn't you call me to help you?' He took her weight.

'I'm fine,' she murmured. 'Tristan, take me home.'

He leant down and kissed her forehead before leading her to the elevator. As Lana sat in the reception area, waiting for Tristan to organize her discharge, she saw Vanessa entering the hospital. She followed her down the corridor, calling her name.

Vanessa turned. Seeing her annoyance, Lana hesitated, feeling embarrassed. Vanessa's face changed to concern as she saw Lana's bandaged head.

'Are you all right?' she asked when they reached each other.

Lana remembered not to nod. 'Yes, I just had a small accident and had to get it tended to.'

As they stood in the corridor, visitors and patients walking around them, she remembered the last time saw her best friend in her other life. They had walked away from Frank's burial with their arms around each other. Only the touch of her best friend had kept her from collapsing.

'What are you doing here?' Lana asked.

'I'm here to visit a sick friend.' Vanessa looked away.

Lana knew that she was lying. Vanessa never could look someone in the eye and lie. She wanted to push her for the truth.

'Well, I have to get going.' Vanessa turned away slightly. 'I hope you feel better,' she said before walking away.

Seeing Vanessa's eagerness to leave, Lana realized she had to let go of her expectations that everything she had lost would be returned to her. She hadn't been given the chance to return in order to replicate her past life, but to have a chance at a better life. She and Vanessa were on two different roads, it was up to fate to decide if they would meet again.

Chapter 16

As Tristan drove them home. Lana fell into a light doze and began to dream of Evan's and Tristan's faces merging into one other. Every time they exchanged faces she heard the words, 'My father ruined my life,' first in Tristan's voice, then Evan's. Yet their mouths never moved.

She woke as they pulled into the driveway. With a sigh, she pushed the dream and the remnants of its uneasiness out of her thoughts.

When the elevator door opened at their floor she blinked in surprise to see Tammy waiting for her. 'Mom,' Lana said.

Her mother smiled at her before they embraced. 'I'm sorry I didn't visit you in the hospital.' She broke eye contact and adjusted her handbag on her shoulder. 'There was something I had to do.'

Tristan had unlocked the door while they were embracing and gestured them inside.

When they were standing in the living room, Tammy shifted uncomfortably. 'There was something I wanted to tell you.'

In the confusion of everything that had happened she had forgotten about Tammy's call the day before, the reason she'd been at the brownstone. She looked at Tristan.

He took her hint. 'Uh, I left something in the car.'

Lana sat on the sofa. Tammy sat too, but quickly stood and started pacing. 'I have—'

Before Tammy had a chance to finish her sentence there was pounding on the apartment door. 'Open up, Alannah, I know that she's in there,' Michael shouted through the door.

Lana looked at Tammy in confusion. Tammy stared at the door with stark fear on her face.

'What's going on, Mom?'

Tammy continued to stare at the door. As the pounding started again, Lana stood to open the door.

'No.' Tammy put her hand out to stop her. 'Sit down.' She stood straighter. 'I'll deal with this.'

Tammy opened the door to a furious Michael.

'What game are you playing?' Michael demanded as he forced his way in.

'I believe my letter said it all.' Tammy nodded toward the paper he was holding in his hand.

'You're divorcing me.' He laughed savagely and shredded the letter. 'We need to work on your sense of humor.' He took hold of Tammy's arm and manhandled her to the door. 'Let's go home.'

Seeing the grimace of pain on Tammy's face, Lana stood to intervene.

Tammy looked at her. 'It's okay, baby.' She looked back at Michael and smiled. 'I'm not going anywhere.' She looked at Michael's hand. 'While I don't need any more evidence of your abuse it certainly won't hurt my divorce suit.'

Lana couldn't see Michael's face, but she noticed his grip had eased.

Tammy pulled her arm out of his grip and stepped closer to Lana, shielding her from Michael. 'You didn't really think I was going to be your punching bag forever? I've submitted the evidence to my lawyers.' Flicking open her handbag, she handed him a business card. 'If you try to block this divorce in any way, the photos of your handiwork will be on the five o'clock news, and it will be the end of your career.'

Michael looked at Tammy as if he was trying to gauge her sincerity. Deciding that she was serious, he put his hand back on her arm, caressing it gently. 'There's really no need for this, is there, darling?' His mouth stretched into a smile that didn't reach his eyes.

Tammy pulled her arm away from him, slowly, making her dislike evident. Michael's lips tightened. 'If you ever come near my daughter or her husband again, I will ruin you.'

He stood above Tammy, his face flushed as he tried to keep himself under control. Just when Lana thought she couldn't take the tension any more, he straightened his lapels and brushed a hand through his thinning hair. 'We can talk about this later.' He quickly strode out of the apartment, closing the door with a muted slam.

Lana looked at her mother with new eyes. With an ache in her heart, she realized she'd never really known her.

Tammy turned around. Seeing that she was trembling, Lana stood. 'Mom, are you okay?' She took hold of Tammy's hand.

'Yeah, baby. I'm fine.' She closed her eyes as tears began to fill them.

Lana reached out and pulled Tammy into an embrace. When she stopped crying, Tammy pulled away. 'Thanks, baby.' She opened her handbag and found a pack of tissues to wipe her eyes.

'Is it true?' Lana wasn't able to contain herself any longer. 'Are you really divorcing Michael?'

Tammy nodded. 'I wanted to do it a long time ago, but...' Tammy stopped herself abruptly, looking down at her lap, where she held the tissue tightly.

'Did you stay because of me?' Lana knew she'd guessed right when Tammy looked at her quickly. She tempered her voice. 'Was he threatening to hurt me? Please, Mom, tell me what happened.'

Tammy glanced at her before nodding. 'I met Michael after my last rehab attempt. My roommate Francine was volunteering at his campaign headquarters and she thought it would be fun if I joined her.'

Her eyes were still on her lap and she was making confetti from the tissue she was holding. 'Michael had been a widower for six months, after losing his wife, Laticia, in a car accident.'

Lana's skin broke out in goose pimples. When Tammy had met Billy, he'd told her he lost his girlfriend in a bike crash. 'He was different to the men I'd met before – he was refined, elegant, charming. I thought he was my Prince Charming.'

Lana swallowed at the coincidences of Tammy's present and past life. When she'd met Billy, she'd realized he was different to the men Tammy was with before. The first time he came over he wore a tie and carried flowers. Usually Tammy's previous boyfriends ignored Lana or made up errands for her to do so they could be alone with Tammy.

'One month after we met, he stayed over. When he left the apartment there was a photographer from the Boston Globe who snapped a photo of him leaving. The next day the photo appeared in the news. I was kissing him goodbye in my nightgown. Well you know what happened after that. They found out about my past and the headline was born: The former showgirl and widowed mayoral candidate. Never mind that I'd never been a showgirl.'

Her voice softened. She closed her eyes and more tears seeped out. 'I was so stupid. He asked me to marry him. He said he was in love with me and was withdrawing his candidacy.' She looked anywhere but at Lana.

But Billy's courtship of Tammy had been slow and insidious. He was charming and affable, slowly insinuating himself in their lives. He moved in three months later when his landlord gave him notice, or so he said. He'd encouraged Lana to take up extracurricular activities at school – the swim team, debating, the drama club – all under the guise of helping her college application. Because she wasn't home much, it was months until she realized something was wrong.

'He hit me for the first time two months after we were married. That's also when he told me it was all a publicity campaign. He'd been losing in the polls, the current mayor was the favorite. After we married, he created us into the picture perfect family.' She met Lana's eyes. 'My past helped him in his candidacy. He was seen as the everyday man who understood the real problems of his constituency.'

In her other life, Tammy became listless and withdrawn, a beaten lock appearing in her eyes, and Lana realized something was wrong. She'd suspected Billy wasn't all he appeared to be, but he was the first man in her mother's life who'd taken an interest in her and filled the space of the father figure she'd never had, so she'd ignored the signs and pretended nothing was happening.

Tammy continued, 'I was willing to give the marriage my best shot but after a year I decided it wasn't worth it. My life wasn't my own any more. I was unhappy and we spent hardly any time together.'

Slowly, Billy had exerted more and more control over Tammy, while showering Lana with encouragement and praise. It wasn't until afterward that Lana realized he'd used her to keep his mother in line. He'd destroyed the bond between mother and daughter, dividing them to conquer.

Lana took hold of Tammy's hand.

'When I told Michael, he laughed. He said that I'd never get custody of you. He had friends on the bench who owed him favors.' She looked at their joined hands. 'That's when I did the only thing I could – I sent you away to boarding school.' Her eyes were full of remembered pain. 'I didn't want you to know what was happening, and I didn't want you to be in Michael's way. By the time you came home for school holidays, I'd lost you.'

Lana realized from reading Alannah's diary that Tammy was talking about when Alannah had returned from boarding school for Christmas. That was eight months after the rape and she'd already started spiraling into anorexia.

'You were distant and moody; wouldn't let anyone touch you. I knew you blamed me for sending you away, but I couldn't tell you the truth. So I accepted your rebuffs and took comfort from the fact that you were safe.'

Lana blinked the tears from her eyes, realizing that her mother had sacrificed herself, just as she had done in her other life.

Tammy had stayed with Billy to protect Lana from his abuse. She'd put Lana in foster care in order to get her out of Billy's reach and then organized her own escape, but Lana's distrust and rebellion had made her return to the apartment and into the clutches of Billy's friend, Rob.

After the near rape she had been so full of rage at Tammy, believing she'd abandoned her and not understanding all the ways Tammy had attempted to protect her, that she'd cut Tammy out of her life, the same way Alannah did to Tammy.

She swallowed back her tears. Now it was her turn to protect her mother. Tammy didn't need to know about the rape. The only thing that had kept her going all those years with Michael was the belief that she had managed to protect her daughter. Lana wasn't going to shatter that belief.

Tammy reached into her handbag and handed Lana a notebook. Seeing the red and white cover, she realized that it was Tammy's diary.

'I wanted to give you this to read.' Tammy handed her the diary. 'After meeting with a lawyer two years ago I've been documenting his abuse and now I'm the one who will be blackmailing him.'

'I'm glad,' Lana murmured. 'You can move into our spare bedroom ...'

Tammy squeezed her hand. 'No, thank you, baby. I have a friend I'm staying with until the divorce is finalized.' She dug through her handbag. 'It's someone Michael doesn't know so he can't try to contact me.' She handed Lana a piece of paper. 'This is my new mobile number if you need to call me.' She smiled softly at her. 'I suspect that you have to put some things in your life in order too.'

Lana nodded, realizing Tammy had picked up on the tension between her and Tristan.

She bent and hugged her. 'I love you, Lana.'

Lana kissed her. 'I love you back, Mom.'

When Tammy reached the doorway, she turned. 'Be happy in whatever you do, baby. Please be happy.'

Lana nodded, holding back her tears as Tammy walked out of the apartment.

When Tristan returned fifteen minutes later, Lana was sitting with the diary in her lap.

'What are you reading?' Tristan asked, bringing her back to the present.

Lana snapped the diary shut and put it on the coffee table. 'Mom gave me her diary.' Seeing his puzzled face, she explained, 'She's divorcing Michael.' She traced her finger over the diary's embossed cover, the smooth gold lettering soothing her. 'She gave me her diary so I'd understand the truth of what happened.'

He sat on the opposite sofa. 'The truth. Now there's a word that has different interpretations.' He smiled wryly. 'Let's talk about what happened between you and Evan.' He quirked an eyebrow. 'Which version are you going to give me? The truth, or what you told the police?'

'You were eavesdropping on my conversation with Evan.'

He nodded. 'Did you really think I was going to leave you alone with that psychopath?'

Lana sighed. She should have known he gave in too easily at the hospital. 'No, I guess not.'

She told him what happened at the brownstone. As she spoke, he fought to maintain an impassive facade, but his clenched fists revealed the truth of his feelings.

'Evan didn't mean to hurt me.' She touched her bandage. 'He was under the influence and didn't realize what he was doing.'

'So that's supposed to excuse what he did,' he demanded.

'No, but —'

'No, Lana. Evan committed a crime and he needs to be punished.'

She knew that Tristan couldn't understand her willingness to lay the ghosts of the past to rest. After reading Tammy's diary, she'd seen the glimmer of who Evan could have been. He had been angry and bitter after Tammy and Michael's marriage. His mother had died just six months before and was already replaced, but when Michael started beating Tammy, it was Evan who ran interference. He and Tammy had learnt to protect each other, until the rape. Then Evan had turned everyone away and withdrawn into a dark place as the drugs obliterated his inherent gentleness.

'Don't you think he's punished himself enough already?' she asked Tristan after telling him about Evan's past. 'Why do you think he's turned into a junkie who can't live without his next hit?' She held up Tammy's diary. 'He used to be a sweet, gentle boy who turned to drugs to escape an abusive household. That boy still exists.' She put the diary down. 'I'm going to give him the chance to discover that boy again.'

'I applaud your Mother Theresa act, but this is a black and white case. He committed a crime and he needs to pay for it.'

She looked at Tristan's closed face in disbelief. She'd known that Tristan was stubborn and had a strong sense of wrong and right, but his coldness was scaring her.

'Like your father did? He committed a crime and he needs to pay for it for the rest of his life.'

Tristan stood. 'This isn't about my father.'

'Yes, yes it is,' Lana insisted, standing up to face him. 'Ever since your mother died and your father went to jail you've been nursing your anger. Your inability to forgive has turned you into a cold-hearted bastard without any compassion.'

Seeing his hurt she regretted at her tactlessness. 'I'm sorry.' She reached for his arm. 'I don't want to hurt you. I just want to try to understand you, and get you to understand me.'

He held his arm rigidly under her hand, but at least he was listening.

'Can't you believe that people are inherently good, but one event can change their life, and change the way they relate to the world? Sometimes all we need is a second chance,' she pleaded.

'I believe that we all make choices. Each choice has a consequence we have to live with.'

She removed her hand. 'So by that you mean that when people make a mistake they should be judged for it for the rest of their lives?' She stepped away from him. 'What hope have we got then? We've both deceived each other,' she said, thinking of her deceit in not telling him about her past life, and his silence about the blackmailer. 'What are the consequences of our choices?'

He flexed his jaw as he met her gaze. Then he turned and walked to the door.

'Where are you going?' she exclaimed. 'Tristan, don't leave, please!' She took hold of his arm and held him back.

'I'm going to see Evan.' He shook her off.

'Please stay and talk to me.' She paused. 'This isn't about me at all,' she whispered, realizing that he was angry about the blackmail.

'That's where you're wrong.' He opened the door. 'This is about both of us.' He walked out, slamming the door shut behind him.

·❤·❤·❤·❤·❤·

Tristan strode through the hospital corridors toward Evan's hospital room like a heat-seeking missile. He didn't know what the bastard had done to Lana in order to make her so willing to forgive and forget, but he was in for a rude awakening.

Evan wasn't going to play him for a sucker. The bastard had been screwing with his life for the last couple of weeks with his little notes threatening to rip his world apart. There were some things that were unforgivable.

As he walked, he could hear Lana's voice as she asked, *What chance have we got then?* He shook off his discomfort. It wasn't the same at all. Evan was a bastard who'd been practicing his deceit to further his own agenda. Tristan had been hiding the blackmail notes from Lana in order to protect her.

Or to protect yourself?, a little voice taunted in his head. He ignored it. This was a simple case of right and wrong, there were no ambiguities to excuse Evan. When he reached Evan's hospital room, he pushed open the door. He saw Michael and let the door close slightly again, but kept watch.

'Did you know what she was planning?' Michael demanded.

Evan lifted his eyebrow. 'She. There are so many she's. I need you to be more specific Daddy dearest.'

Tristan could almost see Michael grinding his teeth. 'Your mother.'

Evan put a finger on his chin as he murmured, 'My mother. Don't you remember where my mother is?' His voice hardened. 'She's in the grave you put her in.'

'Don't be impertinent,' Michael snapped. 'Tammy. Did you know what she was planning?' When Evan didn't answer, he continued, drawing out his words as if speaking to a child, 'Did you know Tammy was planning to divorce me?'

Evan looked taken aback before his face broke into a delighted smile. 'So she's finally done it?' He shook his head. 'I didn't think she had it in her.' He sat back against the bedhead again, his face becoming calculating. 'What is it, old man? Regretting that you'll lose your punching bag? It's okay, I'll buy you a real one. I know that it won't be the same as hitting flesh and blood, but hey, we can't all get what we want.' He shrugged.

Michael's face flushed and he clenched his fists. Taking a deep breath, he pulled up a chair next to Evan's bed. 'Listen, son, I know that we haven't been on best terms in the past, but I really need your help.' He placed his hand on Evan's arm.

Evan looked down at Michael's hand before meeting his eyes, all traces of amusement gone. 'What do you need, Dad?'

Michael stood and started pacing. 'She's been collecting evidence for the past two years.' He looked back at Evan, who nodded, indicating for him to continue. 'She says she'll be presenting the evidence if I don't allow the divorce to proceed and give her half my assets.' He came back and stood by Evan. 'So what I need you to do is help me even the playing field. Tell the courts about her drinking and instability. And tell them about how she made sexual advances to you when you were living at home.'

Tristan watched as Evan looked down, his face closed off. He wanted to go in there and pound both of them into the ground. But he had to know what they were planning to support Tammy.

'So what do you say son? Are you going to help your old man?' Michael laughed jovially.

Evan looked back at him. 'I'm sorry, Daddy-O. I'd like to help, but you see, I've already promised Tammy I'm going to testify on her behalf. I'm going to tell the courts all about your little penchant for discipline. About how you like to hear the sound of popping bones and see your handiwork on bruised flesh. About how you killed my mother.'

There was dead silence. Michael stared at Evan in disbelief.

Evan smiled, his eyes glittering with malicious satisfaction. 'What's the matter, Daddy-O? Cat got your tongue?'

'You little bastard,' Michael shouted, his fist aimed for Evan's face.

Evan twisted out of the way and Michael punched the bed-head. Evan wrapped his arms around Michael's torso and pulled him down, their faces close to each other. 'I want you to under-stand something. I hate you with everything in me. You ruined my life.' His voice was full of disgust. He let go of Michael and pushed him so he nearly fell onto the floor. 'I hope you rot in hell.'

Michael looked at him over his shoulder, his face revealing his fear. He stood slowly, his age showing as he awkwardly held the edge of the bed. He straightened his cuffs and his lapel before heading for the door.

Tristan moved out of the way, standing with his back to the door so that Michael wouldn't see him. He heard his footsteps as he walked away. Looking over his shoulder, he saw the defeat in his walk.

He jerked when Evan's door opened. 'Come in, Walker.' Evan held the door open for him.

Tristan entered slowly, watching as Evan shuffled to the chair on the other side of the bed.

'Lock the door.' Evan sat down. 'I don't think we want to risk any more eavesdroppers.'

Tristan felt his face flush, realizing he'd been caught out. He locked the door and turned around to find Evan's steady gaze on him.

'I was expecting you.' Evan picked up a set of keys on his bedside table. 'I presume this is what you came for.' He held them out to Tristan. 'The newspaper articles are in a box in my study.'

Tristan took the keys and hesitated.

'You don't have to worry about any further copies, or someone else knowing. I hacked into the Registry of Vital Records after a friend thought he recognized you as his old college pal, and found your change of name and birth certificate.'

Tristan nodded, putting the keys in his pocket. 'I'll have them couriered back.'

Evan shrugged. 'It's not as if I'll be needing them where I'm going.'

He met Evan's gaze. Seeing the look in his eyes, Tristan finally understood what Lana was talking about. He was looking at a man who'd been fighting demons all his life, and had nearly lost the battle. Making a decision, he straightened his shoulders and headed for the door. 'I'll send them back tomorrow. I think you'll need at least a change of clothes for rehab.'

Evan's face was immobile. 'So she's got even you believing I'm redeemable?'

Tristan shook his head. 'No. You did that.'

He was halfway out the door when he heard Evan call him back. 'Ask Tammy to call me.'

Chapter 17

Tristan entered the apartment to find Lana sitting on the sofa, reading. It was dusk outside and she'd turned on the lamp and was covered with a blanket.

She sat up as he entered. 'You were a while.' She looked at the wall clock.

He sat on the sofa opposite her. After leaving the hospital he'd gone to Evan's apartment and destroyed all the evidence of his past life. Feeling unsettled, he hadn't been able return to the apartment. Instead he'd driven around for the past couple of hours, trying to put his thoughts in order.

'What happened?' Lana asked.

Tristan opened his mouth to speak, but realized he didn't know what to say. What had happened? Something fundamental inside him had shifted, and he didn't like it. He felt as if his whole life was a house of cards. Seeing Lana's impatient gaze he realized she was waiting for an answer. In the end there was only one thing to say.

'You were right,' he began, 'sometimes people do deserve a second chance.'

She smiled, her eyes filling with tears.

He knelt in front of her. 'I'm sorry, Lana.' He took hold of her hand. 'I've been so stubborn and self-involved that I've been keeping you at a distance.' He looked down at their hands. 'I should have told you about the blackmail. I should have trusted you with my secret.' He looked up. 'Will you forgive me?'

'Oh, Tristan,' she whispered. 'I'm sorry —'

He cut her off. 'You have nothing to apologize for.'

'There's something I have to tell you,' Lana said. 'I've been less than honest with you.'

She was tense, all her muscles clenched. He took hold of her hands and felt her pulse speed up. His gaze narrowed as she bit her lip.

'I... I ...' She gasped for breath.

'Is this about what happened before the accident?'

She nodded mutely.

'Then it doesn't matter. The past is the past.' He gripped her hand tighter. 'All that matters is that we love each other.' Seeing her hesitation he asked quickly, 'You do love me, don't you?'

She smiled. 'Yes, I love you, but —'

He kissed her. He felt this was their last chance. Either they got it right this time, or they were over. She held herself stiffly before melting in his embrace.

Lana pulled away and took his face in her hands. He saw the uncensored love in her eyes. She leant in and kissed him on his eyelids, on his cheeks, his nose, his temple. She met his gaze again. 'I love you, Tristan.'

He rained butterfly kisses on her face. 'I love you, Lana,' he whispered against her lips.

His urgency faded and he wanted to savor her. Leaning into her, he kissed her neck as his arms caressed her. He lifted her hands and kissed her wrists before sliding his hands along her arms to her waist to help her out of her jumper. He moved his hands to her jeans, and she stood as he pulled at their zipper and tugged them off.

On his knees in front of her he kissed her stomach, his fingertips smoothing her soft skin. 'Your skin is like satin.'

She made him stand in front of her and helped him take off his T-shirt. She kissed his collarbone, then his shoulder. Walking around him, she kissed his back as her hands mapped his skin as if he was a classical sculpture. In front of him once more, she pulled down the tab on his zipper and slid his jeans down his legs, kneeling as she did so. He stepped out of them and stood in his briefs.

She tipped her head back and looked at the length of his body. 'You are so beautiful.'

He grabbed her wrists and pulled her up to kiss her. His hands reached under her butt and he lifted her. She wrapped her legs around his waist and he walked them to the bedroom, their lips joined.

He laid her down on the bed gently. Continuing to kiss her, he unhooked her bra and removed it. Her bare breasts pressed against his chest and his hands tightened on her hips.

They rubbed against each other, the friction teasing and tormenting them. When he couldn't take it any more, he pulled her panties down then returned between her thighs. Her hands reached for his briefs and she put her hands under the elastic, stroking and squeezing his skin.

With a groan, he tore himself away from her and tugged his briefs off. He lay between her thighs again and met her eyes. He kissed her deeply as she stroked her hands along his back. She clutched his butt as she felt him shift to enter her. Her eyes closed as she let out a moan as he slowly pushed himself in, filling her. He wanted to lose himself in the rhythm as her heat surrounded him but he continued the slow, tender pace they had set. Her hands gripped his arms as she moved beneath him, her hips rocking in time with his thrusts.

When he felt the tightening inside her, he pressed a kiss to her neck. 'I love you.'

She opened her eyes and met his gaze. 'I love you,' she whispered on a moan. Her eyes lost focus and closed again as she bit her lip. Watching her face as ecstasy ripped through her, he let himself go and followed her over the edge.

Afterwards he lay on his side and pulled her into the circle of his arms. He covered them with a sheet and pulled her tighter against him. For the first time, he could remember he felt pure contentment and happiness. He kissed her on the shoulder and fell asleep.

·❣· ❤· ❤·❤·❤·

Lana sat on the bed in her robe watching Tristan sleep. Sunrise was creeping around the edges of the bedroom curtains, lighting the room. He slept on his side, his face peaceful.

Waking up in his arms, his heart beating under her ear, she had been overwhelmed by happiness. He loved her and he'd shown her with his every touch and kiss. Contentment and peace flowed over her before a small voice inside her asked, *Will he still love you when he knows who you really are?*

She tried to push away the voice, to convince herself that they were happy together and there was no need to ruin it, but she knew in her heart that the time of reckoning had arrived. It seemed her whole existence had been wrapped up in getting Tristan to admit his love to her and let her in, yet now that he was the man she'd always dreamt of she couldn't enjoy it.

She'd had the dream that featured Tristan and Evan changing faces and saying 'My father ruined my life' again. Now she realized the significance of her dream.

Evan was everything that Tristan could be if he didn't forgive Kevin. Evan's bitterness at his father had submerged any good in him and this was the path that Tristan was heading toward. When Tristan had talked about Evan, she'd realized that the hardness went deep down into the core of him. Until he learnt to accept the weaknesses of those he loved, he couldn't make peace with his past and live a full life.

It was up to her to stop Tristan from making the mistakes she had made, because they couldn't have true happiness until they dealt fully with the past. And that included Tristan knowing about her past life. She couldn't live a lie. She needed to know that Tristan loved her for who she was and that she would never have to fear having that love taken away from her.

She looked back at his face and saw he was watching her.

'Why don't you come here?' He flipped open the covers. 'You look lonely over there.'

She lay on top of the covers next to him and held him tightly. She knew this might be the last time she felt his touch. He started kissing her neck and her resolution weakened. She wanted to wish reality away and submerge herself in desire once again.

He kissed the corner of her eye and grazed a tear. 'Hey, what's wrong?' he murmured.

She closed her eyes and breathed in his scent one more time, trying to imprint everything about him in her memory. She pulled away from his embrace and sat on the edge of the bed, her back to him.

'I have to tell you something,' she said. She stood and turned around. 'But first I need a promise from you.'

He watched her curiously.

'I need you to promise me that you will let me tell my story and you won't interrupt me.'

'Okay,' Tristan said.

'No, I need you to promise.'

He smiled at her as if she was a cute three-year-old. 'Okay, I promise, cross my heart,' he said, tongue-in-cheek, as he made the gesture, 'that I will let you tell your story without interruptions.'

'Okay.' Lana breathed out a sigh of relief. Now she had to do the hard part. She bit her lip as she tried to remember the speech she'd rehearsed for weeks. 'You know how you said the other day that I seemed like a different woman since the accident?'

Tristan nodded slowly.

'Well, the thing is.' She started pacing, her clenched hands in front of her. 'I am a different woman.' Seeing Tristan's blank face she realized she'd left out a few details. 'My real name is

Lana Walters.' She turned away from Tristan and pulled back the curtain, peering out the window at the foggy scenery. 'On the day that your wife Alannah had a car accident I ... I ...' Taking a deep breath she pushed the words out: 'Well, I died.'

She looked up to see Tristan's reaction and couldn't decide whether the frown on his face was a good or a bad thing. He nodded at her to continue.

'You see, my real husband was Frank Tristan Walters Junior. Frank was you, but not you.' Realizing she was making a mess of it, she quickly backtracked. 'Frank was you up until the age of eight years old, but when you were eight you had the surgery that repaired your heart after rheumatic fever damaged its valves and that's what set you both on separate paths.' Lana quickly gulped in some air. She waved her hands in front of her hot face, trying to cool herself. 'Do you understand what I'm saying?'

He shook his head.

'On the day I died, I was returning from Frank's funeral.' Her agitation had increased her body temperature and she felt a drop of sweat slither between her breasts. 'I was on Newbury Street with Vanessa,' she tugged at the tie of her dressing gown, but trying to tug it off in a hurry she was all tangled.

Tristan reached for the tie and with two flicks of his fingers it was undone and she was in her nightgown. 'So you were on Newbury Street,' he continued for her.

Seeing the twinkle in his eye, she knew he was finding her fairy tale amusing.

'So I was on Newbury Street and my butterfly brooch fell off.' She touched her chest. 'Frank gave me the brooch for our first wedding anniversary,' she continued. Her stomach was fluttering with nerves and she absently rubbed it. 'The brooch landed on the street so I jumped after it. In my hurry, I didn't check the street first.'

She swallowed hard as she remembered the tingle of warning at Vanessa screaming her name and then looking up, only to be sent flying by the bus. She began to shake as she remembered dying, feeling the sun on her face, the wind lifting her hair, the smell of incense from the relaxation shop next to Vanessa's boutique, and then the eerie feeling of being one with the air.

'Lana, sweetie.' She felt Tristan's hands on her face.

Coming back to herself she met his gaze. He was looking at her with concern.

'After I died, I was carried to Alannah's accident.'

'Shh.' Tristan placed his finger on her lips. Taking her by the shoulders, he walked her to the bed. 'It's okay baby, you're overwrought. This bump on the head has made you confused —'

'Tristan.' Her voice stopped him in his tracks. 'Do you remember your promise?' She jerked away from him. 'Are you scared of what you're going to hear?' Tension had made her voice sharp.

His face darkened but he sat on the edge of the bed and gestured for her to continue. 'I'm riveted.' Sarcasm oozed from his voice.

'I was carried to Alannah's accident. She was trapped in the car and the firefighters were cutting her out of it. Just when they were about to lift her out, she died.' She saw that she now had Tristan's attention. 'They put her on the gurney and started resuscitating her, but she had already left her body. We melded briefly as her spirit passed me, and I felt her guilt and anguish.'

She met his gaze. 'I now know she felt guilty about you. She was coming to see you and tell you the truth when she slid on ice and crashed the car.' She sat back on the chair, the act of recounting the memories exhausting her. 'I was pulled into her body and here we are.'

'Do you really think I'm going to believe —'

'Your parents were alive in my past life.' She interrupted him. 'You have your mother's eyes,' she continued. He watched her like a cornered animal. 'The same golden hazel shade. She wore lavender perfume and whenever she hugged me it was like I was home.' As she spoke her throat tightened. 'When she laughed she covered her mouth, almost like she was embarrassed. She used to knit. She'd make jumpers and woolly socks, gloves and scarves, but only for her family. As she handed the gifts over, she'd say that she was armoring us in love.'

She saw by the look in his eyes that she had struck a chord. 'She'd make your favorite meal, lasagna, every Sunday and we'd all eat together. Your father would tease her about feeling left out because she hadn't made shepherd's pie, his favorite meal.'

'I don't want to hear,' he said, almost as if he was trying to convince himself.

'You have your father's hands,' she continued as if he hadn't spoken. 'The same blunt fingers and broad palms. He was always building something in the house. He said it was his job for eternity to build for his family.

'And you.' She sighed. 'You were different. Your parents said you were your mother's child. Because your heart wasn't operated on, you weren't like other children. Your mother was your playmate and you got her love of art. You used to paint every day. I learnt to love the smell of turpentine.'

She wiped the tear of her cheek. 'I never doubted in the strength of your love. I knew that you wouldn't be mine for long, so I learnt to treasure what time we had, and when you left, I didn't know how I was going to go on without you.' She smiled. 'You gave me everything. With you I had a home, I had parents, and I had a love that I knew was once in a lifetime.'

She took his hand in hers. 'And then I found you again, and you love me the way you used to, but you're not true to who you are. Don't you see, Tristan, you have to make peace with your father —'

He threw off her hand. 'Look, Lana, I know you want life to be a nice little fairy tale where everyone lives happily and loves everyone.' He pulled on his briefs. 'But that's not the way this story is going to end, okay?'

He looked at her and she could see he was fighting to hold in his frustration.

'Honey.' He knelt beside her chair. 'You know I love you and want to be with you. Let's just be happy together.' He pulled her into his embrace and started nuzzling her neck. 'It's just you and me with our whole lives in front of us. Leave the past where it belongs.'

She didn't return his embrace. 'You're doing it again.' When he lifted his head off her shoulder and met her gaze, she continued, 'Brushing aside my concerns. Hearing only what you want to hear.'

He moved away. 'I don't see why this is so important. Not now.'

She took his hand in hers. 'Please,' she said. 'Just listen to what I have to say.'

He nodded without looking at her.

She knew this was her final chance to make him understand and she had to make each word count. 'I spent years keeping Tammy at a distance. I was small minded and cruel because I wanted to punish her for betraying me. For ruining my life and leaving me all alone.' She looked back at him. 'But I was the one who did that.'

She sighed. 'Tristan, we don't choose our families. We just have to accept them and make the best of it. Forgive them their mistakes and the hurts they cause us so that we can move on with our lives without bitterness.'

She squeezed his hand. 'I don't want you to make the same mistakes I did. By not making peace with your father, you're cutting out a part of your life that makes you who you are.'

He covered her hand with his. 'This is my mistake to make. If you want to be with me then you have to accept that.'

She felt chilled to the bone. 'Are you giving me an ultimatum?' Her voice cracked.

'Don't put words in my mouth,' he snapped as he walked away. 'I just don't know why this has to be such an issue. My relationship with my father has nothing to do with us.'

'Yes, it does. You forget, I know who you really are. Not the pieces you let people see, but the real you.' She went to him and placed her hand on his heart. 'And I know that you loved your father and that all your anger comes from that love.'

He met her gaze and sighed roughly. 'Lana, I don't need a therapist. I want a wife.'

'Are you saying it's not a wife's role to share her opinion?' she demanded.

'That's not what I mean. I just want us to be happy together —'

'So do I,' Lana interrupted. 'And if we're going to find some sort of happiness together we need to be honest with each other. And that means telling each other things that we might not want to hear.'

'Tristan, do you believe what I said about living a past life?' She held her breath, needing the answer to be yes. They couldn't have a future together unless they trusted one another.

He looked away for a moment. She saw by his unfocused gaze that he was putting together the pieces. She was full of hope when she saw him come to a decision.

He placed his arms on her shoulders. 'All that matters is that you believe it.' Seeing her disappointment in his response, he snapped, 'What the hell do you want from me? I'm supposed to swallow your fairy tale hook, line and sinker to prove how much I love you?'

'Yes.' She looked at him unflinchingly. 'I need to know that you trust me enough to believe me. That you trust your intuition about what happened between us and accept the truth.'

'Come on, Lana. Who are you fooling? My father was never part of the family and he never could be. It doesn't matter which world you put him in.'

'You don't want to believe me,' Lana whispered, 'because if you believe me then that means that you're wrong about your father. That he's not this evil person you've created in your mind but just a man who lost his way and never got the chance to find it again.'

She saw the torment on his face and knew she was getting through to him. 'If you believe me then you have to believe that he was capable of more and so are you. And unless you believe me we can't be together because I can't spend the rest of my life censoring my thoughts to suit you.'

She stepped back and turned her head away.

'So that's it?' he shouted. 'I tell you I love you and want to be with you, but you're deciding I'm not good enough?'

'You know that's not true, Tristan,' she replied, her voice even.

'Bullshit.' He pulled on his jeans. 'Everything has to have strings attached. You want a perfect life.' He pulled up his zip. 'Well, I'm not perfect, Lana, and I'm not ever going to be. And for that matter, neither are you. Sometimes life is messy and fucked up and you just have to make the best of it.'

'Don't.' She fought to keep her anger in check. 'Don't you tell me about what life is. I spent five years of my life living in constant fear. Every day that I woke up and felt Frank's breath on my neck was a miracle. I know how fucked up life can be. And I refuse to spend this life living the same way.'

'Oh, please —' he muttered, pulling on his boots.

'What proof do you need to convince you?' She frantically backtracked through her memories. 'Did you father tell you about how he met and married your mother?'

He'd stopped in the doorway but didn't turn around.

'Your father was one of the builders hired to construct a pergola for her wedding day.' She knew by the intent way he was listening that he hadn't heard this story. 'As you know, your mother's family was wealthy and she was engaged to marry a lawyer. Her every day would have been full of ease and luxury. Instead, she eloped with your father on what was supposed to be her wedding day.'

Lana smiled as she remembered hearing the story in her past life after a family dinner when they all gathered for story telling. 'That's the reason your father was so consumed with making money. He always felt inadequate that he'd cheated your mother of the life she rightfully deserved.'

She remembered Kevin's voice as he tearfully admitted he'd lost his way, but found it before it was too late. 'Kevin realized that his family was the most important thing after you fell ill. He spent so much time away from the company his partner embezzled the funds and left him bankrupt. But he was never bitter. He said he'd realized love was the only currency that mattered.'

'That's a beautiful story. But my father never told stories.' He glanced at her bitterly. 'He was always at work.' He walked out of the bedroom.

'Tristan.' She followed him. 'Tristan!'

He turned to look at her.

'Please stay.'

'I need to get away, Lana.' He rubbed his neck. 'I don't understand why this has to be so hard.' He left the apartment and got into the elevator, not meeting her gaze as he pressed the button.

When he was gone, she sagged against the wall. She felt as if she'd pushed a heavy stone up hill, only to find it was the wrong kind. Maybe Tristan was right? Maybe it wasn't supposed to be this hard?

Chapter 18

Tristan drove his truck on automatic pilot, his hands clenched on the wheel. Glancing at the speedometer, he quickly eased off the gas pedal. That's all he needed, a speeding fine.

He'd thought that after you told a woman you love her and she told you she loved you back, you moved straight to the living happily part of the deal. But in his case he gets thrown for a loop with stories about a past life. As if life with Alannah hadn't been hard enough he had to deal with this crap. Since the day he'd married her there had been one drama after another. Most people at least got a honeymoon period to cushion them from the hardship that would follow. He got one whole morning.

As he pulled into the car park at his office he shook his head. Life had taken a strange turn. It was as if he was living in the Twilight Zone. Lana was his wife, but not his wife.

Sitting in his truck, he remembered how he'd felt after taking her home from the hospital. He'd felt like he'd taken home the wrong woman, but that had just been a momentary hitch. He'd been surprised at her behavior until Jeremy told him that it wasn't unusual for amnesia victims to start exhibiting behavior that was out of character.

He entered his office and picked up the Rebuilding Boston Together contract. There was nothing stopping him from moving forward in this life. He signed the last page with a flourish, feeling grim satisfaction as he thought of his new future. He would be doing what he'd wanted to do with his life since he was eight years old.

When he'd fallen ill with rheumatic fever, he'd dreamt of houses. As he tossed and turned, all the wondrous designs from an architectural book he'd flicked through in his father's office danced behind his closed eyelids. During his recovery, he'd drawn the designs from memory in his scrapbook.

After his mother saw his drawings she encouraged him by buying the supplies he needed to recreate them as models. He had been fortunate to discover what he wanted to do with his life so young, but unfortunate in not being able to follow through, until now.

Aidan walked into the office and stopped abruptly when he saw him behind the desk. 'I thought you were taking the day off?'

Tristan put the contracts in an envelope and sealed it. 'So did I.'

His assistant, Julie, entered the office. 'Lana's on line one.'

Tristan passed her the envelope. 'Please courier this. And take a message.'

After Julie walked out, Aidan handed him a sheaf of papers. 'I was going to put these in your tray for signature, but since you're here.' He sat down.

Tristan glanced over the papers and started signing. Seeing one of the invoices, he looked up to ask Aidan about it and saw his grim face. 'Something wrong?'

'She's met someone.'

'She always meets someone.' Tristan continued signing. Holly enjoyed the single life and every night was a party. He looked up and caught the unguarded torment in Aidan's eyes. 'This one's different?'

Aidan's eyes answered for him.

'Why don't you tell her how you feel?'

Aidan quirked his eyebrow and glanced at the phone.

'My situation is different. I told her I love her and want to be with her. She's the one who doesn't want to be with me.'

Julie came in and handed him two telephone messages. 'They're both from your wife.' She walked out again.

Tristan didn't have to look at Aidan to know what he was thinking: Lana wasn't acting as if she didn't want to be with him.

Tristan threw his pen onto the table. 'I don't understand why it has to be so hard. There's always something we have to fight through.'

'At least she's fighting alongside you. Holly and I started working at cross purposes a long time ago and we still haven't stopped.' Aidan collected the invoices.

Tristan felt guilty as he realized he wasn't being a good friend. Aidan had his own relationship problems. 'Do you want to get together after work for a beer?'

Aidan shook his head. 'I've got Josh tonight. We're going to play baseball in the park and then watch a video.'

Julie came in carrying another telephone message.

Tristan stood before she could speak. 'I'm going to the work site.'

He heard Lana's voice in his head: You're good at running away. He kept walking.

When he reached the construction site he caught the lift to the top floor. Looking out across Boston, he took a deep breath. It did it to him every time. Being so high without glass obstructing his view he could almost imagine how a bird in full flight felt. As he looked around him he didn't see the empty shell but instead the building as it would look when it was complete. He always felt a mingling of self-satisfaction and frustration at this point.

Working as a builder who specialized in industrial designs, he'd spent the past ten years feeling frustrated at wasting his talent. Each project had been about getting solvent and ensuring he would never again have to worry where his next meal was coming from. His job hadn't been a joy, but at least he had a good life and was doing something he was competent at.

Now that he knew that this part of his life was over, he looked back at his accomplishments with pride. He'd spent so much time focusing on all that he didn't have, he hadn't been paying attention to what he did have. He'd always imagined that when he had the opportunity to build homes, he'd dismantle his company and move on. He caught sight of the sign in front of the building that proclaimed the construction was a Walker and Co project. But he didn't want to destroy what he'd worked toward for the past ten years – it was a part of him and he had to find a way to integrate it into his life.

Hearing his cell phone beeping, he took it out of his pocket and saw he'd received a message. Dialing voicemail he heard Lana's voice: 'I've been thinking about what you said.'

He tried to remember how their conversation had ended.

'When you said it wasn't supposed to be so hard,' she continued, as if she'd read his thoughts. 'Maybe you were right. Maybe it isn't supposed to be. Maybe we're not supposed to be.'

He was struck dumb. It was as if she was plucking the thoughts from his head and repeating them back to him.

'In my past life, things were so easy between us. We met and fell in love and spent every day trying to live happily ever after. Even though we knew it was an impossible dream that we would be together for the rest of our lives, I knew that the strength of our love would be with me always. But now...' She sighed deeply.

'Well, now I wonder if that was all we were supposed to have. Maybe our time has passed and we should move on. So I just want to tell you that I will always love you, but I don't think we're supposed to be together. I'm going to stay with Holly until we sort things out. Be happy, Tristan.'

Tristan ended the call and stared blankly at the view that had given him pleasure only a few moments ago. He had left her seeking a time out from her revelation, assuming that she would patiently wait for him to sort himself out and return to her. Instead she'd taken a page from his book and was moving on while he dawdled.

Anger smothered all rational thought and he wanted to pound something. How could she do this to him? Tell him she loved him one minute and then leave the next? They were supposed to be a team.

So he hadn't reacted that well to her revelation. What was he supposed to say? It's not as if Miss Manners wrote a book about the proper etiquette when your wife confesses to having lived another life.

As he put the phone back in his pocket, he felt the wrinkled phone messages Julie had thrust at him. Okay, so he'd run away and avoided Lana since their conversation, but he didn't know what to say to her. He remembered the pleading in her eyes when she asked him if he believed her, followed by her hurt when he didn't tell her what she wanted to hear.

But how could he believe her? People didn't just die and get transported into another life. And what about the crazy idea that there are parallel worlds where everyone was the same, but living different lives? *Since when are you an expert on after-life phenomena,* his conscience piped up, *Did you even give her a proper chance to talk to you?*

Remembering the way he'd hurried out of the apartment, he felt ashamed at how he'd short-changed her. Maybe there was a reason she believed this fantasy about another life and he should have taken the time to listen to her. It hadn't been easy for her since the car accident when her memory got affected.

But was her memory affected? He remembered all the times she'd made a statement and been surprised to hear that reality was different. She'd believed his parents were alive and that her college roommate, Vanessa, was her best friend. The way she'd recognized Kevin even though she'd never met him or seen any photos of him. It was almost as if she did remember another life.

'Stop it, Walker,' he said aloud. 'Soon you'll be having conversations with little green men.'

So what did that make Lana? She believed that she'd lived a past life. Did that mean she was crazy? He laughed at the absurdity. So why did she believe she'd lived a past life?

Maybe because she did.

His skin raised in goose pimples. What other reason could Lana have for telling him such a story, unless she truly believed it? He remembered all the signs: the feeling he'd had that he'd taken the wrong woman home; how he'd fallen in love with her all over again, as if she was a completely different person.

He absently rubbed at the scar on his chest. His mother had told him that he was very lucky they had insurance so that his heart valves could be repaired, otherwise he would have spent his whole life as an invalid. According to Lana, in her past life he'd died a few weeks ago, his life cut short at thirty.

Yet here he was, healthy and fit with his whole life stretching in front of him to be whatever he wanted it to be. The future he'd been anticipating was empty and lifeless now. In every image, he'd seen Lana beside him as he achieved his milestones, the two of them working together at making their dreams a reality.

Urgency gripped him as he looked at his watch. Lana had left her message an hour ago. He quickly pulled out his cell and dialed their home number. Hearing the answering machine switch on, he ended the call and ran for the lift. He could still catch her. As the lift descended, he called Lana's cell phone and left a message.

He was pushing the key into the lock of his truck when he heard the voice. At first he ignored it. Nobody had called him anything other than Tristan in over ten years– he'd almost forgotten he'd ever had another name.

'Frankie,' the voice called again.

He froze with the open door in his hand, recognizing the voice. Turning slowly, he saw him. He was wearing a yellow baseball cap, his hands thrust in his coat pocket as he watched him warily.

'Hello, son,' his father said.

'It's not a good time.' Tristan turned back to the truck.

'It's never a good time.' Kevin gripped his shoulder. 'But the time has come for our talk.'

'What makes you think I want to hear anything you have to say?' Tristan threw off his father's hand.

'I promised your mother I would talk to you.' His father moved to stand in front of him. 'And I will keep my promise.'

Tristan felt Lana sliding further away from him with each minute that passed. He had to hurry home to her and tell her that he'd made a mistake in not believing her. His frustration boiled over. He didn't have time for this.

'Look, I told you this isn't a good time,' Tristan shouted.

'Please, just hear me out.'

Hearing the desperation in his father's voice, Tristan met his gaze.

Seeing the tired lines on his father's face, the way the skin sagged as if he was ten years older than his true age, pulled Tristan up short. This wasn't the father he remembered from his youth; he was facing a tired old man.

'I won't take much of your time.'

Tristan let go of the door and folded his arms across his chest.

'I know you hate me,' Kevin said. 'Can't say I blame you. I wasn't a good father, or a good husband. The time comes in a man's life when he has to look back and face some truths.'

'Well, I guess I should be grateful it only took you twenty years.' Tristan remembered his mother the last time he saw her at the hospital. Her face creased in lines of pain, her eyes revealing her heartbreak.

'I deserved that. But I can't change the past, all I can do is offer you an explanation and hope I can change your future.'

Tristan's rage exploded. He advanced toward his father. They were exactly the same height and he was staring him straight in the eye. 'Who the hell do you think you are, old man? You weren't any sort of a husband or a father. You left my mother destitute. She died alone in a hospital because you were too busy with lawsuits that your negligence caused.'

'I know I deserve your anger, son.' Kevin placed his hand on Tristan's shoulder.

Tristan shrugged off his hand. 'I'm not your son, old man. I'm no one's son.'

Kevin blinked, his eyes glassy. 'I'm sorry. You'll never know how sorry I am for the pain I caused you and your mother.'

'You're right.' Tristan walked to his truck. 'I'll never know because I don't care how sorry you are. There's nothing you have to say that I want to hear.'

'I told her it wouldn't be easy.' Kevin watched Tristan unlocked the truck door. 'I told her you got my bullheadedness —'

'I am nothing like you, old man,' Tristan shouted. 'Nothing.'

Kevin continued as if he hadn't spoken. '... The last time I saw her in the hospital she said – well, it doesn't matter what she said.' Kevin turned around and started walking away.

'You didn't come to the hospital!' Tristan shouted, so his father could hear him.

'I did see her.' Kevin continued walking. 'I was with her until the end.'

Tristan had unlocked the truck door. All he had to do was get inside and drive to Lana. He looked at his father's back. Even though age had slowed him down, his father's long strides were eating up the pavement and he was halfway down the street.

'Hold on.' Tristan shut the truck door before running after him. His father had stopped in the middle of the pavement and was waiting for him. 'What did she say?'

'She said that you got my bullheadedness but that you got her soft heart. That as much as you blamed me for failing you both, you blamed yourself more for not being able to take care of her.' Kevin's blue eyes watched him calmly.

Tristan turned away, hiding his face as he was taken back to his mother's last days, watching her restlessly shifting in bed, her mouth bracketed in lines of pain.

'It wasn't your responsibility, son.' Kevin moved to stand in front of him. 'It was mine. It was my job to take care of you both and I failed.'

'Why didn't you?' Tristan's voice was hoarse. 'Why weren't you there?'

'It wasn't that I didn't love you and your mother, because I did. With all my heart and soul. But I just couldn't show it the way you both needed.'

Tristan looked at his father. 'Love isn't saying the words. It's actions that speak for you, and yours told the true story a long time ago.'

'I don't know if you mother ever told you how we met —'

'What's the point?' Tristan interrupted as his frustration spilled over. 'You think a trip down memory lane is going to make me forget what you did?'

'I know you think I'm wasting your time, but your mother thought it was important that you hear this. Can I please finish?'

Seeing Tristan's nod, he continued. 'I stole your mother away from her fiancé. She was all set to marry a man her parents approved of and instead I came along with my rough hands and even rougher manners, but somehow she saw something in of me.'

Tristan realized Lana had known the truth of how his parents met. If he hadn't already begun to believe her about her past life, this would have been the final proof that changed his mind.

'You didn't know it, but on her twenty-fifth birthday, your mother came into an inheritance from her grandmother. I was working as a builder and trying to save for our first house. The company I was working for was experiencing troubles and the rumor was they were seeking a partner for an influx of cash. I didn't know it, but your mother used her inheritance and the deposit for our first home to buy into the company.'

Tristan smiled. His mother had always been impulsive, making snap decisions and putting the needs of those she loved above her own.

'When she came home and presented me with the deed, I was so angry. She hadn't told me anything because she knew I wouldn't have let her do it. That was money her grandmother had left her to guarantee her independence from everyone, her parents included. But your mother had a way of getting around my anger. She told me she was investing in our future. She said that if I wasn't happy then she couldn't be either.'

Tristan understood his father's bewilderment. He remembered when he was ten years old and his mother had used the money she was saving to visit her sister to pay for his camping trip. He'd been angry because it didn't seem fair that he was happy at his mother's expense, yet somehow that was always the end result with his mother's love.

'At first we were blissfully happy. Going to work every day was a joy because I wasn't just bringing home a wage, but the promise of a better future.' Kevin sighed heavily. 'I took my responsibility seriously and I wasn't going to fail my Lillian. I was going to prove I was worthy of her belief so I worked harder and harder.'

Tristan remembered all the nights he and his mother waited for his father to come home from work so they could have dinner together as a family. His stomach would be cramping with hunger as their dinner got colder. Eventually his father would call to say he'd be late and he and his mother would eat their cold dinner in labored silence.

'I started spending more time away from the house but what sustained me was the belief that soon all my sacrifices would be worth it.'

Tristan still remembered when they stopped waiting for his father. He'd wanted to ask his mother, but her glassy eyes stilled the questions on his tongue and he ate his dinner in silence. After that it was just the two of them. It seemed his father would only come home to sleep, and sometimes days would pass before they would bump into each other on the way to the bathroom.

'I was close to achieving this when you fell sick with rheumatic fever.'

Tristan's jerked and looked at his father. According to Lana, his life diverged when he fell ill.

'You probably don't remember, but it was a difficult time. I spent less time at the company and my partner was running it by himself. When you recovered I returned to find my partner had gambled his personal finances and was dipping into the company funds.'

Lana had said that in her other life, his father's partner embezzled the funds, leaving his family bankrupt and without medical insurance to pay for the surgery to repair Frank's heart valves.

'Instead of bringing criminal charges against him and bringing down negative publicity on Walters and Green, I took out a bridging loan and bought him out. While I fought to bring the company back from the brink of disaster, you recovered.'

His father had focused on the company to the detriment of his family. As his father's absence became more pronounced, he and his mother turned to each other. Most boys his age were happy to stay away from the house for as long as possible and it would take threats before they would scramble home. But he was different to the other boys. He'd always been conscious that his mother was alone.

'I spent the next two years living and breathing the company. When I was finally able to look around me, I realized you and Lillian had moved on. The two of you had grown closer after your illness and were a firm unit, and I didn't seem to have a place.'

Tristan opened his mouth to retort, but his father stayed him with a wave of his hand.

'I know that it was my fault. I didn't fight to make a place for myself. I was quite happy to continue on with things the way they were.'

Tristan had never wondered why his mother didn't divorce Kevin. As a devout Catholic, her wedding vows were for life.

'What do you want from me?' Tristan asked. 'Do you think your story of woe is going to make up for what you did to us? You destroyed our family.'

Kevin met his gaze unflinchingly. 'I don't expect you to be able to forgive me.'

'How can I?' Tristan demanded. 'Your actions cost a man his life, another one his legs,' he said, remembering his friend Taylor.

'I was careless in trusting the wrong people. I let subcontractors run their own shop, rather than taking charge.' He lifted his hands, stopping Tristan from interjecting. 'I'm not trying to pass the blame. The buck stops with me. I was ultimately responsible and that's why I pleaded guilty.'

Tristan remembered seeing the news headline after his mother passed away, but he hadn't cared to know the details. He'd proclaimed himself an orphan to all and had tried not to think about his father since then.

Tristan looked away, his emotions in turmoil as he tried to get a handle on himself. His hate had sustained him and he didn't know how to feel anything else.

'When I saw your mother the last time she spent the whole afternoon talking of you,' Kevin said. 'She saw that bitterness and anger were destroying you and she begged me to speak to you. To help you heal and move on.'

Kevin tentatively put his hand on Tristan's shoulder, as if expecting him to throw it off. 'Son, it wasn't your fault. You didn't fail her, I did. I was the one who failed you both.'

Tristan blinked, looking down at the ground. Wasn't that why he'd hated his father so much? He'd felt guilty for not being able to take care of his mother.

'Please leave this burden where it belongs, on my shoulders and mine alone. Let me be the father I never got the chance to be.'

Tristan's skin prickled as he realized Lana was right. His father had never had the chance to be the man he could have been. Whichever way life was played, someone had to live and someone had to die. In this life he got to live, but the cost was that he lost his mother and father.

Lana had been searching for the man Tristan could have been. Her belief had awakened in him the desire to remember who he was before his father went to prison, but to do that he had to forgive. Lana was right when she said that no one gets to choose their family. To be able to move forward with his future, he had to lay down the ghosts of the past and forgive his father.

'Okay.' Tristan nodded. 'It's yours.'

His father looked at him and awkwardly offered his hand. Tristan hesitantly took it.

'Your mother and I are proud of you, son,' Kevin said.

As his father held his hand in his frail grip, Tristan thought he smelt lavender. For a moment he could almost feel his mother hovering beside him.

His father let go of his hand and walked away. Tristan stood in place and watched him make his slow way up the street. He didn't know what the future held, whether he and his father would ever be able to bridge the past and reclaim something resembling a father and son relationship. He didn't know whether his heart was big enough to forgive and move on, but the future held the promise of hope.

Chapter 19

Lana picked up her overnight back and looked around the apartment one last time. Even though she had lived in it for such a short time, she had started to think of it as home. Now that she was leaving, each corner echoed memories of her life with Tristan. Her head ached and her eyes were sore from crying, but she felt at peace. She and Tristan had reached the end of their story. There was nothing left to say.

She had known telling him about her past life might spell the end of their life together, but she had no regrets. Either they found a way to accept each other wholeheartedly and build a future together, or they were to learn everything they could and part as friends.

She realized now that Tristan was not able to accept who she was because that would mean having to accept his father's mistakes. She hoped that he found a way to be happy in this life, but they weren't destined to be together. Each time it seemed they were getting themselves together, they faced a hurdle that stopped them short. If they weren't able to learn to deal with the difficulties of life together then they had no future. Life was always full of twists and turns and you never knew where it would take you. She and Tristan clearly didn't have the resiliency to find their way back to each other in a crisis; they were torn apart each time.

The phone rang. Her heart sped up- maybe it was Tristan. The short-lived hope died when she lifted the receiver and heard the taxi driver telling her he was waiting out the front of the building. She walked out of the apartment. It was time for her new life to begin.

After giving Holly's address to the driver, she lay her head against the backrest of the car seat.

'Hmm.' The taxi driver peered into his rear-view mirror. 'Someone you know?' He nodded toward the street.

Lana frowned before twisting to look through the back window. Tristan was running down the street following the taxi, his truck parked askew at the curb.

'Did you want me to stop?' the driver asked.

Lana hesitated. They'd said everything they had to say. She didn't know if she had the strength to rehash the same arguments. She knew that they loved each other, but sometimes love just wasn't enough.

Tristan shouted her name as he stumbled to a stop.

'I think he's got something he wants to say,' the driver said.

Lana sighed and turned back to look at the front. 'I guess you'd better stop, please.' She took a deep breath as she got out and waited for Tristan to reach her.

'Lana, please come up so we can talk.' He touched her arm.

Lana raised an eyebrow. 'That's quite a turnaround. Now you're fired up to talk?'

He ran his hand through his hair. 'You're right. I'm sorry. That didn't come out right.'

'Tristan, I need to go. Holly is waiting for me.' Lana turned back to the taxi's door.

'No, please,' Tristan pleaded. 'Let me just get this out.'

'What about...' She waved toward the taxi.

'Can you please wait?' Tristan asked.

'It's your money.' The driver parked on the side of the road.

Tristan took Lana's hand and walked with her to the footpath. 'Let me just say this and then you can go.'

Lana crossed her arms and looked away.

'I saw my father.'

Her eyes snapped to his face.

'You were right. Who knows what might have been if things had turned out differently? What sort of a father he might have been in another place or another time? I thought about what you said about living a past life and realized I'd known all along.'

'After you spoke to your father and he confirmed my story, of course,' she snapped.

'No!' Tristan shouted. He lowered his voice. 'No. I realized before I spoke to my father that I believed you about your past life.'

'We'll never know,' she muttered.

Tristan grabbed hold of her handbag and started rifling through it.

'Hey, what are you doing?'

He took out her cell phone and turned it on. After dialing her voicemail, he handed the phone back to her.

She held it against her ear and heard Tristan's frantic voice. 'Lana, wait for me. Please, wait for me. I'm coming home. I believe you. I believe you.'

'Oh.' She put her phone back into her handbag as she tried to compose herself.

'But my father did confirm what you said.' He bent and looked her in the eyes. 'He told me about how he met my mother. That he worked so hard because he had to prove himself worthy of her. I never knew. I never wondered why he almost killed himself for that company. I just thought he cared more about the company than us.'

'That's not true, Tristan. He loved you both.' She reached for his hand. 'In my life he spent every day making sure that both Frank and his mother were taken care of and had his full love and attention. Frank and his father were more like best friends than father and son.'

'I'm glad Frank at least got to know him. That he was loved and never had to doubt that.'

Lana stilled. She realized that Tristan had spoken about her past life as if it was real, as if it had happened. She hadn't realized how lonely it had been, being the only one who had a foot in both worlds.

'I'm sorry it took me so long to accept the truth. You were right. It was because I was scared to see my father for what he really was.' He snorted softly. 'I'd spent so much of my time hating him because I felt I'd let my mother down. But seeing him today, I realized he hadn't gotten off easy.' He brushed the hair from her face. 'Please stay.'

Lana shook her head. 'No. It's too hard. It's not that I don't love you, because I do. But it's just not enough. I can't do it any more. I can't believe one moment and then have it ripped away again.' She started walking back to the taxi.

'You're right,' Tristan said. 'It is too hard.'

She turned back. 'What the hell —'

Tristan held her by the arms. 'We've been doing it all wrong.'

'What do you mean?'

'Normal people meet, date, fall in love and then work up to living together or marrying. We jumped straight to the living ever after without the in-between steps.'

Lana stopped pulling away from him as she realized Tristan was right. She had come to this world to find him already her husband. Even though they had managed to fall in love, their relationship had been characterized by one crisis after another because of the pressure they put on each other to get along. The fact was they were strangers.

'I don't think you should come back to live with me,' Tristan continued. 'Just give us a chance to do this properly, to get to know one another and see where it can take us.'

She met his eyes. 'But what if it's too late?'

'Then it's too late. But at least we gave it a shot.'

She looked down at their joined hands. She didn't know why it was so hard to make this decision. She felt as if she'd used up all her energy to get to them to this point and she just didn't know if she had anything left.

'So, can I call you sometime?' he asked.

She realized that the answer was right in front her: she didn't have to do anything. This was their chance to take it one step at a time, without any pressure.

She looked up and smiled. 'Maybe,' she said over her shoulder as she got in the taxi.

She rolled down the window and blew him a kiss. Tristan mimed catching her kiss and putting it to his lips before blowing her a kiss back. She laughed and watched him as she drove away. When the taxi turned the corner she laid her head against the seat and smiled. It was a beginning.

Epilogue

One year later

After getting out of the limousine, Lana fixed the ruffles of her skirt. She walked up the church steps, hearing the murmur of happy voices traveling toward her through the church door.

It hadn't been easy but they had made it, they finally found their way back to each other.

'Are you ready?' Holly's eyes sparkled with excitement.

'Yes.' Lana smiled. Her whole life had been leading to this moment and she wanted to savor each detail.

As the strains of piano started, Lana took her first step toward her future. She'd chosen to walk down the aisle to Des'ree's 'I'm Kissing You.' As she walked, Lana remembered their courtship. They had started slowly, going out on dates the way any couple would do. It had been so effortless. Without the pressure of living together, they had the opportunity to get to know each other, as opposed to assuming they knew the other.

She had learnt not to ascribe reactions to Tristan based on what she knew of Frank, while he learnt that she and Alannah shared superficial differences.

She smiled as she reflected on how her life had changed. She'd been accepted into university and started her teaching degree. Tristan's project with Rebuilding Boston Together had lead to great publicity and he already had clients booked for his new business.

They had worked together and helped each other achieve their dreams and throughout it all, they had taken it one step at a time, enjoying each step of the journey because they knew that they had all the time in the world.

Six months into their courtship, Tristan had taken her to view a house in Roslindale.

'Is this going to be your first job?' she'd asked as she looked at the ramshackle house. It had a sad and neglected air about it, as if it had been sitting unoccupied for years. The paint had peeled and the rot of the wood was showing through.

'The house is barely hanging together and the client wants to knock it down and build a new one.' Tristan's eyes took on a far away look as he turned to look at it.

She knew that he was imagining the new house in its place. 'It's a great area.' She looked down the tree-lined street. When they drove through the area she'd noted the schools and mall nearby. 'This will be a lovely family home.' She kissed him on the cheek. 'I'm so happy for you.'

'Well, actually the client doesn't have a family yet, but he's thinking of the future. You see, the client met this beautiful woman and he can't imagine life without her.' He dropped to his knee and looked up at her.

'Lana Madden Walters, will you marry me?' He took a jewelry box from his front pocket and opened it. 'Will you be beside me every day, help me build a home for us, have babies with me, get old and wrinkly with me as we spend our lives together?'

Lana's eyes teared up. 'Yes.' She took the ring out of the box. He'd had Alannah's engagement ring enhanced. The rose-shaped ring now had a vine engraved on the band with the initials A&T, L&F and L&T set in the leaves.

'I had our story written into it: Alannah and Tristan, Lana and Frank and now Lana and Tristan.' He slipped the ring onto her finger. 'This way the ring represents our past, our present and future.'

Lana pulled his head to her and kissed him. 'I love you.'

'I love you too.' He pulled her to his side. 'I'm going to build you a beautiful house,' he said, as they looked at the derelict house.

'I know.' She kissed his hand before returning it to her waist.

He had kept his promise. He'd built a beautiful home for them and it was waiting for their return from their honeymoon in Florence. After their engagement setting a wedding date had been easy. They had chosen March 21, the first anniversary of their meeting and Lana's transfer to this world. She'd told Tristan she didn't care if the house wasn't finished in time but he'd worked around the clock.

She felt the flower Tristan had given her this morning fluttering against her cheek as she continued down the aisle.

She'd been getting ready at Holly's apartment when she'd felt his hands cover her eyes. 'Tristan,' she'd exclaimed. 'It's bad luck for the groom to see the bride on the wedding day.' But turning around, she'd laughed. 'Your handiwork?' she said to Holly, nodding at Tristan's blindfolded eyes.

'It's all my fault.' Tristan leant down to kiss her and missed her mouth.

'Really.' Lana moved her head so his lips found their mark the second time around.

'Mmm.' Tristan murmured against her lips. 'I'm a very bad boy.'

'I know.' She kissed him back, her hands clutching his shoulders while he pulled her up against him.

When they came up for air, he handed her a yellow tulip. 'I wanted you to have this.' He placed it in her hand. 'Put in your hair.'

Lana smiled as she touched the petals to her cheeks. On their first official date a week after she'd moved out, he'd bought a yellow tulip from a flower stall and placed it in her hair.

'I'd help you put it in, but —' He shrugged helplessly.

Holly stood at a discreet a distance away with her back to them, pretending to be occupied with the wedding dress. She turned and reached for the flower. 'Here,' she said and threaded it through Lana's upswept hair.

When Holly stepped away, Lana took Tristan's hand and lifted it to the tulip.

He smiled and bent down to kiss her again. His lips were sweet and tender on hers, cherishing her.

'Okay.' Holly pulled them apart. 'I'm sure you guys didn't forget why we're here.' She led Tristan away.

'See you,' Tristan called out, narrowly missing the doorway.

Lana laughed as Holly clutched his arm tighter and steered him out of the apartment.

She smiled now and felt the guests shifting in their seats as they turned to look at her. She saw her mother dabbing her eyes gently, careful not to smear her eye make-up. After divorcing Michael, she had embraced the fashion sense Lana remembered from her past life. Her blond hair was puffed out, her eyes bright with the heavy kohl and purple eyeshadow to match her purple suit.

Lana met Tammy's eyes and smiled, glad to see the glow back in her mother's cheeks. Over the past year, they had developed a friendship and Lana felt at peace, their rift firmly in the past.

Tammy's divorce from Michael had been amicable with irreconcilable differences listed as the official reason. With Tammy's evidence, and Evan's supporting testimony, Michael had realized his only choice was to put on a good front and bluster his way through the media furor. After the divorce hit the newspapers, Michael's career became shaky but he recovered, only to be forced to resign when a secretary pressed charges for assault and sexual harassment.

Evan had completed his rehabilitation treatment and vanished. Lana had received a postcard from South America after she and Tristan decided to renew their wedding vows. 'Good luck, sis,' had been scrawled on the back. She hoped wherever Evan was, he was healing and putting the past behind him.

Kevin sat next to her mother. He and Tristan had made some headway to establishing a relationship, but they would never have the closeness that Frank and his father had in her past life. Too much had happened for them to wipe the slate clean, but at least they both had peace.

As Holly reached the altar and passed Aidan, their eyes met. Lana's gaze narrowed as she saw the flash of emotion pass between them.

Then she met Tristan's eyes, and thoughts of Aidan and Holly evaporated.

'Hello,' she whispered.

'Hi.' He took her hand and lifted it to his mouth.

She saw in his face the promise of forever and smiled with joy. Above their heads two butterflies danced before they flew out of the church and into the blue sky.

A note from the author

Return to Me was inspired by a dream in which I was with my husband, but he was different to how I knew him. I grieved for the man I knew and yet loved him in this different place. When I woke up the dream was so real and present, and even as I write this today I remember this feeling of grief that I felt watching the man who was not my husband walk away from me.

The next day I was tormented by questions of 'What if?' What if a woman was transferred to a parallel universe and was married to the man who was her husband, but he was different? What if she knew he was the man she fell in love with, but she had to fight for him to fall in love with her again?

Growing up my favorite TV show was Quantum Leap, starring Scott Bakula as Dr. Sam Beckett, a physicist who involuntarily leaps through spacetime during experiments in time travel, by temporarily taking the place of other people to correct what he consistently discovers were historical mistakes. This show tickled my imagination. I loved how each leap and correction had a ripple effect on everyone Sam met.

And so I wondered, how would Lana's time travel leap affect the people she knew in this parallel universe? Would they feel an echo of her memories, rippling and interrupting their lives?

How would it affect her best friend Vanessa and Jeremy, the man she was fated to be with? Would Holly and Aiden find their way back to each other?

I loved writing this novel because it combined several of my favorite romance tropes: time travel, second chances and star-crossed lovers. If you want to read more of the *Leap of Fate* series, let me know whose story you want next.

In the meantime, read an extract of my next book, *Hollywood Dreams*, from my *Dreams of Destiny* series.

And don't forget to sign up to my newsletter to find out my latest writing news.

About the author

 Mae Archer knew she wanted to be a writer since she was a child. She loved listening to her grandmother's war stories about English maidens falling in love with handsome Yankees while England burnt under the Luftwaffe's blitz.

When she discovered romance novels as a teenager she soon realised that her dream job was to be a romance writer. After many career twists and turns she's making her dreams come true.

Mae's real life is like one of her grandmother's stories. She met a foreigner who travelled through Australia and it was love at first sight. She married him six months after they met and every day since has been an adventure. She lives in Australia with her husband and daughter.

Mae has been an avid reader of romance novels since she was a teenager and her own novels combine some of her favourite romance tropes including time travel, second chances and star-crossed lovers.

Mae Archer is the pen name for author Amra Pajalic. Amra writes young adult contemporary fiction under her own name and dark fiction as A.P. Pajalic.

SIGN UP FOR AMRA'S AUTHOR NEWSLETTER

For news, giveaways, bonus material, and sneak peeks, please sign up to her newsletter below.

www.amrapajalic.com

CONNECT WITH AMRA

goodreads.com/author/show/3310015.Amra_Pajalic

facebook.com/AmraPajalicAuthor/

instagram.com/amrapajalicauthor/

https://twitter.com/AmraPajalic

bookbub.com/authors/amra-pajalic

tiktok.com/@amrapajalic

youtube.com/c/AmraPajalicAuthor

CONNECT WITH MAE

www.maearcherromance.com

https://twitter.com/MaeArcher12

goodreads.com/mae_archer

facebook.com/MaeArcherRomance

PLEASE LEAVE A REVIEW

If you enjoyed this book and would like to show Amra your support, please consider leaving a star rating and/or review on the website you purchased the book from.

Hollywood Dreams
Blurb

She's fallen for his greatest role. But can she fall for him?

Former soap star Tom Calvert dreams of making movies that matter. To get the part of a lifetime he becomes a method actor, living as Beau Tennant, a war hero with a disabling injury. While in character he meets Maree Reynard, a costume designer, and takes her on a date. But when this practice date becomes all too real he realizes that he's made the mistake of a lifetime. Will he be able to get Maree to fall in love with Tom Calvert?

Maree Reynard's father is an actor and she has grown up on a studio lot. She has no illusions about the artifice of the movie-making business and has vowed she would never date an actor. When she meets and falls in love with Beau Tennant she knows that she's found her dream man who is genuine and real. But when Beau disappears from her life she is heartbroken. She meets Tom Calvert on the rebound and sees their flirtation as a way of recovering her shattered confidence. Will Tom Calvert be able to convince her he is the real deal?

Hollywood Dreams
Chapter 1

Even though Beau Tennant was on busy Melrose Avenue in Los Angeles he'd never felt so alone. As he waited for help, he watched the faces of people passing. They stared straight ahead, or craned their necks to the opposite side of the street to avert their eyes.

That's when he saw her, waist-length brown hair bouncing as she walked. She held a phone to her ear, a big handbag dragged on her wrist, and her other hand clutched a box. Her brown eyes caught his and when she didn't turn away he felt a thrill, as if he'd touched an electricity pole.

She stopped beside him. 'I have to go,' she said.

Beau looked up at her, but her eyes were on the box in her hand.

'I'll be there in twenty minutes.' She hung up and dropped the phone in her bag. 'You're stuck,' she said, looking at the wheelchair caught in a crack of concrete on the sidewalk.

'Yes, ma'am,' Beau drawled in his Southern accent.

'Here, hold this.' She placed the box onto his lap and squatted, somehow making the act look elegant in her silver platforms and black Capri pants. 'Mm,' she murmured. 'I need some grunt to get that wheel out.'

'Don't worry—' he started, but she'd walked off, leaving him with the box. What did she think he was, her shelf?

She stood in the path of the oncoming crowd. He saw her zero in on a young man in a tight, white T-shirt that displayed his bulging pecs. Beau knew the moment that White T-shirt caught her eye.

White T-shirt smiled flirtatiously, and slowed. 'Hey,' he said.

'Hey yourself.' She smiled back. 'So I need a hand with something. You got a few minutes?'

'Sure,' the young man replied.

She led him over to Beau. 'I need you to lift the wheel while I push,' she said firmly.

White T-shirt was taken aback, but her tone obviously brooked no argument.

'There's no need—' Beau tried to interject again, but she paid him no mind as she went to stand behind the chair.

'On my count,' she told the young man. 'One, two, three.' She pushed, while he lifted the wheel. 'Thanks. Appreciate you being a good Samaritan.' She patted White T-shirt on the shoulder and turned to Beau. 'Are you good?'

White T-shirt looked at her for a moment, but apparently realizing he was dismissed he merged back with the crowd, a confused look on his face.

'Yes, ma'am,' Beau said, feeling as confused as the young man who'd helped him. When the woman first stopped he'd pegged her for a Looky-Lou; one of those people who thought they could get his life story as part and parcel of small talk. Yet now that she'd gone and blown his first impression out of the water, he didn't quite know what to make of her.

'What happened here?' She looked at his hand with concern.

He'd cut it on the wheel spoke when he'd tried to wrench the wheelchair out of the crack. Before he could say anything, again, she had taken hold of his hand and was looking closely at the cut.

'It's fine.' He pulled his hand back, feeling self-conscious under the force of her attention.

'You can't turn the wheels with a cut in your hand. You'll get an infection.' She went behind the chair and before he knew what she was doing, she was pushing him toward Luna's Café.

That had been his destination—to meet his friend, Carter—but Beau didn't know whether to feel thankful or annoyed that she was hijacking him and his chair without asking.

She chose a table under a green shade umbrella. After she moved a metal chair out of the way and took the box off his lap, she pushed him in. As she sat across from him their knees almost touched under the small table. She placed the box under her chair, and took hold of his palm again.

'It just needs a good clean.' She rifled through her bag.

A waiter appeared. 'Chai latte with skim milk.' She rattled off her order without looking up.

'And you, sir?' The waiter looked at him.

'Black coffee, no sugar,' he said.

The woman pulled out an antiseptic tube and a box of bandages from her bag. As he watched the gentle way she tended to his wound he was puzzled. She was a stranger who'd jumped in to help him when everyone else acted like he was a leper.

He nodded at her supplies. 'You come prepared.'

'I'm a costume designer,' she said. 'In my line of work I find there's always some minor injury or another that needs to be tended to.'

He should have guessed. Prime Studio was only twenty minutes away and a lot of its employees frequented Luna's for breakfast meetings. It was also a café known for celebrity watching and was stalked by tabloid reporters, which is why Carter insisted they meet here.

'So you're in the business,' he said, stressing the word.

Los Angeles was the city of entertainment. Most people were employed in some way by the entertainment industry and if they weren't, then they were just angling for their 'break.'

'I see that we haven't made a good first impression?' she said. 'But I guess that's not much of a surprise. How long were you stuck there for?'

As she looked at him, Beau saw something he hadn't seen in anyone's eyes since he'd sat in the wheelchair. Understanding. 'Half an hour,' he said. 'Shit, I have to call someone.'

She placed a bandage on his hand, gently pressing down to make sure it stuck. He felt his skin tingle.

'Thanks.' He was feeling nonplussed at the sensations her touch evoked. He got out his cell phone. 'Hey, Carter, no need to come down,' he said quickly. 'I'm okay.' He cut off Carter's questions. 'I'll explain later,' and hung up.

'I guess I should introduce myself.' She offered her hand. 'I'm Maree Reynard.'

'Beau Tennant.' As they shook, her hand was enveloped by his much larger one and he realized how small she was. Her presence and manner made her seem much taller. If they'd met while he was standing up she'd only reach his shoulder.

'Lieutenant? Corporal?' she asked.

He was surprised. He was in civilian duds, wearing jeans and a blue short-sleeved shirt. 'Lieutenant. How did you know?'

She reached across the table and lifted his dog tags. He smelled the sweet scent of her hand cream. As she brushed her thumb across the metal he felt a stirring as if she was brushing his skin.

He'd debated about wearing them this morning. A civilian had no reason to wear dog tags, but Beau felt naked without them.

'New to this?' She nodded at the wheelchair as she released the tags, her fingers like the whisper of a butterfly's wings.

'A week stateside.' Beau had joined up with six of his friends after September 11 and had been in the army ever since.

The waiter returned and placed their coffee orders on the table.

'You're the first person I've met, outside of the hospital, who is nonplussed by my wheelchair.' He took a sip of coffee.

'A friend in high school.' Maree lifted the sugar dispenser and poured in two teaspoons. 'She had a car accident after a party. The first six months she got stuck a few times. It's amazing how many people don't know what to do. The whole wheelchair thing spooks them.'

'But not you?'

'Not much spooks me.'

There was a glimmer of flirtatiousness as Maree looked at him. For a moment he forgot himself and responded as the old him, his lips quirking into a smile, his shoulders straightening as he got ready to launch into his move. Then he saw his reflection in the window behind her. His blond hair hung to his shoulders, a beard covered most of his face, and even his eyes were unrecognizable with their brown tint. He looked down at the table as he took a sip of his coffee. He was imagining it. Why would a woman like her be interested in someone like him?

'What are you doing in town?' she asked.

He rubbed his hand across the back of his neck. He'd practiced his story a thousand times, yet now that it was show time, he felt ill at ease. 'I'm meeting with some people. They might be making a movie about me.'

'Oh,' she said.

He cleared his throat. 'Yeah.'

'Did you write the screenplay?' she asked.

'No, a friend of mine wrote it.' He took a sip of his coffee.

'You're a braver person than I am.'

'Why?' he asked.

'Are you sure you know what you're getting yourself in for? After all Hollywood is not known for its accurate storytelling.'

Beau was surprised by her serious face. Usually women were impressed by his movie credentials, but Maree seemed to be concerned that he was naive in getting involved in the business.

'Well, it's based on me, but they're not using my name,' Beau covered himself, not wanting her to think he was a fame chaser, but a regular Joe Blow who just happened to find himself in extraordinary circumstances.

'That won't make much difference,' she said wryly. 'Once that movie comes out you can kiss a regular life goodbye.'

'You seem to know a lot about the negative effects of fame?' he asked.

'My father is an actor.' She said the word like it was a curse.

'You don't sound like you like actors?' Beau asked, guessing from her formal use of father instead of dad that her relationship was strained.

'Maybe I don't.' Maree laughed wryly. 'I've seen too well what fame can do to people. They become arrogant, self-centered, and lose all touch with reality.'

She was looking down at the table, her eyelashes shading her eyes, but her pain was obvious from the sad slant of her lips.

'Not all actors are like that,' Beau said. 'I've met some and they seem perfectly nice.' Even though he'd been thinking cynically about the movie business, now he was feeling strangely defensive.

'Some.' Maree didn't sound convinced.

'Your twenty minutes are almost up,' he said abruptly. She gave him a blank look. 'You told whoever you were speaking to on the phone that you'd be there in twenty minutes,' he explained.

'Yes.' She looked at her watch. 'You're right. I should get going.'

'I've got it,' he said, as she reached for her purse. 'No, really.' He held her hand down when he saw that she was about to argue.

'Okay,' she agreed, a small smile on her face.

He took out his wallet and placed a note on the table.

'It was nice meeting you, Beau.' Maree stood.

He looked up, noticing the way she said his name with an inflection. 'Nice to meet you too, Maree.'

He hesitated. Normally at this point he'd ask for her number, an act that used to be as natural as breathing, but in this new role it didn't seem right. She lingered, and he saw in her eyes that she was waiting, giving him the chance to ask.

'Would you maybe—' he started, his mouth forming the words of their own volition, but he couldn't finish the sentence. 'Never mind. Thanks for everything.' He wrenched his wheels in the opposite direction.

'Yes,' she said.

He stopped and turned his head.

'Call me.' She handed him a card and leaned down, giving him a soft kiss on his cheekbone above the beard.

After she had been swallowed up by the crowd Beau looked down at the business card she'd passed to him. It was plain white and listed her title as Costume Designer for *The Time of Our Lives*, a popular soap opera that had been on television for thirty odd years and whose speciality was love triangles between various family members and their lovers. Beau didn't know if he would call. Pursuing someone who was so close to the business and who could easily break his cover wasn't prudent, but he was intrigued.

He was still thinking about her when he entered his apartment. He'd never met a woman like Maree. It was refreshing to spend time with someone so warm and natural, without an iota of artifice. He got out of the wheelchair, leaving it by the front door, as he walked into the bedroom. He looked into the vanity mirror as he took off the wig and hung it up on the Styrofoam dummy-head sitting on the table. He carefully poked his eye with his index finger and removed the disposable brown tinted contact lenses and put them in the trash.

When he looked back in the mirror, it was now the face of Tom Calvert staring at him. Tom, with his short, slicked brown hair, the blue eyes that a reporter had once described as icy, and the fine features that had helped him launch a career as a fashion model until he became a 'model slash actor', and then finally an actor only.

Sometimes he looked in the mirror and cursed himself. While his good looks had opened up doors, they'd also closed as many, guaranteeing that he would always be seen as a soap actor first and a serious actor second.

He jumped in the shower, momentarily startled as he started to soap himself and saw the black tattoo snaking across his arms and chest. It was in semi-permanent ink, and proclaimed in cursive script 'For those I love I will sacrifice.'

As Tom stepped out of the shower his phone rang.

'So how did you go?' demanded the voice of his agent, Carter.

'Really well,' Tom said. 'Just have to learn to avoid sketchy sidewalks in the future.'

'Ha ha,' Carter said.

Tom heard the sound of rustling paper and knew that Carter was doing his usual and multitasking as he spoke to him.

'We've got a date for the Marco shoot in a couple of weeks.' Carter reminded him of the sportswear line he'd agree to endorse.

'Great.' Tom faked enthusiasm.

He hadn't wanted to do it. He knew that an endorsement was just another cross against him being taken seriously, but it was the only way to scratch the right back in order to get an audition. The *Heroes of Tennessee* director was married to the CEO of Marco and Carter had negotiated the deal. Thankfully it had worked, and Tom had blown the director away and scored his dream part.

'Only a month until shooting starts. Do you think you'll be ready?' Carter asked.

'Shouldn't be a problem,' Tom said. The movie was about six friends from a small town in Tennessee who signed up to the army on the same day, and Beau's character was based on the only soldier who'd survived. Tom had been in character for a week. He'd spent hours every day as Beau, practicing maneuvering his wheelchair in and out of buildings, onto buses, and out on the street, seeing how people related to him. With each day that passed he'd felt Beau settling onto him like an old coat.

'Good,' Carter said. 'Because you know what's at stake.'

'I know.' This part was going to make his career. He would finally be the serious actor that he'd always wanted to be.

After he hung up he caught sight of Maree's business card and smiled. Here was his chance to really put himself to the test as Beau.

She's fallen for his greatest role.
But can she fall for him?

Unbelievable Discounts

https://www.pishukinpress.com/

Memoir

Things Nobody Knows But Me

Growing up Muslim in Australia

Young Adult

The Cuckoo's Song

Sabiha's Dilemma

Alma's Loyalty

The Climb

Romance as Mae Archer

Return to Me

Hollywood Dreams

Dark Fiction/Horror as A.P. Pajalic

Woman on the Edge

9 781922 871022